# Justice Assured

# Justice Assured

DIANE/DAVID MUNSON

# Justice Assured



Cover design by Luisa Pereira.
Cover images from Adobe Stock.
Formatting by Rik – Wild Seas Formatting

Visit Diane and David Munson's website at:
www.DianeAndDavidMunson.com

# ACKNOWLEDGMENT

Many thanks to our dear readers, friends and family who continue to pray for us and our writing. Thanks also to Micah House Media and those supporting them for bringing to fruition this story of courage and faith in such turbulent times. We need God's truth and help more than ever.

Isaiah 9:8 (NIV) is a wonderful promise for us to cling to: "For to us a child is born, to us a son is given, and the government will be on his shoulders. And he will be called Wonderful Counselor, Mighty God, Everlasting Father, Prince of Peace."

John 14:6 (NIV) is Jesus Christ's promise of salvation: "I am the way and the truth and the life. No one comes to the Father except through me."

We give a special thanks to Barbara Breakey of Breakey Acres Proofreading for her expertise in editing and support of this endeavor. And we thank Rik Hall of Wild Seas Formatting for his excellent interior design, and to the creative cover designer, Luisa Pereira. We are grateful and blessed by those who because of the sensitivity of their assignment in the intelligence community, cannot be acknowledged by name.

Each of the Munsons' Stand-Alone Thrillers May Be Read in Any Order.

Facing Justice – ISBN-13: 978-0982535509
Confirming Justice – ISBN-13: 978-0982535516
The Camelot Conspiracy – ISBN-13: 978-0982535523
Hero's Ransom – ISBN-13: 978-0982535530
Redeeming Liberty – ISBN-13: 978-0982535547
Joshua Covenant – ISBN-13: 978-0-983559009
Night Flight – ISBN-13: 978-0983559023 (Young Adult and Grandparent Suspense)
Stolen Legacy – ISBN-13: 978-0983559047
Embers of Courage – ISBN – 13: 978-0983559061
The Looming Storm – ISBN – 13: 978-0-983559085
North by Starlight – ISBN – 13: 978-1-732582309
The Breach – ISBN – 13: 978-1-732582323
Justice Assured - 13:978-1732582347

# Justice Assured
## Prologue

O n another hot and humid night in Washington, DC, rookie ICE Special Agent Eva Montanna knew there was nothing unusual about high temperatures in July. Rather, she felt a heat of a different kind. She sat in the unmarked government-owned car (G-car), checked her watch, and couldn't help thinking, *Tonight will surely test my worth!*

But, with a shaky hand, Eva simply wrote in her surveillance log: 8:17 p.m.

She forced herself to ponder what was at stake with a new attitude. Success was within her grasp if she kept a cool head, and Eva refused to believe whatever happened next would be her undoing. Or that Special Agent Hector Santos would be either.

Parked on the street near the restaurant and hyper-alert, Eva rehearsed all that was expected of her in providing backup surveillance for Hector, who was at this precise moment, ensconced inside a swanky eatery meeting with a crooked attorney named Paulus.

Eva knew that though her boss was the lead agent on their team, Hector was posing as an unsavory businessman in league with a crooked financial guy who wanted to invest in drug smuggling to rake in huge investment returns. Hector was wired, and his device was now recording every word Paulus said. Their team of agents hoped to discover if the corrupt lawyer was the sole investor, or if other criminals were also putting in illicit money.

A looming problem brought beads of sweat pooling on Eva's forehead in the stifling car. Where was Regina Spire, another rookie federal agent on the team? Eva craned her neck to see out the window of the unmarked Impala, but her assigned partner was nowhere in sight. This was bad.

"Regina," Eva said forcefully into the microphone of the two-way radio in the G-car. "Where are you?"

*Crackle crackle* pierced Eva's eager ears. No reply came from Regina. Mere static met her on the other end.

Adrenaline rocketed through Eva's veins. Had something happened to Regina?

Eva fought for calm. Forty-five minutes had passed since Hector had gone in. He and Attorney Paulus would appear on the street at any moment. Eva hadn't endured all the grueling months of training in Glynco, Georgia, to fail.

No!

She'd recently become a Special Agent for Federal Immigration and Customs Enforcement (ICE) and vowed this stake-out would succeed no matter what happened to Regina. While Eva wasn't responsible for Regina's actions, her partner's erratic actions had the potential to adversely impact Eva's future.

Eva checked her watch again, and figured about now, Hector would be convincing Paulus about all the cash he'd raised from investors to rent an airplane and buy fuel for a flight to Colombia and back, loaded with illegal drugs. With Hector's years of experience posing as a drug dealer, there was no way he'd end the meeting until he recorded enough of the conversation for Attorney Paulus to incriminate himself.

In fact, Hector had stressed in their pre-op meeting several times that Paulus was *not* to be arrested until he took delivery of the satchel containing three hundred grand in one-hundred-dollar bills, all to further prove his guilt.

Eva tried again. "Regina! Where are you? Are you ready?"

Her radio crackled, and once again there was no response. Had Paulus' goons assailed Regina? Or had her radio simply quit working?

Eva's buzzing cell phone made her jump. She quickly answered and barked, "Regina, where are you?"

"Shh … I snuck into the ladies' room. Hector and Paulus are getting ready to leave."

"You'd better get out here then," Eva shot back.

"10-4."

Eva's phone went dead. Just then, she spotted Regina rush out of the eatery, head toward her own G-car, but then swerve toward Eva's; she practically dove into the front passenger seat. Eva glanced over at her fellow rookie agent.

Regina was wheezing and glancing around like a cat in a strange neighborhood.

"Did the suspect see you?" Eva demanded, her lips pursed tightly.

Regina shrugged her shoulders as if she couldn't care less if she'd been spotted.

Eva battled against her rising angst. Rather than lash out at Regina for her reckless behavior, she sought common ground. She'd backed into a diagonal parking spot on Pennsylvania Avenue, giving them a view of the Willard Hotel directly across the street, just east of the White House.

She gestured outside the window. "It's amazing how quiet these streets get once the commuters beat feet for home."

"Yeah, if it weren't for this dumb operation," Regina replied, pointing at the historic hotel, "we'd be in there enjoying some pretty fine dining."

Eva jerked her finger into the air. "Wait!"

In her earbud, she heard the undercover agent inside the Willard say, "Negotiations are over. We'll be walking to my car to get the money. After I give him the satchel, y'all can make the arrest."

"Did you get that?" Eva asked, glaring at Regina. "Hector must have enough evidence on the recording with Paulus to arrest him."

With a sharp nod, Regina shot out of Eva's G-car and ran to hers, which she'd parked closer to Hector's. Tension mounted within Eva. She lacked confidence in her partner but could do nothing about it. The next few minutes were critical.

Besides making the arrest at the right time and in the proper way to ensure the conviction of Paulus and his cohorts, Eva's next posting depended totally on this operation's outcome. Both she and Regina would receive new assignments to major cities in the U.S., and Eva knew Regina also wanted to remain in the nation's capital. Only one of them would receive the plum assignment. The other would be sent to Los Angeles, Miami, or some other large city in between.

The Willard's glass doors opened, and Eva's breath quickened. An unknown woman dressed in a long coat left the hotel and slid into a cab out front. Eva stayed on alert for

Hector to leave with the greedy lawyer. She would have no trouble recognizing him, as she'd followed Paulus from his office to a local bank, and also before he'd driven here to the Willard Hotel in a luxury car. Although he'd made a few evasive turns, hopefully he hadn't spotted her surveillance. She couldn't speak for Regina, who had parked her G-car too close to the suspect's, in Eva's opinion.

From the corner of her eye, Eva spotted Hector emerging with the attorney. She spoke hurriedly into her radio microphone, "Undercover agent and suspect have left the hotel. Be prepared to make the arrest after the UC gives him the satchel."

A different unmarked car driven by Supervisory Special Agent Cedric Foster, the lead ICE agent, zoomed by Eva's car and then Regina's. Eva noted Cedric glancing briefly at Regina before coasting into an empty parking spot in front of the Willard.

Cedric's voice whispered over the walkie-talkie, "Be alert. Target and Hector are walking toward us."

Eva spotted the undercover agent striding beside the well-dressed attorney. Both men stepped off the curb behind Cedric's car before crossing the street. They walked toward a Mercedes, the one in which Hector had arrived over an hour earlier. Eva watched the undercover agent press the trunk remote to retrieve the satchel, the expected fruits of the crime.

She expected him to hand over the satchel and was prepared to leap out of her undercover car when something shocking happened before her eyes.

Without warning, Regina roared up in her G-car and screeched to a halt, nearly striking Attorney Paulus. She jumped from the car and, pointing her service weapon at Paulus, screamed, "Federal Agents!"

She grabbed him and folded him over the hood of her car.

Eva bolted out of her car. Seeing the undercover agent gawking at Regina, Eva said sharply, "Regina, what are you doing?"

Regina ignored Eva. Instead, she quickly frisked the attorney for weapons hidden beneath his suit jacket. Cedric Foster and two other surveillance agents ran up at full speed.

Regina continued ranting, "And if you can't afford an attorney, the court will appoint one for you."

"Are you all crazy?" Paulus turned toward Eva and the undercover agent, his neck muscles bulging against his shirt collar. As Regina cuffed his hands behind his back, he yelled, "I've done nothing wrong."

"Save it for the judge and jury," Regina scolded, leading him to her car and shoving him into the back seat.

Eva fumed as Regina turned around. All the team members began hollering at once.

To be heard above the din, Eva shouted at Regina, "Why didn't you wait until he took the satchel full of cash?"

"Did someone screw up here, or did I miss something?" Cedric shook his head from side to side as if incredulous at the turn of events.

Regina balked. She stared blankly at her team members. The awkward silence was split by two Capitol Police cars skidding to a stop, their lights flashing. Both uniformed officers hustled over.

"We just got a report of a woman with a gun," one said. "What's going on here?"

Hector stepped forward. "We're Federal ICE agents on a training practicum. I'm the lead instructor." Gesturing to the others, he added, "Our rookie agents just completed a surveillance exercise with an arrest."

The uniformed officer stared first at Hector and then at Eva and the others. "You got any identification?"

Paulus, the attorney, slowly reached inside his suit jacket and carefully removed a leather credential case with a gold badge affixed to the front. "The arrest occurred prematurely. Not as we instructors had expected."

The officer handed back the IDs. "You're too close to the White House for your operation. Makes the Secret Service folks nervous. Better scram before more citizens make complaints and we're forced to take action against you."

Both officers waved before hopping into their cars. They turned off their flashing lights and drove off. Eva shoved her hands into her pockets, reliving the horrible outcome in her mind.

"I want you all to follow me to Pershing Park, across the street from the Willard," Cedric ordered, pointing fiercely.

When he stalked away with an angry look, Eva envisioned the worst. Her career as a federal agent was fizzling before it ever got off the ground.

**AS INSTRUCTOR CEDRIC FOSTER STOOD BEFORE** the group of six special agent trainees assembled on park benches at Pershing Park, Eva sat as far from Regina as she could, hoping Cedric wouldn't remember she'd been the failed rookie's partner in the training exercise gone wrong.

Cedric folded his beefy arms across his massive chest. "Today, you've seen why we brought you here from Glynco, Georgia. We wanted each of you to apply what we've been teaching you about metropolitan surveillance. Anyone care to comment?"

"Other drivers and the buses made it super difficult," the rookie agent sitting beside Eva offered.

"Good observation." Cedric flashed a lopsided grin. "Most of you did quite well on the surveillance aspect."

He nodded at Paulus, the instructor who'd been pretending to be the crooked attorney, and said, "The team managed to stay with our fake suspect the entire time. Let's ask the hare what insights he has for the hounds."

Paulus pointed to the rookie sitting next to Eva on the hard bench. "I marked you as surveillance the moment I entered the revolving door at the bank. You followed me much too closely. When I stayed in the revolving door, panic flooded in your eyes as I came back out."

The rookie shifted on the park bench. Eva waited to hear how she'd messed up, like letting Regina run wild. But when Instructor Paulus smiled at the rookie in the hot seat, Eva relaxed her tense shoulders.

"Good thing the agent didn't follow me back out," Paulus said. "If I was really doing something illegal, I'd have been spooked by his reaction."

Paulus' eyes scanned the group before he explained, "Another time when I drove into a cul-de-sac in the residential neighborhood, I noticed a couple of your surveillance cars."

Here, he jabbed a long finger at Regina. "I first spotted you in your car near the bank. Then, I saw you again on foot inside the Willard Hotel, which was too great a distance from the bank to be a coincidence. Your being in the hotel after I saw you at the bank would have alerted me had I been up to no good."

Eva couldn't believe it, but Regina started giggling. Eva failed to see any humor in the ghastly situation and wondered what Paulus might say next.

He fixed a hot glare on Regina's face and erupted, "The meeting was being recorded. Why risk foiling the operation by showing up in the hotel?"

"I had to use the bathroom, Sir," Regina replied, wearing a smirk.

Paulus shook his head. "They make absorbent adult undies for times like that, Agent Spire. You might want to carry some with you in the future."

To her incessant giggles, he told the others that over all, they did well. "All except Agent Spire. She arrested me sooner than she should have."

"Right," Cedric snapped, stepping closer to the group. "Spire, you made an awful mistake. What were you thinking?"

Eva saw Regina wring her hands as she croaked, "Sir, I can't say why I didn't wait for the attorney to receive the package of currency."

"Whatever your reason, ineptitude or too much adrenaline, you not only spoiled things for yourself, you failed your entire team."

Cedric stared at Eva with his piercing blue eyes. "What's the impact of this mistake, Agent Montanna?"

Eva blinked as if that would erase the disaster. She knew it could not. How much of Regina's hot mess would stick to her?

"Sir, I believe that because the lawyer never accepted the money, the prosecutor would have a hard time proving his guilt."

"True," Cedric replied with a curt nod. "There's another impact I was thinking about."

"Ah ... We should all learn to follow instructions in the

future?" Eva added, hopefully.

Cedric flexed his jaw. "Of course. I had something else in mind. You all know the agent who graduates from the academy with the highest GPA can select his or her assignment to the ICE office of their preference. Agent Montanna and Agent Spire are tied for the highest GPA. That's why I assigned them both to the same practicum, so neither would have an advantage over the other. By Agent Spire making a premature arrest, her GPA will take a major hit."

"And so," he fixed a penetrating gaze upon Regina. "The impact of tonight's case gives Agent Montanna a great advantage."

Regina moaned, and she flashed Eva a dark look. Eva stared back, unwilling to be caught up in Regina's shenanigans.

"Enough for now," Cedric announced, checking his watch. "We'll resume our critique in the morning. You're all dismissed for the night."

As Regina headed toward her car, Eva thought she heard her mutter, "You'll be sorry for crossing me."

Eva shook off Regina's negative vibes. She headed toward her G-car with a sigh. The coming days until graduation promised to be even more difficult. Her mind jolted with a new awareness. There was something she could do to help, something she'd neglected and would remedy immediately. Car keys clenched in her hand, she lifted up a silent prayer for God's help in navigating her new career and her future.

The 'hot-seat' rookie agent caught up to her and whispered, "Hey, Montanna. Regina Spire better buy a new wardrobe for her new duty assignment in Anchorage."

Eva could only smile and pray that Regina was sent that far away from Washington, DC where Eva fully intended to stay and start her fabulous career.

# Chapter 1

The years since that rookie fiasco had flown by for Special Agent Eva Montanna. She left the negative thoughts behind as she dove inside the Metro car in a subway tunnel beneath Washington, DC. She made it one second before the doors swished close.

With the car jammed with people at lunchtime, Eva had nowhere to sit. She wrapped an arm around an upright post and juggled her cell phone, trying to text her husband, Scott. The Metro jolted forward, then stopped, tipping Eva against the cold pipe, forcing her to tighten the crook of her arm around the post. She dropped her cell phone.

Loud moans and groans from other passengers echoed around Eva's ears. She detested running late for her rare lunch with Scott. These days, they barely spent alone time together, and here she was trapped on a stalled Metro, without a clue how long she'd be stuck underground.

Eva tried to stay upbeat. At least she hadn't fallen down. She steadied her balance before bending to snatch her phone. Swinging her left arm around the post again and holding her phone in her left hand, she typed with her free right hand: *Scott, I'm on the Metro. Stalled, again! Hope to see you soon!*

She hit send. Fuming, Eva recalled how last evening at the kitchen sink, she'd whispered to Scott, "Kaley wants to bring that Dylan Webb guy to dinner tomorrow night. He's arrogant and negative. I'm troubled because our daughter is much too serious about him. Can we meet for lunch tomorrow to strategize?"

"I hear you," Scott had said, nodding. "He gives me the creeps. I'll try pushing back my conference with the CentCom commander."

He'd successfully changed his meeting to two o'clock this afternoon. Eva checked the time on her phone, 11:58 a.m., and rolled her eyes. It was beginning to look like their lunch date was going to be a bust. She exhaled slowly.

Why had time and everything else suddenly become her

enemy?

Eva looked at her phone for Scott's reply or even a thumbs up. Nothing.

She pictured him sitting alone at the café, waiting for her. Frustration rose within her. If only she could flee this Metro car. Escape wasn't possible, so she turned her mind to Dylan. Kaley was too young for a boyfriend, especially this not-very-nice one, who also happened to be two years older. Could she ever convince her daughter to see him more clearly?

When the Metro lurched forward, Eva wanted to shout, Yay! Instead, she clung to the post as the subway began edging along at a crawl. Roughly ten minutes later, she reached her stop, and Eva burst free from the crowd of people, bolting up the escalator.

She'd just reached the sidewalk when a tall man jostled her, forcing her big shoulder bag against her side. Eva couldn't help but wonder if her government-issued Glock pistol bruised his arm as it probably did her ribs. She began running toward the historic Old Post Office, quickly dashing past Pershing Park.

Memories again assailed her mind of the night years ago when she'd sat with rookie ICE special agents on benches being debriefed on their surveillance practicum after Regina Spire had wrecked their undercover case.

It was surely some kind of miracle and evidence of God's fingerprints in her life that Eva hadn't suffered any repercussions from Regina's failure. She kept running along the sidewalk, with the realization that she hadn't once thought of Regina before today, not since Eva's rival had been packed off to Anchorage.

Breathing hard, Eva finally reached the former Old Post Office. The sight of Scott sitting beneath a large umbrella by the outdoor café table warmed her heart. They had attended several events here in various restaurants as the building transitioned from the Old Post Office to the Trump International Hotel and finally to the Waldorf Astoria Washington Hotel, which was a hop, skip, and a jump from FBI Headquarters.

Eva eyed her fabulous husband. On this beautiful spring

day, fresh love for him soared through her, reaching deep inside. Tension vanished, and she smiled widely. With his long legs stretched out and a slight smile on his handsome face, he seemed content to watch Washington tourists and business types rush along Pennsylvania Avenue, the street stretching from the Capitol to the White House.

She shouldn't have worried about him.

Eva slid into the seat across from him, ignoring the view of the majestic Capitol to focus on his eyes. When Scott's didn't meet hers, she knew he was distracted. Did he even see her?

"Honey." She lightly touched his forearm. "Did you get my text?"

His eyes finally snapped toward hers from the Treasury Building, which blocked his view of the White House. "I just saw someone run across the street and nearly get hit by a car. I did receive your text and sent a message not to worry."

"I never received it," she replied, gathering her wits. "My meeting at NCIS ran late, so I took the Metro, which ground to a halt for some unknown reason. I'm starving."

A waiter came to take their order. The words, "I'll have crab cakes with sweet potato fries," had left her lips when Scott's eyes darted toward the sidewalk behind her.

A man yelled, "Stop! FBI!"

Eva spun in her seat.

Scott hollered, "Those two men grabbed a guy, but he broke loose!"

Eva jumped from her seat, leaving her purse, badge, and gun for Scott to guard. A thin man with cropped black hair, wearing green pants and shirt, sped straight to the Waldorf. Two men wearing business suits were in hot but distant pursuit.

She joined the chase after the suspect. Going after bad guys was no problem for her. A seasoned federal agent, she worked out regularly. She was almost to the runner when he suddenly swerved, avoiding her grasp.

Eva dove at and hit his knees. With her arms wrapped firmly around his thighs, they both collapsed in a heap on the sidewalk outside the hotel entrance.

"I'm a federal agent! You're under arrest!" Eva shouted at him.

He ranted in what sounded like Chinese. She didn't understand what he was saying and struggled to stand while trying to pin her prisoner to the ground. Eva glanced over her shoulder for backup from those agents who had been pursuing the man.

To her shock, both men turned and ran in the opposite direction, speeding west on Pennsylvania Avenue. The man at her feet shoved her hard, jumped up, and disappeared into the Waldorf. Confusion pierced Eva's mind.

*Who are these people? Should I keep chasing the guy in green?*

A jagged tear in the knee of her slacks made her pause. And brought a possible answer. Perhaps she'd just interrupted a surveillance practicum for a team of rookie FBI special agents!

Scott hustled up and, reaching toward the ground, said, "Hey, what's this? Your guy dropped something."

When he leaned down to pick up what looked like a business card, Eva gazed over his shoulder and decided it was unlikely she'd interrupted a practicum.

She turned around, but a seed of doubt crept in. "Scott, I shouldn't let the runner slip away. He's probably a wanted fugitive."

"Eva," he said, straightening. "Forget him. He's not your concern."

He nudged up her pant leg to reveal a bloody scrape. Pedestrians walking by gave a wide berth to the woman they'd just seen tackle a man. Frustrated at the crazy turn of events, Eva hobbled over to her seat, where she rubbed the back of her knee. It was starting to pulse oddly.

A well-dressed woman approached with a cell phone pressed to her ear, asking Eva, "What just happened? Are you okay?"

Eva began cleaning her knee with an antiseptic wipe she'd gotten from her purse and didn't answer.

She did look up when Scott exclaimed, with a lilt in his voice, "Help has arrived."

"Did one of you call 911?" a uniformed officer asked, hurrying over from her squad car.

The woman with the phone pointed at Eva. "She's hurt."

"Officer, I had a dustup with a man fleeing from two FBI agents." Eva said, trying to stand before quickly sitting down again. "After I tackled him, all three ran away."

"Should I call the EMTs?" the officer asked. "Seems you've had a pretty bad scrape, or maybe a fracture."

"I'm okay." Eva waved her off. "Mostly a bruised ego. I'm with ICE and thought I was helping. I think I've landed in the middle of a drug deal gone wrong or a domestic spat."

The officer pulled out a small notebook. "Maybe imposter FBI agents?"

"When they grabbed the guy, he broke free. They yelled 'Stop FBI,' but when I identified myself as a federal agent, they all three fled."

The officer tapped her pen on a small pad. "Maybe they were all undocumented. Let me get details for my incident report."

"That's unnecessary. I have a short lunch break and am hoping to share it with my husband." Eva pointed to Scott.

The officer smiled grimly. "I'd like to see some ID so I can account for the dispatch."

After seeing Eva's badge, the police officer wrote down Eva's name and address to the local ICE office before stuffing the notebook into her pocket.

"Thanks, Agent Montanna. Enjoy your lunch." The officer turned and left along with the lady pedestrian.

Lowering his voice, Scott quipped, "Eva, I sense you have other ideas about what just happened."

"You know me very well," she admitted. "What I have in mind definitely does not require Metro PD's attention."

"Yet, you have it, thanks to that bystander." Scott lifted up the business card he'd found, holding it by the edges. "Oh, look. It's a Metro pass."

He tried handing it to Eva, which she refused to take.

"No, I don't need it. Besides, I'm hungry. Hope you haven't forgotten our need to talk about Kaley."

Scott fluttered the card in front of her face. "The guy you

tackled dropped this. I thought you might want it, just in case. He's apparently been riding the Metro."

"All right. You convinced me."

She took it and absentmindedly slipped it into her purse.

# Chapter 2

Eva returned to the FBI's Joint Terrorism Task Force (JTTF) office after the harried lunch with Scott, her knee aching. She passed slowly by the various FBI special agents and others on loan from Homeland Security and Alcohol, Tobacco, and Firearms without stopping to chat. Instead, she shuffled directly to Griff Topping's cubicle.

Her longtime FBI partner looked up. Concern lit his eyes as she limped in with her soiled and torn pant leg flapping.

"You look like you've been in a fight. What does the other guy look like?" he asked, scowling.

Eva pulled an empty chair close to his desk before flopping down.

"Can't tell you," she said glumly. "He got away."

Griff studied her face for a long moment. "You're serious, aren't you?"

Eva pulled up her pant leg to display the bloody token of her battle. "Yes, which is why I'm here, hoping you can help me solve this weird puzzle."

For the next few minutes, she briefed Griff on how the two men who identified themselves as FBI agents had turned tail and run once she announced herself as a federal agent.

Eva shook her head. "And the runner got clean away."

"What do you make of it all?" he asked, drumming his fingers on his desk.

"My torn-up knee prevented me from continuing the chase. So, Scott and I took a rare chance to talk about our three kids, Kaley in particular."

Griff ignored her family comments and went right to the heart of the matter. "Is it possible the two guys were bounty hunters chasing down a bail jumper?"

"Not likely." Eva stuck out her jaw. "They wouldn't run from an ICE agent. Here's what I want to know. Were the guys in suits really FBI agents? If so, why hightail it from me?"

Because she'd worked lots of cases with Griff through many years, she knew when he ran the palm of his hand across his moustache, he was puzzling over the strange scenario.

"Did you get a good look at any of them?" he finally asked.

"Yes, for the guy I tackled. But he fled into the Waldorf. Because the two suits looked more professional, I discarded the idea they were drug dealers trying to collect a debt."

"Eva, that might explain why they ran when you shouted, 'Federal Agent.' Or maybe ..."

Griff paused. Raising his bushy eyebrows, he offered, "Maybe the runner was on his way to FBI Headquarters. You know, it's just down the street from where you and Scott were sitting outside. Perhaps those two suits were trying to keep him from going there."

"Never thought about that possibility," Eva mused, rubbing the back of her neck as if it might result in the final answer.

Griff got up and began to pace his cubicle. "Understand, I'm not saying our government's done this, but in some countries around the world, their counterintelligence agents are assigned to watch the embassies of foreign nations. If they see their own citizens approach a foreign embassy, they try to identify them to ensure they're not their own scientists or military personnel trying to become spies for the foreign government."

"But there's only one embassy near the Waldorf, and Canada's not our enemy," Eva replied, frowning. "So, your theory makes no sense."

"I know, but isn't it possible some foreign intelligence services try to keep their citizens from contacting the FBI?"

Eva's eyes widened. "You're onto a possible motive: fearing their people will reveal national secrets to us. The runner looked like he could be from Asia. The guys in suits were farther away, so I can't be sure."

"If I'm right, that might explain why all three ran away from you just a couple blocks from FBI Headquarters," Griff said, leaning against the wall.

"I'll type a summary and describe the three men the best I can. We can determine the time pretty well, and there might be video surveillance of people entering the front door." Eva rose to her feet. "Maybe your Counterintelligence Division is interested in the incident."

Griff dropped his voice to say, "I trust one guy over there. Write it up, and I'll pass it along to Bruce Sterling. He and I have known each other for years. He's a member of my flying club."

"I approve. Knowing who to trust around DC gets harder with each passing day."

Eva headed back to her cubicle. She had plenty of thinking to do before writing her report. She turned on her computer, and with her eyes closed, she lifted up thanks to God that she hadn't been seriously hurt.

"Please God, guide me and help me in these strange and trying times," she whispered.

**EVA STOPPED FOR TAKE-OUT** at their favorite Italian restaurant on the way home. No way she wanted to cook tonight despite the fact Kaley's friend Dylan was coming for dinner.

*Or because of him?* she wondered.

That thought didn't sit well with Eva. While she certainly didn't want to encourage Dylan to become a regular in their home, she did want to be kind.

The problem was the disturbing dream she'd had about him and Kaley last night. Eva had wanted to share the details with Scott at lunch, but her hopes had been dashed by the Runner.

Waiting for the order to be delivered to her car, Eva recalled how, during her life, some of what she had dreamed came true. In these instances, she believed God was working through her mind to prepare her. Eva decided she'd share this dream with Scott tonight and get his opinion.

To distract her mind, Eva toggled through her emails.

One from Griff caught her eye: *Is your report done? Bruce is anxious to follow up.*

Before Eva could type a reply, Kaley called.

"Hi Mom," she chirped. "After supper, Dylan is taking me to a concert at Wolf Trap."

*Oh oh.*

Eva's protective mode pulsed on full alert. In the dream

last night, Dylan took Kaley to a play, and on the way home, they were in a bad car accident because he talked nonstop on his cell phone.

"Who is playing at this concert?" she managed to ask.

Kaley answered quickly, as if prepared for an inquisition, "A swing band playing hits from the forties."

"Ah …" Eva considered how to answer. "Forties isn't really your kind of music. Is it his?"

Kaley quipped, "It's a cheap date. I think they're family season tickets no one wanted."

Trying to put aside anxiety from her dream, Eva considered this was the first Friday of the month, when the Montannas gathered as a family to play games or watch movies together. Because Kaley would soon be a freshman in college, Eva and Scott had decided to allow her certain freedoms. Within limits.

Oh, the chaotic speed of her kids growing up. The pace zoomed faster with each passing day.

"Andy and Dutch hoped to beat their sister on the new foosball table tonight," Eva said.

"I know it's last minute, but Dylan's cousin backed out."

Eva gripped the wheel, feeling forced to relent. "Okay. Don't forget we eat at five-thirty."

"Thanks, Mom. You're the best!"

Mother and daughter hung up just as the server brought out four giant bags of food, a triple order of spaghetti and meatballs along with large salads and garlic bread. Second thoughts nagged. Scott had made it clear at lunch that they should discourage Kaley's relationship with Dylan.

Eva downed the last of the tepid coffee in her travel mug and sped out of the parking lot. What did she really know about Dylan? Kaley met him through a friend. He claimed to be pursuing a major in philosophy and political science at George Mason University. From the few times Eva interacted with him, he seemed overly fascinated by his oddball ideas and showed no support for Kaley's views. He'd never spoken of his family or having faith in God.

Eva drove home to tempting smells of garlic and sauce, all the while pondering why Kaley was always available to

Dylan. Eva pressed the brake hard, jerking to a stop at the red light. She wanted her daughter to become independent and pursue God's plans before involving herself in a serious relationship.

Something else seemed glaringly obvious. With all his modern talk, Dylan was no swing-band, forties-music kind of guy. No, he was glib, self-absorbed, and a creature of the latest social media influencers.

Eva pulled into their driveway, resolving to run Dylan through the website for conducting a background check. The one Griff had given her. First, she cajoled Andy into helping her unload the car, and then headed straight for their tiny home office. She couldn't be too careful with her daughter's future.

# Chapter 3

Eva recruited Andy and Dutch to help set the table in the dining room while Kaley stayed in her bedroom getting ready for her date.

The moment Dutch, his younger brother, dashed into the kitchen looking for more napkins, Andy blurted, "Before Kaley's bizarro boyfriend gets here, you need to know something. I don't like him or his attitudes."

"What don't you like about him?" Eva asked, setting an empty glass at Scott's place.

Andy dropped forks with a clatter and stared at Eva. "Couple things, Mom. Sure you want to know?"

"What is it, Andy? You can tell me," Eva said, concern flashing through her mind over what her oldest son might say.

"Well …" Andy swallowed before telling the tale. "You know the last time he was here?"

"Okay, it was Saturday." Eva nodded to hurry him along before Dutch came back.

"Yeah, well, I overheard him on the phone. Kaley had gone back in the house to find her purse. I happened to be in the garage dustin' off Dad's old Mustang. Dylan didn't see me. He got a call, and he told whoever that he was bringin' a date to a concert. The guy must have thought he meant someone besides Kaley because Dylan laughed and said, 'No, I'm taking the other girl on my dad's yacht on the Chesapeake.'"

"What does that mean?" Eva asked, her hands on her hips.

"Duh, Mom! Dylan has another girlfriend."

"Maybe you're assuming something. He could have been talking about a girlfriend from his past."

Andy lifted his shoulders sharply. "Okay, but listen to this. I'm not assuming he's eighty and too old for Kaley. Why else does he have a handicap parking pass hangin' from his mirror?"

"He does?" Eva was incredulous.

"Yeah." Andy sounded certain of his facts. "It was danglin' there the other day, and he's got no cast on his leg."

Just then, Dutch roared in to dump a pile of napkins on the table before running out again, crying, "Dad's home. Can't wait for foosball!"

Eva put a hand on Andy's shoulder. "Son, let's keep this between the two of us while I give it more thought. Meantime, you finish here while I go check something on my computer."

"You'll see I'm right, Mom."

Eva hurried to their office and closed the door. Her fingers flying across the computer keyboard, she entered Dylan Webb into the background search engine for information on any Dylan in Virginia.

*Bingo!*

Dylan Webb was the son of Maynard and Gloria Webb of Fairfax, Virginia. Eva continued searching and learned Gloria Webb was a criminal defense attorney made famous by achieving an acquittal of Raymond Atlas, a court-appointed conservator who embezzled more than two million dollars from three elderly Alzheimer patients. Dylan's father, Maynard, was a financial advisor and CEO of his own investing company.

Eva remembered reading about the Atlas case. One victim died during the trial, leaving the man's widow penniless. Some local Christian churches started a crowd-funding appeal to help her. Eva wanted to launch more research sites, but in glancing at the wall clock, she saw it was time for dinner. She shut down her computer, appalled to think her precious daughter was dating a young man whose mom profited by freeing an embezzler.

Scott opened the door, treating her to one of his brilliant smiles. "Why are you holed up in the office? Trying to avoid Dylan? He's here now."

"Our Italian supper is ready, but I'm not ready for our daughter to be involved with this kid. Scott, what can we do?"

He reached out a hand and pulled her up from the chair. "We'll keep loving her and praying she discovers his deficiencies before he hurts her. Let's eat. Our lunch this noon seems as distant as the moon."

**SCOTT ASKED THE BLESSING ON** their dinner. In the quiet aftermath, Dylan launched a bomb.

"I don't eat meat," he said, waving a hand over the dinner table. "Or dairy."

Kaley blinked. "Sorry, Mom. I forgot."

"Give me Dylan's meatballs." Dutch held up his plate to Eva.

Sharp retorts blazed through Eva's mind. She pressed her lips together, flashing Scott a doubtful look before telling Dylan, "You are welcome at our table. Pass the spaghetti and meatballs, Kaley."

"Why don't you eat cheese?" Andy asked, reaching for the bowl of parmesan.

"Plants hold the best hope for our future." Dylan lifted his square chin.

Eva studied him as she took the platter from Kaley, who sat smiling beside him. Her friend looked different from the last time Eva saw him. The entire back half of the curly black hair covering his head was now bleached blond.

She couldn't believe it when he slid only a few spaghetti noodles onto his plate. With the tongs, he placed several pieces of lettuce and tomato slices into a small bowl.

The platter was passed around, with everyone else helping themselves to spaghetti and meatballs, all except Kaley. Eva noticed her daughter, who usually loved Italian food, mimicked Dylan. On her plate were a few noodles covered in tomato sauce. She also skipped the parmesan cheese.

Eva's appetite shriveled to nothing. That awful dream floated through her mind, bringing scenes of flashing lights and Kaley crying in pain. This wouldn't do! She must get a grip!

And not be swayed by emotions. She needed to find out more about Dylan, and fast.

She picked up a basket of hot bread, and handing it across the table to Dylan, she enthused, "Perhaps you'll like this fresh bread. The chef uses a recipe from his Italian grandmother. Tell us about your family."

Dylan removed a tiny slice of bread.

Leaning back into his chair with a lopsided grin, he began, "Kaley met my folks. We live in Great Falls. Our summer home's on the Chesapeake near Annapolis. Dad just bought a new boat, a yacht, really. I hope to take Kaley and you all on it one day."

"Do your grandparents live near you?" Eva hoped to keep Dylan revealing his family connections.

"Mom's folks lived in Seattle, where she grew up. My dad's family resides in Manhattan. He grew up near Central Park. Kaley told me she's never been to Central Park, and I want to take her there soon. Maybe this summer."

Eva sipped her water and then asked, "You used the past tense about your mom's parents being in Seattle. Have they moved?"

"Sort of," Dylan said, winding a spaghetti strand around his fork. "When my grandfather died, my grandmother came to live with us."

"I didn't know your grandfather died," Kaley said sharply. "Why didn't you tell me?"

Dylan shrugged. "A guy has to keep some secrets to be interesting, don't you think?"

# Chapter 4

Monday morning started differently than most. Scott fixed an early breakfast for the boys, while Eva headed to the dealership in the family's van for an oil change and service. Kaley followed behind in her bright green VW Bug, which thankfully was still roadworthy. Kaley's summer break before college allowed her to shuttle Eva back home to retrieve her G-car in time to head for work.

After dropping the van and key in the cramped office smelling of grease and oil, Eva jumped in with Kaley for the ride home. Already, Kaley had become a capable driver, and Eva felt comfortable in the passenger seat.

"Thanks for being my chauffeur today," Eva said. "Remember, you're taking your dad to the Metro after you get home. Stay by your phone when he calls to be picked up later today. I'll stop and pick up the van on my way home. I can leave my G-car in the lot, and your dad can take me back after dinner to retrieve it."

"You make it sound complicated. I've nothing else planned for today, so I can do everything, even fix supper."

"I thawed out some chicken thighs. You could put those in the slow cooker with mushroom soup."

Kaley turned sharply at the corner. "Ugh. Chicken. How about I make a brown rice casserole with mushrooms instead?"

"You may have given up meat, but the rest of your family hasn't. Put the chicken in the cooker with the soup, and use the fresh mushrooms for your rice as a side dish. Don't forget to log into your George Mason account and select your first-semester classes. You don't want to be miss the deadline."

"Okay." Kaley checked her side mirror. "I'll work on it later."

"How was the concert at Wolf Trap? Did you like swing music?" Eva asked carefully.

Kaley glanced quickly at Eva. "Not exactly my kind of music. A lot of white-haired people in the audience."

"Did Dylan like the music?"

"Not really. That's probably why his parents gave him

their season tickets. They don't like swing either."

Eva wondered if she and Scott might have enjoyed the music. "Was it well attended?"

"No."

"Then you probably didn't have to park a mile away and walk."

Kaley grinned. "How did you know, Mom? We parked in the front row."

"Someone left a choice spot?"

"No. Dylan got lucky. When his grandfather passed away, he was able to get his grandfather's handicap parking pass."

"How is that a good thing?" Eva probed.

Kaley arched her eyebrows. "Because we didn't have far to walk and weren't late."

They were nearing home. Saddened to have Andy's suspicions confirmed, Eva wondered how best to use this teachable moment.

She cleared her throat. "Kaley, your great-grandmother Montanna had severe arthritis in her hips. It was painful for her to walk in from the parking lot, so she got one of those passes, which helped her greatly."

"I didn't remember that." Kaley admitted, turning into their neighborhood.

"When Grandma died, we destroyed the permit. We could have used it unlawfully, but didn't want to deny a handicapped spot to somebody who needed it."

"Wow. I never considered that. Dylan shouldn't use it either."

"I agree, Kaley. He doesn't sound considerate of others. Maybe you should be alert to other such evidence in his life."

Kaley pulled into the driveway and parked. They sat in silence for a few moments. Eva could almost hear Kaley's mental gears turning.

With her lips drooping, Kaley admitted, "I barely heard any music. Dylan talked constantly about how this weekend he's boating on the Chesapeake. The boat is out of this world. You know, the one he boasted about it being a giant fancy yacht."

"Are you going with him?" Eva asked, worry edging into

her mind. "The weather report predicts strong storms rolling in."

Kaley sniffled and wiped her eyes. "You know what, Mom? He never asked me."

"Fancy yacht, huh? Sounds like his family has money to burn."

Kaley shrugged in silence.

"Have you told him about your mom being a government agent?" Eva asked.

Kaley's head snapped to the right. "No way, Mom. There's a kid in class who admitted his dad's a DEA agent. Everyone avoids that kid like he's the narc. My friends all think you work for the Census Bureau."

"Okay." Eva immediately understood that her daughter was in a precarious place with Dylan Webb. She avoided saying anything more, seeking to encourage Kaley.

So, she reminded her, "Good thing we have the church picnic on Saturday. If he asks you last minute, you made plans of your own."

"I forgot about Saturday's picnic," Kaley said, with no enthusiasm. "Probably will be rained out."

"Didn't you promise you'd play on Dad's baseball team against the church team?"

At Kaley's sullen face and sad shrug, Eva suggested another idea. "What do you say to speeding up our family vacation? Grandpa Vander Goes texted last night. It's calving time, and their calves are due any day. They've invited us to Florida to see their new farm."

"Baby calves?" Kaley squeaked, a new light shining in her eyes. "How soon can we leave?"

**AT THE CHURCH PICNIC ON SATURDAY**, Eva sat beside Scott and their three children gathered on benches across from each other at a long wooden table. Tantalizing smells of burgers and brats sizzling on the grill made her mouth water and her stomach growl.

When Dutch whined, "Can we eat soon?" it was like her youngest son just echoed her thoughts. Too bad she'd chosen this day to skip a hearty breakfast; she'd eaten only an apple a few hours ago.

She dug a peppermint from her fanny pack, which she handed to Dutch. "Okay buddy, this should tide you over until everything's ready."

"We're fading fast." Eva elbowed Scott. "Find out what's causing a delay, please."

He groaned slightly. "I hear you. My stomach feels hollow after working in the yard this morning."

He hurried off to the grills. Her husband must have worked his magic because five minutes later, he let out a whoop and yelled, "Grab your plates, everyone, and bring your appetites."

"Yahoo!" Dutch cried.

He snatched his plate and roared off, snagging the first place in line.

*Such innocence. Such happiness,* Eva thought as she piled extra tomato and lettuce on a burger. She skipped macaroni salad to make room for two ears of sweet corn slathered with butter.

After the delicious meal, Eva drank a large iced coffee while rooted for Kaley and Andy playing baseball with their dad. Although Dutch wore a jersey, he cheered on the sidelines for his dad and siblings. Just when Andy whacked the ball to the outfield, Eva felt her cell phone buzz in her fanny pack. She unzipped the pack and pulled out the phone. It was Griff.

She answered, "We're at the church picnic. Hold on."

Eva hurried over to their van to take his call. She didn't want to miss the fun and told Griff so. He laughed, passed along a brief message, and hung up before she could say good-bye.

She dashed back to watch the final two innings. Kaley ran in from the outfield, all smiles.

"We won!" she chimed, pumping her fist. "Mom, I'm so glad you talked me into coming. Did you see me hit a double?"

"Yes, and you were great!" she said, savoring the victory.

Scott clapped Andy on his back, praising his base hit, and led the family to the dessert table. The pastor and his wife were serving strawberry shortcake to the throng. After squirting a dab of whipped cream on her berries, Eva found a quiet spot to talk with her husband.

"I'm having a blast." He dipped the plastic spoon into his confection. "We should do more fun things as a family."

Eva squeezed his free hand. "That's exactly what we need to decide. I'd like to move up our family vacation this summer."

"Where should we go? Out West to Yellowstone and the Tetons? Or Alaska?"

Eva pointed out that both of those would be too pricey with Kaley starting college. "How about we drive down to see my folks' new farm in Florida?"

"They're in the Panhandle, right?" he asked, stopping his spoon midair.

"Near Panama City. I mentioned baby calves to Kaley, and she's over-the-moon excited. Besides, Mom's been asking me to come. She sounds lonely."

"Okay with me," Scott said good-naturedly. "Call your mom when we get home and decide a good time. I'll need some time to finish up important issues at Defense."

Eva's smile beamed down to her toes. "Scott, you're the best man I've ever known. Let's head to Florida before work heats up too much. Griff just phoned and needs me to write a report for the FBI about those two FBI agents chasing the Runner."

"I'm ready to leave for home, and you can start packing." Grinning, Scott stood and reached out his hand to help her up. "Seriously, do you need my input from what I saw outside the Waldorf that day?"

She nodded, taking his plastic, empty bowl and nestling it into hers. "Yes. I value your input. It's strange how all three guys fled and vanished. I may never know who they are or what I interrupted, but you know me. I sure want to solve the mystery."

# Chapter 5

On Sunday, after an inspiring time of worship and teaching at church, Eva and Scott took the kids out for a fun afternoon at Nottoway Park near Griff's house in Vienna. They picked up grilled chicken sandwiches, spicy fries, and chocolate shakes from a local eatery on the way.

Eva spread a tablecloth over a picnic table beneath the shade of a maple tree while Scott put out the paper plates. He prayed over the meal, and then everyone dug in, with Dutch slurping his chocolate shake loudly. Andy nudged his sister for more room on the bench seat.

When she complained, he shot back, "How did Dylan like going out on his dad's fancy boat yesterday without you?"

Kaley's cheeks turned pale. She thrust her sandwich down on the plate and dashed back to the van. Disappointment filling her heart, Eva reached across the table and touched Andy's arm.

"Son, you knew what you said would hurt your sister. Why say it?"

"Kaley started it by saying she wouldn't move over," Andy looked satisfied with himself.

Scott interjected, "Perhaps Kaley should have given you more room, but instead of asking her, you just banged her with your arm. When she objected, you hit her again, this time with barbed words."

"Kids at school taught me a song," Dutch said, and he sang out, "Sticks and stones may break my bones, but words will never hurt me!"

With an innocent grin, the boy ate his french fries. To Eva, what should be a happy time with her family was turning into a free-for-all. She and Scott traded pained looks.

"I'll talk with Kaley," she announced, getting up from the table.

She picked up her shake and also Kaley's before speeding over to the van, where she found Kaley slumped in the front passenger seat, door open. She swiped at her eyes.

"At least drink your shake," Eva said. "You love

chocolate."

Kaley took it from her, disdain etched across her pretty face. But she sipped the cold drink. Eva finished hers, waiting for her daughter to open up.

"Andy acts mean towards me," Kaley grumbled. "He was never like this before. Is he starting to hang around weirdos?"

"I'm not sure. Dad is talking with him. Tell me what you're thinking about his comment."

Kaley's bottom lip trembled as she explained, "Dylan didn't ask me to go on the yacht. I told you how sad that makes me feel."

"I don't agree with what Andy said or how he said it, but I have an important question for you. You're getting ready to start college with your entire future before you. Perhaps you're too serious about Dylan, who is two years older. Why not step back and consider your options?"

After drinking her shake in silence, Kaley finally climbed from the van.

"You're right, Mom. I had so much fun yesterday playing ball with Dad and my brothers. I won't let Dylan ruin our Sunday time together."

Eva patted her shoulder. "That's my smart daughter. Let's go finish lunch."

They walked back to the picnic table, where Andy slid over, saying, "Kaley, sit here by me. I'm sorry for what I said."

"Okay, I forgive you, and I'm sorry I didn't move down," Kaley replied.

"I almost ate your fries, Kaley, but Dad said I couldn't," Dutch chimed, and everyone burst out laughing.

Eva lightly clapped her hands. "Okay, we've settled back into the loving family that we are, so Dad and I have an announcement. How would you all like to visit Gramps and Gram in Florida and meet some new baby calves?"

"Yay!" Dutch cried. "I wanna see calves and fly kites on the beach!"

"Hoorah!" Andy hooted.

Kaley nodded her head and piped, "I'm in. Hope we go there soon!"

Scott wadded up sandwich wrappers, making crunching

sounds. "Amen to all you said. We'll leave after Kaley's graduation and school gets out."

"Kids, gather your sandals, swimsuits, kites, and flashlights, and we'll have a fun adventure together," Eva said, and cautioning, "so long as you each stay on your best behavior. Any more griping, and we may rethink our plans."

The thought of the kids arguing in the back seat on the long and tedious drive to Florida was not what she or Scott wanted.

"I'll throw away the plates," Andy announced, scrambling up to clear the table.

Kaley grabbed the empty shake containers. "I'll help too."

"Dad, I'll help you wash the van and try not to get you wet like last time!" Dutch said, making a funny face.

On the way home, Eva rejoiced that her family seemed back to normal. And she hoped their trip to Florida would be a blessing to them and her parents.

**AT NOON ON THE FOLLOWING MONDAY**, Eva chose to eat a quick lunch in the conference room rather than go with Griff and colleagues to the café around the corner. Wanting to clean up old files, she finished her PBJ sandwich and carrot sticks and was about to return to her desk when Griff appeared in the doorway.

Eva put her phone in her tote bag, asking, "I thought you were going out for lunch?"

"Yeah, we grabbed a sandwich. Sorry if my call disturbed you at the church picnic."

"Nope. We all had a good time letting off steam." She motioned for him to sit. "How about your weekend?"

He waved off joining her. "Sunday after church, I flew Dawn in my flying club plane over to St. Michael, Maryland. We ate a fabulous crab dinner at a marina."

"You feel refreshed?"

"Yeah, it was good for us both."

"Scott and I are planning a Florida getaway to see my folks."

Griff turned to leave but stopped. "Come to my office. I want to find a digital file. There's something for you to see."

Eva seized her tote bag and followed Griff to his cubicle, where he sat at his computer, his fingers flying over his keyboard.

"Remember the report you wrote after your non-arrest in front of the Waldorf?"

Eva glanced at his computer, questions bombarding her brain. "The one I filed last week?"

"The very one. It's been assigned to Bruce Sterling, my flying buddy. He's the agent on the FBI's counterintelligence squad at the Washington Field Office I told you about."

Seeing no clues on Griff's stoic face, Eva asked pointedly, "And?"

"He's preparing to send you a lead, which he said he'd do first thing this morning."

"So, you're checking to see if you can find it."

"Right. Why wait for Sosa Garcia to discover the lead as part of his supervisory function? If I locate Bruce's report, you'll have a head start working on it."

"I don't want Sosa thinking we've gone behind his back," Eva observed.

Griff continued scrolling. "Bingo! Here it is. I'll print Bruce's synopsis and report. Hey, he also sent a bunch of photos captured off the Waldorf's video surveillance system."

"Here, Eva." He stood from his chair. "Comb through these pictures while I snag the report from the printer. Bruce wants to know if you see any men in the photos involved in your chase."

Eva slid into his chair and began scrolling through surveillance camera pictures. She could see the hodgepodge of photos included multiple angles of people entering and leaving both of the Waldorf's front entrances and service entrances. Eva concentrated first on Asian-looking men in hopes of finding the Runner.

She kept a close eye on the digital clock that showed on the pictures while it advanced. Near the time of her meeting with Scott, she saw a picture of a young Asian man in full stride approaching the hotel's main entrance.

"It's him!" she blurted. "The guy I tackled."

Griff hustled in, carrying several pages of stapled papers.

"Let me see."

"Look at this guy approaching the front entrance," Eva said, fidgeting with the mouse. "When I enlarge the picture to show the background, you'll see Scott with me on the sidewalk, and he's examining my injured knee."

"Wow, once again technology presents us with fantastic evidence," Griff said, leaning forward to look at the photo. "Eva, he looks quite young and in good shape. You may not have been able to catch him in a foot race."

She shrugged. "You may be spot-on, but after he fled, I didn't feel it to be urgent. In fact, I still don't."

"You don't know everything yet," Griff reminded her.

"I can't disagree." She pointed to another of the captured photos. "Look, the same guy is hurrying out an exit. The clock shows it's only forty seconds later."

Griff stood up straight and arched his back with an audible sigh. "I suspect he wasn't a guest and used the hotel for an escape route."

"Hmm … I wonder." Eva scrutinized his features on the screen. "Where was he headed when those other two guys grabbed him?"

"If he was an American suspected of selling secrets and headed toward the Russian Embassy, it's possible the FBI agents might nab him."

Eva interjected, "Russia's embassy is nowhere near there. Only the Canadian embassy is on Pennsylvania Ave. Besides, our suspect looks Asian, not Russian."

"Yeah, you're right," he admitted. "But, there is a large Asian presence in Vancouver, Canada. On the other hand, he was a mere two blocks from FBI Headquarters and headed toward it when you tackled him."

Eva forced her mind to think. She felt like she was stuck in neutral as she tried to piece together this peculiar puzzle. An idea occurred to her.

"Griff, let me ask you, if those two guys were indeed FBI agents, why run when I helped them?"

"That's the million-dollar question. If it was a dark operation, they might be trying to avoid publicity."

Eva tapped her fingers on the keyboard. "Valid point.

However, the FBI would know then who he is, and they wouldn't ask me to identify him in these security photos."

Griff edged toward the screen and, with his cell phone, snapped a picture of the young Asian man.

"There, we have his picture. Bruce and the Bureau can begin checking other nearby surveillance cameras to figure out his route and perhaps get photos of the men claiming to be FBI, like checking the bus and Metro stations."

"Griff, you just reminded me!" Eva began digging through her tote. "Scott found a Metro Smart Trip card right at the spot where I tackled the guy. I stowed it in my purse."

"That could be a huge lead."

Eva tossed the contents of her purse onto Griff's desk, and searching through the miscellaneous mass, she finally gasped, "Here it is."

She picked it up deliberately by its edges and handed the small pass to Griff. "The card might have a latent print and also might show the Metro stations where it was used."

# Chapter 6

Eva poured coffee into two travel mugs, one for Scott and one for herself, early the next morning. He lightly kissed her cheek and reached for his mug.

"I'm off to the Pentagon, sweet pea," he said, his eyes holding Eva's with his. "If we're truly heading to Florida soon, I've got a mountain of paperwork to move."

Eva leaned her head against his shoulder. "You head out. Kaley offered to drive the boys to school, so I'm right behind you. I hope my work doesn't heat up and prevent our leaving for vacation."

Scott pulled out of the driveway, and Eva went to remind Kaley to take her brothers to school. Eva sped in her G-car to the JTTF office in Fairfax, guzzling her coffee at every red light. The first one into the office, she was making a fresh pot of coffee when her desk phone rang.

Who was calling her before 8:00 a.m.? Eva hurried to answer it.

"Agent Eva Montanna," she huffed into the phone.

A monotone voice on the other end said, "Thought I'd get your voicemail. Montanna, be at Headquarters for a meeting with OPR this morning at eleven. Don't be late."

"Ah … who is this calling, so I can make a note in my ledger. What's the meeting about?"

"I'm Director Whidbey's assistant. You'll know what it's about when you get here."

The assistant hung up.

A burning question battered Eva's brain. Why the sudden summons for her to appear at OPR?

When Griff arrived a few minutes later, she told him about being ordered to the Office of Professional Responsibility.

"Can you believe it? Heard scuttlebutt of what's behind this request?" she asked.

He shook his head, narrowing his eyes. "Eva, you know I'm not on the inside at your agency. I have enough trouble keeping up with what's going on at the FBI."

"I wondered if you heard more from Bruce Sterling, your

agent buddy who's working on the Runner. The timing with OPR is suspicious."

"Oh." Griff shifted the subject. "Bruce processed the Metro pass for prints. He has an FBI intelligence analyst checking with Metro to find where it's been used and when. Hopefully we can get security camera data to show who used it and who else was in the area at the time."

**AN HOUR LATER**, Eva's journey to ICE Headquarters brought her a toxic mixture of emotions. Doubt collided with confidence in her thoughts. During her many years of federal service, she'd always been assigned to law enforcement in the Washington, DC area and usually paired with joint agency teams while on loan from ICE. She was perfectly happy working in the JTTF's detached office space with Griff and other colleagues.

She dreaded this venture into her agency's headquarters building. It seemed like she was heading to a foreign nation. She parked her G-car, wondering what she'd face at the upcoming meeting. More than leaving behind the familiar surroundings of the work-a-day investigators who she knew sought justice daily, Eva was entering the cutthroat environment of the executive class, many of whom had limited law enforcement experience in ICE's Field Offices throughout the country.

Eva pocketed her keys. Unease dogged her steps through the front door and as she passed the security gauntlet. A continual question peppered her mind.

*Why am I being ordered to OPR?*

Meeting any OPR Inspector, or headhunters, as they were commonly called, could go awry in a millisecond. ICE Inspectors were the highest ranking of the agents, and each was on a career path into upper management.

After reporting to the reception desk, Eva sat on the edge of an uncomfortable hard-backed chair, trying to figure out if someone she had worked with was being investigated. Or, worse, did OPR have their sights set on Eva?

Soon, she was approached by a man dressed in a dark business suit, knotted tie, and a white shirt. He looked every bit the professional as he extended his hand.

"Agent Montanna, I'm Inspector Ken Conway," he said in an icy tone.

Eva rose to give him a firm handshake. She didn't recognize his name and steeled herself to enter his lion's den as he beckoned her toward the door.

"We'll talk in our conference room," he said over his shoulder.

Eva walked behind Inspector Conway into a smallish room with gray walls and a rectangular table surrounded by six chairs.

Conway pointed to a chair at the end of the table and ordered Eva, "Have a seat."

She noted the woman in a black blazer sitting at the other end of the table.

Conway introduced her as "Inspector Gwen O'Leary."

Inspector O'Leary stood and walked over to Eva for a handshake before returning to her seat. She took the lead in questioning Eva.

"Agent Montana, you're here because we have an issue with an incident in which you were recently involved."

She removed papers from a file lying on the table. She glanced at them and then peered at Eva through her extremely large tortoiseshell glasses.

"This report from the Metropolitan Police Department states you made an arrest on Pennsylvania Avenue and that your prisoner escaped. What surprises us here at ICE is that after checking our entire record system, we can't locate any record of you reporting the arrest. Why not?"

Ken Conway sat mute. So did Eva.

O'Leary intoned with a wry smile. "Perhaps it's because your arrestee escaped. That is embarrassing, but when an agent fails to document the arrest, there's less to be embarrassed about."

Eva felt her blood pressure and temperature rise. Sweat accumulated on her neck beneath her long hair. For the next five minutes, she gave an accurate account of how she tackled the sprinter running from apparent imposters claiming to be FBI agents.

"So, in conclusion," Eva said, running her wet palms across her slacks to dry them off, "it seems strange that in my many years assigned to the FBI Task Force, I've never written a report to ICE of arrests I've made for the FBI. This has always been acceptable under the memorandum of understanding, which exists between the two agencies. Now, for an insignificant incident, I'm summoned to OPR."

Both inspectors shrugged as if they couldn't enlighten Eva in any way. Their stern faces gave her not one clue as to why she was being called on the carpet.

Inspector Conway offered, "Maybe it's because the MPD report can't be matched up to any of our ICE cases."

"I can understand that," Eva replied. "Try and see the facts from my position. I only agreed to give the MPD my name and agency so they could clear their dispatch."

Inspector O'Leary closed the file and stood. "Are you willing to send us a copy of the report you wrote for the FBI so Ken and I can close *our* file?"

Eva was puzzled but also relieved by what seemed to be the sudden ending of the inquisition.

"Absolutely. I will forward it this afternoon."

As Inspector Conway stood, so did Eva. He led her out of the office and to the elevators. He gave her hand a final wimpy shake and left. After pushing the call button, Eva waited, deep in thought. What a baffling interview. For experienced investigators, Conway and O'Leary acted uninformed and unprepared.

Suddenly, the elevator doors swished opened. Eva stepped forward, but then she halted as a smartly dressed woman stepped out.

"Eva Montanna. Long time, no see!"

The years melted away as Eva recognized the woman with coal-black hair and in a matching black suit standing in black heels before her. Unpleasant memories of her ICE Academy days with Regina cascaded through her mind.

"Regina Spire," Eva sputtered. "It's been a long time. Last I heard, you were an ICE Supervisor on the West Coast."

Regina looked Eva up and down, as if disapproving of Eva's casual skirt and blouse.

"Yes, and you were the fair-haired girl who picked the Washington, DC field office after placing first in our academy class. Where else have you served, Eva?"

Feeling the point of a knife in her ribs, Eva replied, "I'm blessed to have remained here ever since."

"Oh, that's unfortunate. I've been in five different offices across the country, but each move was career-enhancing."

Regina's arm swept broadly toward the office from which Eva had come. "Now, I'm in command of all the inspection functions and fifth in command of ICE."

Immediately, Regina spun on her heels, bidding Eva farewell with a wave.

Eva pressed again for the elevator. She hopped on, and when she began her descent, she realized an important fact. Regina hadn't inquired about Eva's reason for being in the building. She had a sinking feeling Regina already knew.

# Chapter 7

Early on Thursday morning in mid-June, Eva and her family loaded the family's van with their gear, snacks, and bottles of water and set out for Florida with Scott behind the wheel. Their destination was the home Eva's parents had recently purchased near Panama City on the Gulf.

"Dad, did you pack our kites for the beach?" Dutch called from the back seat.

"Sure thing, buddy," Scott answered. "We'll do fun things with your grandparents. You know, being on their farm will be lots different from their Richmond townhouse."

"Sounds like work," Andy grumbled.

Miles passed along in silence until Andy asked, "Why do Gramps and Gram raise goats? Do they sell goat milk?"

Eva turned in her seat. "I think the goats came with the farm, but there's only a few."

"So, it's not really a farm?" Andy asked.

"Yes, it is a farm," Scott replied. "They raise cattle and timber. Pine trees. Row after row of tall pine trees. There's not much work to do. They don't feed or milk any trees."

Eva chuckled at Scott's joke, adding, "The property sellers planted sixty acres of tiny pine trees fifteen years ago. In five more years, your grandparents will have them cut down. They'll sell them to a paper mill to make paper or cardboard, and then plant new trees."

"No wonder they bought the farm," Kaley quipped. "All they have to do is put their feet up and watch them grow."

"None of you will be asked to water them or anything," Eva promised.

"Oh no!" Kaley suddenly shouted. "Is it too late to turn around and go home?"

Scott looked into the rearview mirror. "Why? Did we forget something?"

"No," Kaley grumbled. "Dylan just texted and wants me to go with him on his family's yacht on Saturday."

"You already know the answer to that invite," Eva said.

"Your grandparents are expecting us, and we're going to enjoy our family time together."

Andy reached over and touched Eva's shoulder. "Mom, please tell Kaley that Florida is supposed to be a Dylan-free zone."

"I know." Kaley sighed. "I texted him that I'll be on the beach in Panama City, Florida. Don't worry, Andy, the last person I expect to hear from is Dylan, since we'll be so far down in the sticks."

**EVA AND FAMILY PLAYED THE ALPHABET GAME** along the highway, keeping track of various states' license plates.

At noon, Scott announced, "Time for lunch. Who is hungry?"

"Me!" everyone cheered.

Scott drove into a fast-food parking lot, where they piled from the van and stocked up on chicken sandwiches with spicy pickles, waffle fries, and icy drinks. They hadn't been back on the road very long when the sky darkened. The oncoming cars were driving with their lights on.

Scott gestured toward the windshield. "Looks like rain up ahead."

The words were barely out of his mouth when the torrent began. The wipers went from intermittent to full blast. Scott's speed dropped from the usual seventy-four miles per hour to fifty-five in a flash.

After an hour of heavy rain, Scott grunted and sighed. "If this keeps up, we'll arrive at the hotel after dark."

Eva needed to introduce a diversion in a hurry.

"Hey, how about we each think of one thing we'd like to do on this vacation? Start with Dutch, and we all get a turn."

"Search for lost treasure!" her young son chirped.

"Where would we do that?" Andy burst out.

"In the sand," Dutch insisted. "Great Grandpa Marty told me all about pirates being in Florida."

Sounding unconvinced, Andy sneered, "Yeah, hundreds of years ago."

"Be nice," Eva insisted. "Andy, your turn."

"That's easy. Watch the Thunderbirds fly at Tyndall Air

Force Base," was his swift reply.

Kaley laughed. "Shows what you know. The Thunderbirds fly out of Pensacola Naval Air Station. I looked it up last night."

She leaned toward her father, asking, "Dad, you flew for the Navy, right? Tell Andy I'm right and he's wrong."

"Well, Andy's right and you're wrong," Scott said, glancing at the kids in his mirror. "The Thunderbirds are the Air Force exhibition flying team and occasionally fly out of Tyndall Air Force Base. The Blue Angels are the Navy's hotshots, and they're based at Pensacola."

Andy shot back. "That's not super far, is it?"

"No, son, it's not. And it sounds super fun."

Kaley chimed, "My turn. I want to visit the campus of some local colleges."

"Really?" Eva spun in her seat. "You're not thinking of going to college in Florida? My little girl has to stay closer to home."

"Hahaha, Mom, you should encourage her to get away from Dylan," Andy offered.

"More like getting away from you!" Kaley cried.

"I'd like some peace in the car with all this rain pouring down," Scott objected.

"I can take over driving," Eva said.

Scott shook his head. "No, I'm okay."

"I searched the web for schools near Gramps and Gram's. I could be at college but still near family," Kaley went on to explain.

Thoughts of Kaley attending college so far away took Eva by surprise. Given the back and forth in the car and Scott's request for quiet, she'd postpone any more counseling of Kaley until they were alone.

"Mom, what's your fun idea?" Dutch asked, interrupting Eva's worry about her kids growing up too fast.

"Everything you guys just said," Eva answered, tossing a sideways glance over her shoulder. "And Gram hinted they've got a special day trip for us. That sounds great, right?"

"Yes, honey, it does," Scott replied, flashing her a brilliant smile.

# Chapter 8

As they left the hotel early the next morning, the sky was still overcast. At least the roads were dry, permitting Scott to recover some lost time. The family acted more subdued after eating a full breakfast of waffles, eggs, and fruit from the buffet. Eva relaxed against the seat back, enjoyed the time of quiet and introspection, and not once thought about work.

"Yay! The sun's out," Kaley announced hours later as they approached the Florida Welcome Center.

Scott glided into a parking spot, and everyone headed for the restrooms. Eva waited for Kaley, who dried her hands by waving them in the air.

When they came out, Kaley asked, "Where are the guys?"

"Probably in the welcome center," Eva suggested. "They typically serve food in there."

"Sweet, Mom. Let's see. I can't believe I'm hungry again."

Eva and Kaley joined them in sampling free orange and grapefruit juice and collecting coupon brochures for theme parks, pristine beaches, and restaurants. On the way back to the van, Kaley removed her sweatshirt and twirled around.

"Wow! We're in a different world. We should move to Florida."

Scott laughed and handed out granola bars. "The tourism board would love to see the effect of its free OJ on you, girl."

Back on I-95, the van stayed quieter, as Eva had put Dutch in the middle seat to ease the constant friction between Kaley and Andy. The teens perused the brochures for places they wanted to visit on vacation.

Andy read out a warning to the others, "Says here, wherever there's standing water, ponds, and lakes, alligators are lurking."

"Great," Dutch added. "Maybe we can catch one."

Scott looked into the rearview mirror. "Not so fast, Crocodile Dundee. You stay away from them. They get as long as twelve feet and are very dangerous."

Their drive transitioned to Interstate-10, heading west

toward Pensacola, but Dutch still had alligators on his mind. Suddenly, he pointed down the road ahead.

"Dad! Look out! An alligator's in the road."

Eva pointed too. "He's right. Cars are swerving around it."

When the entire family strained to get a good look, Scott started laughing.

"That's no alligator. It's a tire tread from a blown truck tire."

"Dutch's imagination goes wild," Andy griped.

Eva jumped in. "We all saw it and thought it was an alligator."

"Those tire-gators are dangerous if a car runs over one," Scott said. "It can damage car tires or the bottom of a car."

Not much time had lapsed before Scott announced, "Look! Another tire-gator on the road."

After that, Eva and her family rode through the Florida Panhandle, each lost in their own thoughts, with Dutch occasionally interrupting the silence to add another tire-gator to his count.

"Yikes!" Andy exclaimed, "See all those trees blown down. They're in huge heaps!"

Eva turned to look out the side window and saw the giant logs and trees that had once stood tall and proud.

"Wonder what happened?" she mused aloud.

"It's from the hurricane that hit Panama City a few years back," Scott answered in sober tones. "Remember, our church helped raise funds to rebuild the church down here."

Eva nodded. "Yes, which is the church where Mom and Dad attend."

"Hey, is that big bird an eagle?" Dutch asked from the middle back seat.

Andy shrugged off his younger brother's question. "Nah. It's a dumb crow."

"Will we see any eagles, Dad?" Dutch insisted on knowing. "My teacher showed us a nest someplace in Florida with baby eagles."

"We'll be sure to look," Scott promised, as he drove along a winding road.

"Look at those giant spider webs hanging from the trees,"

Andy said. "Do they have huge spiders here or what?"

Dutch gasped. "Giant spiders? Yuck!"

"That's Spanish moss," Kaley corrected. "It's a plant that grows in the air and attaches to trees."

"Are we moving to Florida, Mom?" Dutch asked. "I heard Kaley say so back there."

"We're here for a visit," Eva answered calmly.

Considerable time passed, and then she announced, "Okay, kiddos, get your things together. We're almost there."

Andy peered out the window. "Can't be. I haven't seen a single house in the last twenty miles."

"Put on your shoes," Eva ordered. "It's three more miles."

"Mom, look for yourself. There's nothing around us but forests," Kaley differed.

"Did you forget your grandparents live on a timber farm?" Scott countered. "This isn't forest land."

Eva nodded. "Your dad's right. Look at how these trees grow in straight lines. We're surrounded by timber farms."

"There's no houses around here," Andy insisted. "Are we camping out? I forgot my new flashlight."

They passed a two-track drive leading into the woods between rows of trees, and Eva pointed, explaining, "See the mailbox? It means a timber farmer lives way back off the road amid the crop of trees."

Scott turned sharply and then slowed as they continued down a paved, narrow county road. When he set his turn signal for a right turn, Eva said excitedly, "Look, everyone! There's Gramps and Gram's mailbox."

Scott turned onto the hard-packed gravel two-track drive, aiming their van down the drive hugged by tall pine trees that were as straight as telephone poles. For as far as Eva could see, the driveway continued.

"At the tee intersection ahead, we turn there," she told Scott.

They turned, and a wide, grassy opening appeared among the pines. There in the meadow stood a beautiful brick ranch home with a three-stall garage. Several purple flowering trees dotted the yard.

"Wow! There is civilization here," Kaley exclaimed. "Look

at the pretty lilac bushes.”

“Those crepe myrtle trees are really lovely,” Eva said softly.

Scott nodded to a modern pole building. “Gramps even has a barn.”

“And a tractor,” Andy added, sounding like he wanted to drive one.

The gravel driveway transitioned into asphalt, and Scott stopped in front of the house. Before they could even get out of the van, Grandma Vander Goes was already standing by the passenger side, waving. Eva hopped out and fell into her mom’s arms.

“Mom, it’s been too long since I’ve seen you,” Eva said, tears fluttering on her lashes.

Her mother returned a warm hug. Then Eva’s dad rushed over from the direction of the barn.

After many hugs all around and a happy reunion, he said brightly, “You’ve been driving all day. Before we feast on Marcia’s supper, who wants to see the new calf born last week? She’s a tiny thing still.”

“I do!” Dutch chimed.

“Me too!” Andy said without missing a beat.

Scott pocketed the car keys. “Count me in.”

And so, the Montanna and Vander Goes families hustled to a rich, green pasture behind the barn, where a white and brown speckled cow grazed, her calf lying in the grass beside her. Eva’s heart filled with joy at the tender scene.

This trip to the Panhandle of Florida and escaping the snarls and hurly-burly of Washington was exactly what her spirit needed to be refreshed and restored. She lifted a silent prayer of thanks to God for His wonderful blessings.


**DINNER AROUND THE TABLE** gave them time as a family to catch up and enjoy a splendid meal of homemade meatballs piled atop spaghetti mixed with sliced mushrooms and thick marinara sauce. The aroma of toasted garlic bread with bits of garlic wafted around the large farmhouse table.

“Dad, this new table is stunning,” Eva said, reaching for another slice of bread. “And Mom, everything is delicious.

Wish I had gotten here sooner to help with dinner."

"Our neighbor Zion made this table from an oak tree," her father explained. "Wait till you meet him. His background is similar to yours."

"In what way?" Eva asked.

Grandpa Vander Goes lifted an eyebrow, his eyes sparkling. "He might tell you about it when he stops by. When not at his part-time job, Zion spends his time building furniture in his workshop or out among the trees. He's taught me and your mom much about raising pine."

"Gramps," Dutch interjected, smacking his lips. "Can I have another meatball? They're really good!"

They all chuckled in good humor, including Kaley, who asked for another meatball, too. When Eva glanced at Scott, he smiled at her with warmth in his eyes.

*He must also see our daughter is becoming more like herself, being away from Dylan's clutches,* Eva thought.

"Even more than this wonderful homemade meal," Gramps quipped. "I'm enjoying being all together as a family."

"Here, here," Scott replied, twirling spaghetti on the end of his fork.

Finally, after the last crumb was eaten, Gramps pushed his chair away from the table, "Boys, how about we leave the cleanup to the ladies? I've got things to show you in the barn."

"Wait," Kaley wailed. "I'm not a lady yet and want to see what's in the barn."

"Be sure to come back for dessert," Gram said, flashing a smile.

Gramps led the way, pointing toward a clearing beyond the rows of pine trees. "See those cattle? They're Florida Cracker cattle, and are rare and somewhat protected."

"Do they eat crackers?" Dutch asked, with wide eyes. "I'll go ask Gram for some."

Their grandfather laughed heartily. "No. They mostly graze on the grass in the field. Here, I'll show you why they're called Crackers."

They entered the pole barn, where he strolled to a large timber post rising toward the roof. From a peg, he removed a coil of braided leather.

"Follow me," he said and stalked outside of the barn.

Here, he uncoiled the whip, and with the straight handle in his hand, the six-foot whip dangled on the ground and trailed behind him. With a quick jerk, he extended his arm forward and cracked the whip in the air, like the sound of a firecracker popping.

"Wow!" Andy shouted. "That's cool."

Again, Gramps swung the whip behind him and out to his side. Each time the whip reached its full extension, it cracked loudly.

"Whips like these were used by Florida cowboys to move cattle like mine. They didn't strike the cows, mind you. But, the sound of the crack caused the animal to turn in the intended direction of the cowboy."

"So, that's why your cows are called Crackers?" Kaley asked.

"Yes. You see, these cattle are descendants of cattle brought by settlers from Spain in the sixteenth century, which gave the settlers a food source. Since then, they've been crossbred with other breeds because they're healthier and parasite-free."

He pointed to a lone black cow in the distance. "They can be brown, tan, dappled mixes, or even black. These have been purchased through a state-run program to assure the Cracker breed remains from the bloodline of the original Spanish imports."

He cracked the whip once more. "You kids can practice with this whip, but be careful because it can really hurt if it hits someone."

"Your farm is amazing," Scott said, adding, "and it looks like your trees are unharmed from the hurricane."

"It's a blessing to us. This week, y'all can explore the farm and animals. We'd better hustle back for some of Gram's favorite treat, some black cow."

After hanging the whip back on the post, he led his Scott and his grandchildren back toward the house.

"Is that why there's only one black cow left in the field?" Andy asked.

Gramps roared with laughter. "Oh no. You'll be surprised. She'll have to show you."

# Chapter 9

After everyone returned to the house, Eva scooped vanilla ice cream into a large frosted mug, with her mother pouring cold root beer over the top, making a frothy confection. Gram dipped in a long spoon and straw before handing the creamy treat to her youngest grandson.

"Where's the black cow?" Dutch looked around. "Gramps said you're making us some."

Gram chuckled. "Look in your hands. That's what you're holding!"

"We also call it a root beer float," Gramps explained. "A soda maker from Colorado invented this fizzy dessert after seeing the snow-capped Cow Mountain. So, he named it a black cow. Try it, buddy."

Dutch hurried to the table where he spooned out some of the ice cream. Then he drank from the straw, proclaiming, "It's super good."

"Dad, you used to make these for us on hot summer nights," Eva said softly, her heart touched by such happy memories.

The sun set and dusk settled onto the farm. Kaley went to one of the guest bedrooms to unpack, and the boys dragged their suitcases up the steps in the garage to what Gramps called 'the barracks.' For the first time since their arrival, Eva and Scott had some alone time to visit with Eva's folks. Her dad explained why he bought the sixty acres, with forty acres of nearly harvestable, disease- and pest-resistant pine trees.

"It appears you are both loving Florida," Scott said.

Clifford and Marcia both nodded as one, with her mom adding, "Of course, we miss you all, but not the zooming traffic or high crime that's happening in DC and Virginia."

"I should check on the boys to make sure they're settling in."

Eva strode from the living room, and at the top of the garage stairs, she opened the door into the finished attic. She looked out the dormer over the nearly-dark expansive lawn and driveway leading back through rows of tall pines back to the road.

"Look, Mom." Dutch pointed to his upper bunk bed. "Next time, we can bring four friends."

Eva admired the spartan military décor, which did resemble a barracks. Three military-type upper and lower bunks were lined up along the rear wall. Small dressers were placed on each side of the dormer. Air Force and Army insignia added to the ambiance.

"I don't see a bathroom for you guys."

Andy pointed out the door. "The bathroom's down in the garage and even has a shower. Dutch is right, we could bring friends here."

"Better not let your sister see this, or she might want dibs on it." Eva stifled a yawn as she headed for the stairs. "You two get to bed. Gramps has big plans for us tomorrow."

Eva felt her phone whirl in her shorts pocket as she descended the stairs. The message on the screen was from Griff: *No hurry. Phone me when you have time for an update.*

Knowing Griff, she thought now would be a good time. Eva slipped into the house and retreated to the other guest bedroom. She plunked down on the custom-built wooden chair she remembered from her youth. She called Griff, and he answered on the second ring.

"Is this a good time to talk?" he asked.

"We arrived at my folks earlier, and I can talk," Eva said. "What's up?"

"Where exactly do your parents live?"

"Near Panama City. Remember, I told you they bought a sixty-acre timber farm here."

"Panama City is where Dawn and I met and began courting. She was a federal probation officer, and I went down there to interview one of her parolees in Apalachicola."

"How could I forget?" Eva chuckled. "Your text said you have an update."

"Agents have determined your runner purchased the Metro card at Reagan International Airport, forty minutes before you tackled him. He then took the Metro to the Federal Triangle stop next to the Waldorf. He was most likely heading for FBI Headquarters."

Eva was impressed and told Griff, "It's great you found all that out. Sounds like he'd just flown in from somewhere."

"That's what we suspect," Griff said. "Agents are checking manifests for all flights landing within the hour before he bought his card. They're looking for Asian names and reviewing security video to match the guy pictured at the Waldorf."

"I'm happy to hear the investigation is moving along. Any other developments?"

"Yeah, two things. They found a latent print on the Metro pass, but have nothing to compare it with."

"And the second thing?" Eva stifled another yawn.

Griff dropped his voice a notch. "Eva, a call came into our group from ICE OPR wanting to speak to the supervisor. The call was given to our boss, Sosa Garcia, and the female inspector wanted a copy of the report you wrote about the Runner. What do you make of it?"

Eva thought she detected a note of concern in Griff's voice.

"Not sure," she replied, thinking over the implications. "I told the inspectors I'd get them a copy but failed to do so before our trip. I wonder why they didn't simply remind me?"

"Sosa told me something else that I didn't like hearing. The inspector said she couldn't understand why you were even detailed to our task force and asked if you were critical to our mission."

Eva drew in a sharp breath. "That's weird."

"Sosa and I agreed, but he told them your report went to the FBI Counterintelligence Division. He'll get a copy for you, so you can give it to OPR."

"Have any good news?" she snapped back.

"Eva, it's not really bad news. She's probably just a rookie inspector still feeling her way along."

Eva shook off any gloom. "You're probably right, Griff. Thanks for the heads-up. Keep me advised, okay?"

"I've got your back as always, partner. My eyes and ears are staying wide open. How long will you stay in Florida?"

"I should be back next week and can speed up the time if

things heat up. Let me know."

He promised to keep her in the loop. Eva hung up, setting aside her phone, and wondered what power plays were going on behind her back in Washington. She'd barely mentioned to Scott the summons to OPR, not wanting to worry him with all they had to do to get ready for vacation.

Should she tell him about Griff's info or keep the inspector's unnerving questions to herself?

**TEMPTING SMELLS OF FRYING BACON** wafted through the house on Saturday morning. Eva gathered with her family around the long dining room table. Eva poured freshly squeezed orange juice for everyone, and a praise song erupted from her lips.

"Eva, we sang that song last Sunday in church," her mother said as she set out pancakes and syrup. "By the way, where's my youngest grandson?"

Andy pulled out a chair to sit at the table. "Dutch is zonked out. He's that way at home too most Saturdays."

"He'll miss his breakfast," Gram objected.

Eva slipped into her chair. "He's fine. He needs rest after the long trip. We'll save pancakes and sausage for him."

They closed their eyes as Gramps prayed, "Lord God, thank You for keeping our family safe on the roads and for the bountiful food before us. Your mercies are new each morning. Show us Your presence as we will soon be exploring Your Creation. Amen."

No sooner did Eva open her eyes than Andy started gushing over the neat barracks. "Gramps, can my buddies and I visit the farm some—"

His voice was drowned out by a tremendous roar that shook the entire house.

Andy bolted from his chair to look out the window, shouting, "Where are they?"

"I'd like to see those jets." Scott hustled out the front door.

The loud sounds of several low-flying jets waned, and Scott returned to the house. Suddenly, Eva heard a loud thump from the direction of the garage and the pounding of running feet. The door from the garage burst open, and a pajama-clad Dutch ran into the room, his eyes as big as saucers.

"Dad! What was that?" he cried.

Laughter rolled from Gramps, and he held his belly. "That's our alarm clock."

He walked over to his grandson Andy, who was still gazing out the window, and asked him, "Sure you want to bring your friends here to stay at the barracks? Now you know what it's like to live close to a military base."

Dutch ran to his mother for a hug. She patted his back, telling her dad, "You should have warned us. Who are they?"

Gramps pointed toward the rear of the house. "Tyndall Air Force Base is a few miles away. It's the home of the 325th Fighter Wing, and their F-22 fighter pilots frequently fly over us."

"Cool," Andy chimed. "Can we go see them?"

It must have been part of Gramps' plan because he jumped on the idea.

"We'll take you kids for a ride this afternoon and show you around town while your folks settle in here and relax."

Scott objected. "I don't need settling in. I'm going to see the fighter jets with you."

"I stand corrected. Your mom can settle in with Gram," Gramps added, smiling.

Later at dinnertime, the afternoon venture was all the talk. Gramps, Scott, and the kids had driven around Panama City. The kids were impressed with the beach and overwhelmed by how close the public streets were to Tyndall Air Force Base.

Kaley was really wowed. "Mom, did you know one of your favorite actors served at Tyndall during the Second World War?"

"Who's that? Greer Garson?"

"No. I mean male actors."

"Oh. That would be Clark Gable. Did he train there?"

"Yeah," Andy interrupted. "It was a gunnery base, named after a World War One vet from Florida. He won a Silver Star."

Eva smiled. "Sounds like Gramps is a professional tour guide."

Andy announced, "Yeah, our tour guide parked across

the road from the Air Force Base, and we saw a bunch of fighter jets. We parked so close we could see a pilot climbing into his jet, but we waited and waited. He never did blast off."

"Wrong!" Kaley objected. "I think I saw a bun. She was a lady pilot."

"It was really cool. Brought back many memories," Scott intoned.

Kaley reached for the basket of bread. "The beach is nice, Mom. This is a fun place to live. Doesn't ICE or the Pentagon have jobs down here for you and Dad?"

"One has to wait for retirement to enjoy all God has bestowed upon us, right, Marcia?" Gramps said, passing around a dish of rice.

"Oh, I'm not sure," Eva's mom answered. "Maybe Scott could get reassigned to Tyndall as the Public Information Officer."

Eva interjected, "With a big pay cut. You kids would have to set up lemonade stands."

Kaley ate the last of her chicken kabob and then changed the subject. "I'm thinking of applying to Florida State University in Tallahassee."

"Seriously?" Eva set down her empty glass of lemonade.

Doubts invaded her mind. Was Dylan Webb somehow behind this? But how could he be? He went to college in Northern Virginia.

Kaley looked at her mom, determination burning in her eyes. "Mom, it's something I've thought of since we got here, like it's my future. I can't explain it."

"I like you considering your options," was Scott's reply.

*So much for his support*, Eva thought.

"Here's an idea." Gramps refilled Eva's lemonade. "FSU has a campus in Panama City, not far from here. Gram and I can drive you to see the local campus one day while you're here. It's right on the Gulf."

Eva noticed Kaley sported such a genuine smile; she didn't have the heart to pour cold water on the idea.

# Chapter 10

Sunday worship at her parents' country church was inspiring for Eva as they praised God together as a family. Pastor Dobson and his wife greeted Marcia and Clifford's daughter with enthusiasm, saying how thankful they were for her parents and their giving service at the church.

Scott grilled steaks for lunch on her dad's grill, and then they all headed to walk the fishing pier at the beach, making sure to apply sunscreen and wear floppy hats. Boats sailed by, giving Eva a peaceful feeling.

Her father arced his arms across the sparkling ocean beneath them. "We're all signed up to take a dolphin cruise tomorrow after we tour the FSU campus."

"Will we really see dolphins?" Kaley asked, a smile spreading across her face. "I can't wait to tell Dylan. He doesn't see dolphins in the Chesapeake!"

"Dylan, Shmylan," Andy grumped, folding his arms.

Eva sought Scott's eyes, but he was engrossed in telling Dutch how the tide came in and out. Later, after supper, Gram fixed her famous black cows for dessert. Eva refused to worry over the extra five pounds she was sure she'd already gained. As the kids played board games with their grandparents, Eva asked Scott to join her on the porch.

They sat next to each other on wicker rockers, watching the Master Painter paint the sky into vibrant shades of gold and orange.

"I haven't given work much thought these past few days, which feels weird and wonderful at the same time," Eva admitted.

Scott reached for her hand. "These quiet and joyful times together will give me the fuel to keep on going at the fast pace when we're back."

"Well said. I am concerned that Kaley keeps talking about Dylan. I'd hoped the distance would cause her to forget about him."

"Give her a chance to sprout her wings, Eva. We've raised her right, and I believe she'll soon come to her senses."

"From your lips to God's ears," Eva said softly. "I mean that seriously. Tonight, let's pray more for Kaley and all our children to walk the narrow path and keep their faith in God strong."

**MONDAY TURNED OUT TO BE A FULL AND FUN DAY,** with the grandparents driving the kids to the FSU Campus and Eva and Scott following behind. They stopped at the admissions office, where Kaley and her parents met with a friendly advisor who gave them an application and her email address for questions.

She gave Kaley a map of the campus, so afterward, they walked around and scoped out the various lecture halls, the Center for Innovation, and the bookstore. By the time they were finished, Kaley was convinced this college was for her.

"Especially with Gram and Gramps inviting me to stay in the barracks above the garage," she told Eva, her eyes twinkling.

"We'll have a good long talk later with your dad," Eva replied.

They stopped for soup and sandwiches at a bistro near campus. Dutch ate every bite of his pancakes with strawberries and whipped cream. Then they sped home to get ready for the dolphin cruise on the double-decker, glass-bottom boat.

When they were settled onboard, the captain explained, "We'll be motoring through the Grand Lagoon, into St. Andrews Bay, and then out the Pass to the edge of the Gulf. These waters are home to common dolphins and bottlenose dolphins."

"Dolphins swim in pods of about ten, so keep a lookout," Gramps added.

Eva sat next to Scott on a cushioned seat large enough for two. She watched the buildings along the shoreline grow smaller. They must be heading into the Pass. She inhaled the crisp, salty sea air, feeling as free as one of the seagulls floating above her head.

Scott tucked her hand into his, whispering, "Eva, this is marvelous. I'm glad work pressures didn't keep us from taking a vacation together."

"I agree. And I can better understand why Mom and Dad moved here."

"Something's swimming!" Dutch cried, hurrying to the side of the boat.

Eva joined him at the railing and, through the plexiglass beneath the railing, spotted the water breaking beneath the bluish-gray backs and dorsal fins of two swimming mammals.

"Dad! They're leaping!" Andy hollered.

The dolphins played and jumped over the wake created by the boat plowing through the calm water. They kept pace with the boat for a few minutes before disappearing as quickly as they had arrived. Eva enjoyed the rest of the cruise and watched the sunset with Scott.

"Tonight, the sky is turning purple and pink," she said. "It's so breathtaking out here on the water."

Joy filled her heart, and Eva vowed to remember this moment as one of the most blessed of their family time away.

**TUESDAY DAWNED SUNNY AND HOT.** Eva and Scott drank coffee, the two of them relaxing on the veranda. Her mom called them in for breakfast. After Gramps said grace for the meal, Andy asked if more fighter jets might fly over the farm.

"I hope so, son," Scott replied. "I enjoy being reminded of my days as a Navy pilot."

Eva understood his desire for flying and the memories of his years in the service. The words had barely left her husband's mouth when a loud roar erupted outside, sounding to Eva more like the roar blasting from the race track her dad took her to as a teen.

Dutch stiffened. "Are the jets back?"

"Nope." Gramps shook his head. "Marcia, put on more coffee. Zion's coming."

"It doesn't sound like the trumpet of the Rapture," Kaley quipped.

"Hah! That's a good one, Kaley." Her grandpa slapped his knee. "Nope, Zion's our neighbor from the tree farm across the road. He loves to drive his noisy quad. It has no muffler."

Gramps opened the door before Zion could knock and said, "Hey, neighbor, come in and meet my kids. They're here from the seat of government."

A tall, thin man wearing jeans and a tee-shirt, a straw cowboy hat, and cowboy boots squeezed past Gramps. "As I offered, I brought my quad over so your family can buzz around these parts with you."

"Many thanks. Let me introduce you." Gramps turned to the others, wearing a grin. "This is my across-the-road neighbor, Zion Adelman. He, like you, has spent his share of time in Washington."

Zion lifted his hands in the air and smiled.

"Our daughter, Eva Montanna, is the Special Agent with ICE," her father enthused, pointing to Eva. "And my son-in-law here, Scott Montanna, is the Press Secretary for SecDef at the Pentagon."

Zion squared his shoulders and snapped an exaggerated salute to Scott. "Glad to meet you."

Pointing to the kids, he inquired, "Are these the quad drivers for the week?"

"Indeed." Gramps smiled upon his grandchildren. "Meet Kaley, Andy, and Dutch."

"I've heard so much bragging about y'all; it's good to finally meet," Zion replied. "I started out my adult life in the Air Force and finished my career here at Tyndall as a colonel, but Scott, I too spent time at the Pentagon along the way."

Gramps added, "Zion tried out retirement by growing timber but found watching trees grow is boring. So, now he's back working as a civilian at Tyndall."

"Only as needed." Zion turned toward the door. "Nice to meet and hope to see y'all some more with my wife, Noelle. Meanwhile, enjoy this area and the quads."

Soon, the guys were on the quads, zooming along the trails. Eva stayed behind to help her mom make chili for dinner, which turned out to be a rousing time as the kids talked nonstop about their adventures among the trees.

"Way up in the sky, I saw a bald eagle," Andy announced proudly.

Kaley pushed out her bottom lip. "Eagles aren't around

here."

"Yes, they do live in Florida," Gramps said, laughing. "And that was an eagle your brother saw. I spotted its white tail feathers as it soared overhead."

"The eagle was too high up to see," Dutch exclaimed before chiming in a sing-song voice, "Kaley has a boyfriend."

All eyes turned to Kaley.

"Anything you want to tell us?" Scott asked, crumbling crackers into his chili bowl.

Kaley flipped her hand dismissively. "Not true. Dylan called this afternoon. He's nearby to see his uncle and wants to know if we can get together."

"What's he doing around here?" Eva asked, her nostrils flaring.

Kaley shrugged, and Gram offered, "We'd love to meet him. Invite him to dinner."

"Don't get the wrong idea, Mom," Eva objected. "This kid is older than Kaley and not her type."

"What is Kaley's type?" Gram asked, raising her eyebrows.

Eva was quick to respond, "I haven't decided yet, but it's not him."

"Good. Let's get Dylan here, so we can all examine him," Gram quipped.

"Okay, Mom." Eva gave in. "Kaley, invite him so he can spend more time with your family."

Eva drank the last of her sweet tea while thinking of ways to best quiz Dylan without making it an inquisition. She also intended to talk with Scott and her mom to be sure they didn't miss any of his disqualifying faults.

Somewhere in the back of Eva's mind, a piercing thought lingered.

Was she being too hard on Kaley's friend? After all, he was coming all the way to Florida to see Kaley. That might be a positive thing. Or was it?

# Chapter 11

On Wednesday, Gramps let out a "Whoopee!" as he took off on Zion's noisy quad with Andy sitting on the back. Meanwhile, Scott drove Dutch around on Gramps' smaller quad. Eva was gone, helping Marcia pack up meals at church for a family whose father was injured at Tyndall AFB.

"Gramps, can I drive Kaley on the quad? Please!" Andy asked more than a few times.

Eventually, he gave in to his grandson, warning, "Stay on my property."

Gramps kept an eye on them from his seat on the veranda. Andy and Kaley had just returned and hopped off the quad when a young man driving a Ford Mustang convertible pulled close to the house.

"Ugh, Dylan's here," Andy grumbled.

Gramps walked down the steps to greet him. "Dylan, you're welcome to help Kaley and her brother Andy with their chores. Here, I'll show you what I mean."

"Um … " Dylan frowned. "I wanted to take Kaley for a ride in the convertible."

"Did you drive all the way here in that car from Virginia?"

"No, I flew into Panama City and rented the car. Isn't it a beauty?"

"No, siree! Kaley stays here," Gramps insisted. He raised his arm, "Come on."

At his instructions, the kids and Dylan walked among the rows of tall pines and raked long pine needles into piles, which would be spread around planting beds along the house.

Gramps leaned on his rake. "Kaley, if you'll take Dylan on the quad and zip across the road to Zion's farm, you'll find a small trailer. Zion isn't home, but said we can use it. Just hook it to the quad and bring it back here for hauling this pine straw up to the house."

**KALEY JUMPED ONTO THE QUAD**. She drove down the long drive to Zion's, Dylan holding on behind her.

She asked Dylan loudly, "Why are you visiting your

uncle?"

"My mother asked me to," Dylan said, clinging to the seat behind Kaley while the quad bounced along. "Since you're here, I figured now's a good time."

Kaley liked the sound of that. "Have you seen him yet?"

"Yeah. I'm staying with him, but wanted to see you."

Kaley skidded to a halt near Zion's small barn.

"Is that the trailer?" Dylan pointed beyond her face. "It's hooked on the back of that tractor."

Kaley stood beside Dylan, staring as she considered the large bolt and nut securing the trailer to the tractor.

"Now what should we do?" she muttered.

Dylan walked straight for the pole barn. "Must be a wrench in there."

Kaley helped Dylan slide open the door to the rich aroma of alfalfa and hay. The light from the skylights above was dim, but a switch on the wall provided enough light for them to search among the tools.

"In all these tools on this giant work table, I don't see any wrenches," Kaley declared. "Do you?"

Dylan shrugged. "Not really."

"You keep looking," Kaley said, heading for the door. "I'll run back and get some from Gramps."

Only ten minutes passed between the time Kaley sprayed gravel leaving and then skidded to a stop back at the barn. Dylan raised his empty hands before sliding the barn door shut behind him.

Kaley raised two wrenches in the air, proclaiming a victory shout, "Yahoo!"

"Let's see if I can get this thing to work." Dylan reached for the biggest wrench.

Kaley supervised over his shoulder, watching him work the wrench and free the small utility trailer from the tractor. Soon, the pair were back on the quad with the trailer bouncing behind them. Kaley giggled all the way back across the road. She liked Dylan being here.

*Perhaps going to college here in Florida isn't in my future after all,* she thought.

**LATER THAT EVENING,** when Gram was making chicken tender salads, Eva's phone whirled in her pocket. She slid it out. Surprisingly, her partner, Griff, had texted her photos.

Eva read his brief message: *Photos of the Runner in Panama City and Atlanta airports on the way to Reagan airport in DC.*

She scrutinized the airport security camera photos and saved each one onto the camera roll in her phone. She then toggled back to the earlier picture of the Asian man who had fled into the Waldorf Hotel to escape her clutches. Bingo! The possibility that her prey had actually been in Panama City collided with her memories of the recent family frivolity.

A thought popped into her mind at the speed of light. The photos showed that the Runner appeared to be Asian. However, Eva could not ignore the fact that he might be an Asian American pilot in the U.S. Air Force. The man was slender and lean, built like a fighter pilot.

Eva was back in investigative mode. She must find out.

"Dad, did you say Zion works with Air Force pilots who are training at Tyndall?"

Clifford looked up from the map he was showing Scott of his favorite fishing spots.

"Right. He's retired Air Force, now working for a defense contractor who trains pilots on fighter simulators."

"I'd like to talk to him about an idea I have. Do you think he'd agree to see me?"

Her dad left the map with Scott and walked toward his office, saying, "I'll call and ask."

Eva didn't learn anything from her dad as dinner was about to be served. She decided to put aside work concerns and relish another yummy family dinner. After the dishes were done, she and Gram challenged the kids to a board game. Scott seemed content with his feet up, reading on his tablet, when Eva's father approached her.

He leaned over to whisper, "Zion's off work tomorrow. He'll expect you mid-morning."

With a nod, Eva whispered back, "Thank you, Dad."

# Chapter 12

The final week of Eva's vacation was quickly evaporating. It was already Thursday morning when she drove her dad's quad across the road. Adrenaline spiked in her veins as she sped up the long drive to Zion's house. What might Zion tell her?

He responded to her knock and beckoned her inside.

Yet Eva hovered near the door. "Zion, Dad told you that I'm a Special Agent with ICE. I'm assigned to an FBI Terrorism Task Force in Washington."

"Clifford's very proud of your service to the country." Zion gestured toward his living room. "Come in and meet my wife, Noelle."

"Honey," he said, turning, "Eva is Clifford and Marcia's daughter."

Noelle stood from her easy chair while holding a knitting project. "Eva, it's nice to meet you. I see you resemble your lovely mother. We're glad your folks moved in across the road."

"Please have a seat, Eva," Zion said, pointing to an upholstered chair.

Eva looked around for a private place to talk. "Is it possible you and I can talk business?"

"I understand. Come to my office."

Inside his tidy den, he shut the door and motioned for her to take a chair next to his desk.

"How can I help you?" he asked while remaining standing.

"Dad mentioned you work with the Air Force pilots. I have a photo to show you."

As she scrolled through pictures in her phone, Eva explained, "I had an encounter with this man in DC, but I have reason to believe he may be from Panama City."

Eva found the picture of the Runner entering the Waldorf Hotel on that fateful day. She centered him in the middle of the screen before handing Zion the phone.

"Have you ever seen this man?"

Zion gazed at Eva with serious eyes. "I have. In fact, I was with him today."

To Eva's chagrin, her whole body jumped. She was too skilled an interrogator to let her surprise show like that.

"What? You saw him today? Where?"

Zion nudged a chair closer to Eva and sat down. He turned her phone toward her.

"The man is Captain Yang Ming, an F-16 pilot with the Republic of China Air Force."

Eva's heart began to race. "Is he a ChiCom?"

"No, no." Zion fiercely shook his head. "The Republic of China is *not* the People's Republic of China, which is Communist China. Captain Ming is from Taiwan, which withdrew when China went Communistic."

"Yes, I understand," Eva said, calculating her next move. She decided to be direct and asked, "How do you know him?"

Zion straightened his shoulders. "Eva, even though our government doesn't have diplomatic relations with Taiwan, we have respected their democracy and trained their pilots. Taiwan has older F-16 fighters, and we have a simulator on which they train."

Eva's brain could hardly process such a discovery. "He's at your base! Can I assume the Captain is friendly toward our government?"

"Certainly," Zion said with assurance. "All we instructors have top secret security clearances. Captain Yang Ming has his military's equivalent."

Before Eva could forge ahead with more questions, Zion told her, "You said you encountered the Captain in DC. He's been here at Tyndall for about four weeks. This photo must have been taken some time ago."

"Let me think of the exact date." Eva paused before confirming, "It was three weeks ago."

Zion shook his head. "Can't be. He's been here four weeks."

"Maybe it's not him." Eva thumbed through her camera again. "Look at another photo."

He studied the small screen, spread his fingers to enlarge the picture, and then with a coy smile, Zion said, "I see you've been onto him for a while. That's Ming. No doubt in my mind."

"Why do you say we've been *onto* him?" Eva coaxed.

Zion jabbed a finger at the photo. "I see he's at an airport other than Panama City, and he's being followed."

Eva snatched her phone to examine the picture. "He's not being followed."

"Oh, yes he is. I know your type is secretive, but I recognize one of your colleagues behind Captain Yang Ming."

Handing the phone back to Zion, she intoned, "Please show me."

He enlarged the screen and plunked his finger upon a fiftyish man carrying a sport coat over his shoulder. "That is Danny Boyd. He was the Panama City FBI agent who used to come to the base. That is, until he retired some years back. At least, I thought he retired. Maybe he's been transferred elsewhere."

Eva wasn't about to admit Zion knew something she didn't. "Can we come to an agreement here?"

"I'm listening," he countered.

"Our conversation, and any further ones, must remain between the two of us."

Zion became stern. "Is this a national security matter? If so, I should advise my superiors."

"Perhaps Ming is a highly-trained American plant sent here to evaluate the quality of our simulator instructors," Eva added, smiling.

Zion simply stared at her, so she continued, "I'm sure you wouldn't want to do or say anything that would interfere with FBI Agent Danny Boyd."

"No," he cupped his chin in his hand. "But you've got me concerned about security matters at the base. There are too many crazies out there. I'm watching my own back every day. Noelle and I moved here to get away from the insanity, and so did your folks. Now, it's looking like it's stalking me in my own backyard."

His eyes downcast, Zion gave Eva back her phone.

She sought to further enlighten Zion without telling what she knew. "You said Captain Ming has been here four weeks. I assure you that four weeks ago this Friday, which would be tomorrow, he was in my presence in DC."

"You could be right." Zion frowned. "He and some other

Taiwanese pilots arrived here four weeks ago from Luke Air Force Base in Arizona. They spent three days for orientation, then they were free that Thursday and Friday. We've had them busy ever since."

"Are you suggesting Captain Ming is one of the crazies, as you put it?"

Zion pointed to Eva's phone. "He's always been polite and attentive. It does appear he might have flown to DC, which makes me wonder."

Eva had heard enough. Before she divulged confidential information, she pocketed her phone and stood, reaching out to shake Zion's hand.

"Thank you for the information about the Captain."

"Anything for Clifford. Your dad's the real deal, so you must be, too."

Eva grinned at his praise, and stopping in the living room, she told Noelle it was nice to meet her, adding, "I'm glad to know my folks have neighbors that are like family. Scott and I will keep you in our prayers."

"We'd like to see you again before you travel home," Noelle replied sweetly.

Zion followed Eva down the front steps, and raising his burly eyebrows, he asked, "Would you like to be in Captain Ming's presence again?"

She spun around. "What?"

"I usually invite the pilots to the house for bar-b-que. I'll try getting them here, so you and he can visit again."

Eva inhaled deeply. "Speaking of bar-b-que, Zion. What's that I'm smelling?"

"You are smelling something, Eva." Zion turned his head skyward and inhaled deeply. "It's not bar-b-que."

He sniffed the air. "Someone is burning something. Barn fires are common around here, but those fires usually have a sweet smell. There's a lot of cattle raised in the area. They supply the Grass Fed Beef Processing Plant about four miles down the road. You've probably bought their beef in your supermarket."

"You know, we do eat their beef." Eva inhaled again. "Do you think that smell is a cattle farm burning? Maybe we should call 911."

Zion whirled around as he looked skyward. "It could be a farm. That would explain the odor of roasted meat. I don't see any smoke. It could be ten miles from here."

Eva's thoughts returned to the possibility of meeting Captain Ming. "Zion, if you think you might plan a bar-b-que for this weekend, I'll stick around and attend."

"Does Saturday work?" Zion gave her a friendly smile.

"Yes. But remember, not a word to anyone. Especially the Captain."

Zion pulled out his cell phone. "Give me your cell number. I'll check with Noelle and get back to you."

Eva gave him the number to her cell phone, which Zion typed into his phone. When he placed a call to her number, she felt her phone vibrate in her pocket.

"There, now you have my number," he said.

Eva thanked him, and mounted the quad to zoom back to her parent's farm. As she rode, her mind was consumed by thoughts of meeting the here-to-fore unknown Captain Yang Ming.

Back at the farm, Eva walked into the kitchen.

Her mom was making banana bread and said brightly to Kaley, "And your mom and dad could spend a few hours together at our beautiful beach. I'll pack them a picnic lunch. Gramps and I want to take you kids to the water park. Does that sound like fun?"

Scott, stepping in, must have heard about the beach plans, because he put his hand over Eva's resting on the table and said, "Sea and sand sound perfect."

"Count me in," Eva replied. "I plan to leave my cell phone here."

"I'd like to take you for a spin before supper," Scott said, winking at Eva.

"Kaley and I have to wait for the banana bread to cool, but she's helping me make baked gulf grouper. Be back in about an hour," Marcia declared.

The drive among the trees and green pastures relaxed Eva. She leaned forward and wrapped her arms around Scott, causing him to go a bit slower.

"Honey, I like being on the quad more than your motorcycle!" she cried. "We have four wheels!"

"Grab the side arms!" he shouted back to her.

In a burst of speed, they were off. Eva laughed and laughed all the way back to the house. She wanted such jolly times to last forever.

**FRIDAY NOON AT THE BEACH,** the emerald-colored sea lapped beyond Eva's toes. She lounged beside Scott on colorful beach chairs, holding his hand. They had shared a delicious picnic lunch, and she didn't want to leave. The sky had never seemed so blue. Fluffy clouds floating above their heads had never seemed so merry.

As the sun's rays peeked out from behind the cottony clouds, Eva suddenly felt intense heat on her bare feet.

"The sun is getting hot," she said. "I should put on more lotion."

Scott held fast to her hand. "Wait a sec. I need to ask you something."

At the note of concern in his voice, Eva turned in her chair. "I'm not sure I like the sound of that. Is something wrong?"

"Nothing bad, I promise." Scott raised his voice above the chattering seagulls. "Here's what I want to know. Are you truly relaxing here? Letting the peace soak in?"

"Hmm ... good question. Are you?"

He squeezed her hand. "More than I thought I would driving down here in the rain. I'd like more times like this with you."

"Me too. How do we go about doing that?"

Seagulls leapt into the air and circled overhead. The idyllic scene reminded Eva of the wonderful trip to Austria she and Scott went on soon after they were married.

"Remember our days in the high mountains near Maria Alm?" she asked Scott. "We talked for hours getting to know each other."

Happy memories rose in Eva's mind, bringing light to her heart like the noonday sun above.

Scott laughed. "Boy, do I! There I was, resting the camera

for our self-portrait on my wallet on a big rock by the historic church. I never discovered I'd left the wallet behind until I tried paying for dinner later."

"Good thing I had enough cash so we didn't have to wash dishes," Eva said, smirking. "I haven't forgotten how God answered our prayers, because the next morning we found your wallet untouched."

They were silent for some moments, each listening to the sea birds calling and feeling the breeze rustling their hair. Eva slid sun lotion onto the tops of her feet before gazing at her husband, whom she found even more handsome than the day she'd met him. This was the time to share her true feelings.

She squeezed his hand. "I love you more each day. Work has taken up so much of my thoughts and energy lately that I realize, sitting here with you, I should tell you more and show you more. You are my everything, and I thank God for you with all my heart."

"And I'm crazy in love with you," Scott said, his eyes shining with tenderness. "Forever."

Eva kept looking into his eyes. Time passed to the sound of playful waves along the shore.

She leaned back into the canvas chair. "Sweetheart, let's remember this special moment. We could make a date night once a month. Kaley is heading to college. Andy's old enough to watch Dutch."

"I have another idea. Maybe the kids would like to stay here and enjoy a few weeks in Florida with their grandparents."

Eva reached over and tousled his hair. "I've always said you were a genius!"

# Chapter 13

Before dinner, Eva phoned Griff at home. She was determined to be most circumspect while talking over her cell phone. Eva knew U.S. intelligence assets and their foreign allies, with whom the U.S. government had mutual assistance agreements, intercepted phone traffic, and listened for people speaking or texting suspicious words or phrases.

Eva and Griff rarely bothered each other during off hours, so she was hopeful he'd answer. The call rang a few times before he answered.

He sounded out of breath, saying, "Eva, has something happened?"

"Sorry to disturb you on a Friday evening," she said.

Griff insisted it was no problem, adding, "Dawn and I are working on a house project. I paint, and she supervises. I can use the break."

"You and she will need a vacation pretty soon yourselves. Home remodeling can be grueling."

He chuckled lightly. "Should I be concerned about this call?"

"Listen, I'm going to carefully explain some happenings without much detail. At the end, I need your recommendation of what I should do. Remember the day I scraped my knee and encountered the Runner?"

Griff paused before hesitantly answering, "Ye-es."

"Keep in mind the city where I am. I met a source who works at a large airport here where drivers are trained. Hopefully, you get my drift."

"Yikes, not really."

"You know what you do on weekends if your club members haven't taken the vehicle for a ride."

"Okay, I'm following you, sort of."

"Well, the Runner is here learning to drive fighters. Based on his picture, you can figure out what friendly country he's from."

"I get your drift. This is amazing."

"It's too weird, Griff. But the source has invited me to meet the Runner casually, at a picnic. I'd have the chance to gather more info if I feel the Runner is approachable."

"Hmm … let me think about this and call you later."

"Exactly what I was hoping you'd do. Be super careful. No texts."

"Right."

"Oh, and Griff. Scroll through the pics you sent me of the first airport encounter. I'll wait while you do it."

"Okay, I am looking now."

"Be alert for a photo of the Runner with a guy in the background holding a sport coat over his shoulder."

"Yes, I see him."

"The source saw that photo and identified the guy as Danny Boyd, one of your colleagues who is supposed to be retired from this town a couple of years ago."

"That's even more strange," Griff groaned.

"I led the source to believe he was transferred instead. But I wonder if he was shadowing the Runner and is working privately now."

"Or if he's working for some other group similar to ours."

"That's why I need you to call back with your advice, sooner rather than later."

"Oh, I assumed it could be a serendipitous meeting at the picnic ."

Eva hesitated before saying, "I'd like it to be, but I don't want to interfere with others."

After Griff promised to check on Danny and get back to Eva, the line went dead.

Eva stared at her phone, hoping she wasn't making a mistake by stepping on someone's toes. Depending on what Griff found out about Danny Boyd, Eva would have a better sense if she could trust Zion's evidence.

**EVA WAS HELPING** her mother finish supper preparations when Andy and Dutch came running into the house.

Andy was panting. "Whew, we're done helping Gramps with chores and are starving."

"As you see, it's in the making," Eva replied with a grin.

Dutch wiped his forehead with his sleeve. "We earned a

big meal, but no beef. They all got cooked up."

"You need to get cleaned up." Eva pointed to the bathroom. "What's this about Gramps cooking hamburgers?"

"Nope," Andy interrupted. "Gramps isn't cooking burgers. Dutch thinks there won't be any more beef because of the big fire yesterday."

Eva turned to her mom. "What are they talking about?"

"Yesterday's big fire at the Grass Fed Beef Processing Plant near town," Marcia replied, tossing her head. "Heard it was bad and wiped out hundreds of cattle."

"Oh no!" Eva exclaimed. "Zion told me yesterday about the farmers around here who raise cattle for Grass Fed Beef. He and I thought we smelled smoke."

Her mom handed Eva a basket of rolls for the table. "This morning's news revealed the fire began in the night and burned through much of yesterday. Burned to the ground. It's sad because so many in this community rely on those jobs at the plant just to survive."

Their conversation was interrupted when Eva's cell phone chirped. She looked at the screen and wiped her hands on a towel.

"Excuse me, Mom. I need to take this work call."

She walked out onto the veranda and made her way to a rocker while connecting with Griff's call.

"Hey, partner. How's it going?"

"Very interesting," came his reply.

Eva tried to keep her voice low. "Should I accept the bar-b-que invite?"

"Yes, if you can make it appear unplanned."

"Oh? Do I need to know more?"

"Hold on."

Eva could hear muffled talking as though Griff had placed his hand over the phone receiver.

"I'm back. Dawn is asking for my help in the basement. Remember the sport coat guy?"

Eva prepared for the unexpected. "Yes."

"He's one of my former colleagues and is now retired in the Atlanta area. He's working privately for a group of other retired colleagues."

Eva marveled at how much Griff had learned. "Is it an Atlanta-based group?"

"No. This is why you must proceed carefully, Eva. They are a major, worldwide group."

Eva tried envisioning the scope of what she was dealing with. In what kind of national security mess had she gotten herself entangled?

"Take advantage of all the hospitality while you're there," Griff said, adding in a serious tone, "but we shouldn't talk further until you're here in the office."

"Understood. Give our love to your dear wife. I plan to see you there on Monday."

Eva returned to the kitchen, concern plaguing her. Had she stumbled into another agency's investigation? But what agency used only retired agents?

As the family assembled, her father sat down at the table and straightened his chair. Eva decided to call Zion after supper. Her mother passed around a large platter of chicken that Scott and Clifford had cooked on the grill.

"We have fresh corn on the cob, sliced tomatoes, and baked potatoes," Gram said. "And save room for the peach pie. Kaley peeled all the peaches."

"It's fun helping you in the kitchen." Kaley was all smiles. "I have news. Dylan called and wants to hang out. He plans to take me to the local FSU campus to look around some more."

"How wonderful," Gram chirped. "We'd love Kaley going to college close to us. Wouldn't we Gramps?"

"Wait a minute, Kaley," Scott interrupted. "Let's talk after we eat about you spending more time with Dylan. We have only a little more time here together."

Andy jumped in. "I think it's a great idea. If Kaley likes FSU, then maybe I can attend there after high school."

Throughout supper, college chatter continued. Eva's mind jumped from Kaley's possible move to Florida, to Zion's picnic and the hope of meeting Captain Ming. She barely picked at her food. Scott sought out Eva as the kids helped with the dishes.

"I don't want Kaley or the kids staying down here this

summer without us," Scott proclaimed, his brows creased. "Especially with Dylan hanging around like a spider. We will all head back together. I haven't said anything to your folks about them staying longer, have you?"

"No, I had an urgent call from Griff, and I've been too busy plotting my next strategy for what's turning out to be a working vacation. I need to call Zion."

Eva entered Zion's cell phone and took a brief walk into the pine forest to phone him.

"Hello, Eva," he answered.

"Sorry not to have called earlier. Your offer to attend a bar-b-que and meet our friend might be to everyone's benefit. If you get my drift."

"Hold on, Eva, while I close my door."

Eva heard a door latch, and then Zion was back on the line,

"Perfect. I expected as much and had already invited the four guests to our home tomorrow for an afternoon meal. Noelle and I are smoking the meat."

"Sounds perfect."

"Should we plan on your folks and the kids, Eva?"

"Zion, without knowing where these peculiar circumstances may lead, it's better if I come as your neighbor, helping Noelle with the meal. I'll bring a dessert."

"Ah, yes. Much better. Also, I'll look for ways to involve the guests so you'll have a lone opportunity to be reacquainted with the Captain. He is their team leader. Come about one o'clock."

Their call ended. Eva took a moment to study the photo of Captain Ming in her phone. She wondered what might come from meeting him at Zion's luncheon. Would he become a runner again?

# Chapter 14

On Saturday, before Eva left for Zion's bar-b-que, she took from Dutch the inexpensive cell phone she and Scott had bought him to reach his parents in case of an emergency.

"Mom, do I have to?"

Eva nodded. "Buddy, Dad and I will buy you a new one when we're back home in Virginia."

"Okay."

He shrugged and dashed off outside. Meanwhile, she reset the phone and typed in the owner's name in the settings as "Runner."

A little after one o'clock, after lunch was done, Eva heard a horn honking. That was Zion's signal that he was arriving back home with the four Taiwanese pilots from Tyndall. She checked out the front window in time to see his minivan disappear through the rows of tall pine trees between the road and his house.

She fastened on her fanny pack, which now held two cell phones and a charger, and gave last-minute instructions to Scott and the kids, who were getting ready for an outing at the beach. Her mom gave Eva a container of chocolate chip cookies she'd made that morning.

"We'll miss you at the beach," she said softly.

Scott gave her shoulder a squeeze. Eva waved good-bye and then jumped onto her dad's quad. She sped toward Zion's house, her mind awhirl with questions.

*Will the Runner recognize me from our collision in DC? Am I putting my family in danger by plunging deeper into this case?*

Eva knew what she had to do next before zooming into Zion's yard. She slowed the quad, lifting up a prayer to her Heavenly Father for guidance.

She passed by Zion's stopped minivan just as the four pilots climbed out. She coasted to a stop and dismounted. Zion was introducing the pilots to Noelle as Eva approached. Each of the pilots was dressed in jeans and collared polo shirts, while Eva wore a white cotton blouse and navy slacks.

"Meet our neighbor, Eva," Zion told the group. "She's helping Noelle with the meal."

"Hope you all like cookies." She smiled, holding up the goodies with her left hand.

"Eva, this is Captain Yang Ming, who we refer to informally as Captain Ming," Zion said, grinning. "He's the team leader."

She noted Ming's firm grip as he shook her hand and saw an intelligent gleam in his eye. He didn't seem to recognize her face, which was a step in the right direction. Zion continued introductions, and Eva shook hands with each pilot.

She was astounded that less than a month ago she'd wrestled with Ming in front of DC's Waldorf Hotel, and here they were in Florida, both being welcomed by her parents' new neighbors. It was truly miraculous.

Eva hurried into the house to help Noelle. Soon, she carried out a tray with plastic cups, ice, and pitchers of both sweet and unsweetened tea. Zion had settled the pilots at two picnic tables beneath a low-hanging live oak tree. Eva poured the tea of their choice.

Meanwhile, Zion shared with the pilots what happened during his first tour of duty at Tyndall. "It didn't take me long to develop a love for the vast forests and the close proximity to the beautiful sandy beaches. Does anything about the Panhandle of Florida remind you fellas of back home?"

Ming spoke first: "Nanwan Beach also has turquoise water. Lots of families go there."

"Sounds lovely," Eva told him before heading back to the kitchen.

Noelle handed her a tray of smoked cream cheese and crackers, along with a bean salad.

"My hubby spent the morning on his smoker making this cream cheese. I hope you'll also enjoy the brisket."

Eva trailed behind Noelle, who carried the main entree of smoked brisket. Eva's mouth watered, and her stomach growled in anticipation. Good thing she'd eaten just a tiny salad at her folks. Zion assigned seats around the table, conveniently sitting Captain Ming beside Eva.

He stood at one end and explained to the group, "While

the U.S. was founded predominantly by Christians, my family migrated here from Europe just before World War Two. We were Jewish, and I knew little about the Christian faith."

Noelle smiled and nodded as if urging him to continue telling about his family history.

Zion obliged her. "When I fell in love with this lovely woman in college, I began studying about my Jewish heritage and discovered Jesus Christ was actually Jewish and was the promised Messiah, which most Jews at the time wouldn't accept."

"So today," he said, gesturing over the table of goodies. "We thank God for how he has blessed us with a great marriage and with the good food we are about to share."

After praying a blessing for the food, Zion made sure each guest took plenty to eat, telling them, "What you don't eat now, you'll get to take with you to the base."

As they ate the delicious food, Eva was surprised at how friendly Captain Ming seemed and his command of the English language.

"Are you attached to the military?" he asked her.

She thought about how best to reply, deciding she'd be as truthful as possible. Hopefully, she could turn their conversation to her advantage.

"No. I'm employed by our government as a civil servant, but my husband is the public spokesman for our Secretary of Defense."

She noticed Ming's eyes drift toward the wedding ring on her left finger. Keeping her voice low, Eva asked, "How about you? Is your family back in Taiwan?"

Instead of replying, Ming raised a fork in the air and spoke to Zion, "Colonel, this beef is most delicious. Thank you."

"You're all most welcome in our home," Zion replied. "Be sure to help yourselves to everything."

When the three other pilots began talking with Zion and Noelle, Ming returned to his conversation with Eva. "You asked about my family. I am divorced, which makes my trips to the U.S. less stressful. My son is in the Taiwanese Air Force officer training academy. My daughter is in her last year of college."

"You must miss seeing them," Eva said, trying to calculate Ming's possible age.

He suddenly asked, "What is it you do for your government?"

Well, she hadn't expected Ming to be so direct, but she didn't want to lie to him.

"I work for the Immigration and Customs Enforcement agency. We deal with issues of border security."

Ming nodded. "We have a similar agency in our government."

"You mentioned previous trips to the U.S. Have there been many?"

In between munching on crackers with smoked cheese and salad, Ming explained he had a successful career in his military, and when not flying patrols between Taiwan and China, he would bring junior pilots to the U.S. for flight training.

"I am what you call a chaperone," he said with a sharp laugh.

They spoke briefly of the Florida Panhandle and Arizona, as well as Ming's homeland in Taiwan.

Zion then stood to announce, "We have cookies and chocolate cake for dessert, but let's first enjoy yard games. Horseshoes and ladder golf are both available."

Eva helped Noelle clear the table and prepare for dessert, while Zion showed the pilots the art of pitching horseshoes. When Eva noticed the Captain sitting alone at the table, she decided it was most fortuitous, so she joined him the moment Noelle finished wiping down the tablecloth.

Eva had barely seated herself across the table when Ming folded his hands together and asked, "Through your work, are you acquainted with the FBI?"

"Yes. In fact, I am on loan to a task force of other federal law enforcement agents to combat terrorism. Several colleagues are FBI agents."

"Do you know any FBI agents?" Eva asked lightly.

He looked in the direction of his colleagues, then shook his head.

"I sense you want to know one," Eva offered. "Am I correct?"

Ming focused intently on her eyes. "Why do you ask me that?"

Eva felt her being forthcoming with Ming was working, so she explained, "My husband and our family are visiting my parents on a neighboring farm. It's really no accident that I'm here today. I believe God in Heaven has ordered our steps."

Captain Ming studied her face but didn't speak.

"You might not realize it, but we've met before," Eva said, watching his eyes flicker.

Then, he shook his head. "No, I would remember your pretty face."

"You are kind." Eva smiled. "However, we did meet before."

She looked over at the pilots, who were still playing horseshoes. They seemed clueless about her meeting with Ming, so she pulled out her phone to scroll through the pictures.

She stopped at one and turned the phone so Ming could see it. "This is Scott, my husband. Four weeks ago, on Friday at noon, I was supposed to be having lunch with Scott."

Raising up her knee slightly, she pointed. "You can't see it, but that's when I got a scab on my knee."

Eva carefully observed Ming. It was as though he was counting days. Still, he said nothing.

"Scott and I were two blocks from FBI Headquarters in DC," Eva continued, "when I saw two men wrestling with another man. Because I'm a law enforcement officer, I interceded and tried to end what I thought was a fight. When I announced I was a federal agent, all three men ran away, but I ended up injuring my knee." She again pointed.

Ming's intelligent stare changed as fear swept across his face.

Eva quickly scrolled through her pictures until she found the ones from the date in question.

"Surveillance cameras at the hotel took these pictures. Here you are hurrying through the hotel to escape. See these other photos of you."

Ming's voice quivered as he said, "Have I been invited here so you can arrest me?"

"Why should I?" Eva countered. "It looked to me like you were the victim of an assault. Do you want to tell me about this?"

He quickly glanced over his shoulder toward the pilots. "It might not be safe for me to talk anymore here with you."

"The others are enjoying the game," Eva replied evenly.

"You are right." He pointed to her phone. "Show me the picture of the assault."

Eva found the picture in front of the hotel on the street and turned it toward Ming. He pointed to the blurry image of an Asian man in glasses who was struggling with him.

"You cannot see his features clearly, yet I know this man. He is a Chinese Communist agent. I was on my way to the FBI to report him. I do not know how he found me, but he pretended to be FBI and tried to stop me."

Relieved that Ming was opening up about what happened, Eva asked quietly, "What were you going to report?"

He peered again over his shoulder. Because the other pilots were entertaining themselves, he told Eva, "My sister lived in Hong Kong, where she worked in banking. The Chinese government totally controls everything there. My sister disappeared not long ago, and my family is trying to find her. A Communist agent showed up at my home in Taiwan to warn me they had my sister. They expect me to pass military secrets to them for her release."

Listening intently, Eva nodded to keep him talking.

"I do not know what to do," he admitted. "After I arrived at Luke Air Force Base, the same Chinese agent in your picture threatened me. He insists my sister will be executed if I do not get back in touch with him and pass along military secrets about Taiwan."

"I'm so sorry," Eva said in soothing tones. "I may be able to help. I work with the most trusted of FBI agents."

Ming shook his head. "I trust nobody. How can Chinese agents know how to find me here in the U.S.? How could the same Chinese agent find me in Arizona and then in Washington when I am trying to go to FBI? Maybe your FBI is working with the Chinese Communist Party."

"I understand your concerns. We and the FBI often refer to the Chinese Communists as ChiComs. Captain, will you let me help you?"

Ming dropped his head as if deep in thought. "Tell me how you found me here."

"Fair question. Again, it is the hand of God. How do I know that? Because my parents moved to this neighborhood last year, and this is my first visit. After I arrived, I met the Colonel and learned he works at the base. Around the same time, I learned you'd flown from Panama City to DC. You wear a military haircut and I remembered you were the right height and size to be a U.S. Air Force pilot. So, I showed him the photo of you, and he recognized you immediately."

"Does Colonel Adelman know of my situation?"

"No, only that we met previously."

Ming nodded and scrolled through the contacts in his phone. He pointed. "This is the phone number in U.S. given to me by, as you call them, the ChiCom who threatened me in Arizona."

Eva set Ming's phone on the bench beside her. While he continued checking on the other pilots over his shoulder, Eva snapped a picture of the contact number before handing him back his phone.

"Captain, the key is not to use your phone. The ChiComs may be tracking you through social media, games, and travel apps in your phone. They're probably tracking your every move and phone conversation using spyware in your phone."

He gulped as he stared at his phone. "This is also my enemy."

Eva removed Dutch's phone and charger from her fanny pack and slid it under the table toward Ming.

"I reprogrammed this phone under the name 'Runner.' There are only two contacts. My phone number is listed as 'Coach,' and my partner, FBI Agent Griff Topping, is listed as 'Assistant Coach.'"

Captain Ming took the phone, immediately stuffing it into his pocket.

He said, keeping his voice low, "I do not know what else to do. I must help my sister, but I am not a traitor. I need your help."

"I will do everything I can," Eva promised. "You must use your phone for normal everyday uses only and never use it for arranging travel. Leave it behind if you don't want to be tailed. Keep the one I gave you turned off most of the time. Check it daily for messages from me. If I have news, I will contact you through that phone. If you have an emergency, call me. If you can't reach me, then call my partner, 'Assistant Coach.'"

Ming's gaze lingered on the three other pilots for whom he was responsible. "Who can I trust?"

"My guess is, it's more likely the ChiComs know your movements from your phone than from the pilots you're traveling with. What are your requirements to notify your own military chain of command?"

"Yes, I am supposed to, but am afraid to do so while here. That is why I tried to make it to FBI. The ChiComs are so bold, they operate right by FBI Headquarters."

Eva weighed the risks to him going forward. She wanted to give him some assurance based on everything she knew.

"Sir, you have much to consider. We may ask you to repeat your attempted travel to the FBI, but won't do so until we determine who else might be involved. How much longer do you remain here?"

He swiped at his chin. "These three pilots are nearly finished, and we usually head home soon. My command asked me to remain so they can send another three over here."

"Will you? That may not resolve the situation with your sister."

"Yes, because the longer I am in the U.S., the ChiComs will believe I have greater value to them because of what I might access while here. Therefore, they will keep my sister alive."

"I see this puts additional pressure on you to provide military secrets, which I do not like."

Ming reached toward her with both hands. "You should know what the Colonel said about being a Christian; I am one, too. My parents introduced me to Christian missionaries after my wife divorced me. When I was hurting, they gave me a

Bible and invited me to study it in their home with others. They showed me the way to Jesus. I want to honor my Savior with my life, and I am not a risk to your national security. My sister believes in Jesus, too. So, I pray for her each day to be set free from prison like Peter the Apostle."

"Captain, you and your sister will also be in my prayers," Eva replied with feeling. "The others will return soon to eat their dessert. I'm glad we talked and that I could meet you *again*."

Eva scrolled to her phone contacts and opened a new page. "Griff and I will help you as much as we can. Remember, the phone I gave you is your lifeline. You should give me your sister's name."

"Type in her name and address." She slid her phone to Ming. "Find a picture in your phone for me to copy."

He busied himself typing in his sister's data. When finished, he found her picture and snapped a photo of it using Eva's camera before handing it back. She heard footsteps behind her and turned to see Noelle carrying a tray of cookies and chocolate cake. Eva went to fetch everyone more tea and motioned to Zion. Soon the horseshoe pitchers were back, telling stories of their prowess.

Before she could be questioned by anyone about her conversation with Ming, Eva slipped away to her quad. Driving back to her folks, her mind became consumed with "what ifs" for the Captain and his sister going forward.

What if she and Griff could not help her in time?

# Chapter 15

As the sun streaked the dawn sky with light, the Montanna family ate a hurried breakfast on Sunday morning before hugging Gram and Gramps good-bye. Eva's mother sent banana bread and fruit for them to eat on the way home.

Scott and the kids started loading the van while Eva filled their travel mugs with coffee for her and Scott and water for the kids. She dallied on the veranda, finding it hard to leave her parents.

"Mom and Dad, you've given us all such a marvelous time. I feel your love. We all do."

"And we feel your love," her mom said, wiping tears from her eyes. "You have blessed us by coming all this way. Our hearts and home are open to you all coming again. Let us know what Kaley decides. We'd so enjoy having her stay with us for her college years."

Her dad nodded vigorously. "Amen to everything your mom said. Have a peace-filled and safe trip home. You should have clear weather for the long drive."

Eva started out behind the wheel, and thankfully, the kids fell asleep until she switched with Scott at a gas station to purchase fuel, food, and more coffee. He drove the remaining trip, arriving home just after the sun had set.

The first thing Eva did after helping Scott unload the van was to text her boss, Sosa Garcia, and Griff: *Just to advise, I'll be taking tomorrow morning off as annual leave.*

Her mind and body were both tired. Lights out came pretty quickly, and with it, a blessed night of sleep.

**EARLY MONDAY MORNING,** Eva fixed breakfast and saw Scott off to work. She then enjoyed some coffee before starting a load of laundry. The kids were busy getting reacquainted with their friends. While Eva considered all the needs for groceries, her thoughts were interrupted by worries about Captain Ming.

Was everything he said true? If so, his fears were justified by how boldly the ChiComs were operating in the United

States.

She arrived in the office by one. Griff instantly showed up at her cubicle.

"How about an update on what happened with your Taiwanese pilots?" he asked.

Eva had just spotted a curious message on the screen of her computer, so she promised to meet him in the conference room in thirty minutes.

She toggled to the message section on her computer screen, managing to ignore the myriad of messages that piled up during her vacation. These could wait until tomorrow.

Instead, she went straight to the one piquing her interest: *Eva, it's Cedric Foster, ASAC, ICE Chicago. Call me ASAP.*

How strange. Eva hadn't heard from Cedric in all the years since she'd been trained by him in Basic Agent Training. Because his message sounded so urgent, Eva looked him up in the ICE system. He was the Assistant Special Agent in Charge (ASAC) of the large ICE office in Chicago, which meant he supervised as many as four or five groups and as many as sixty other supervisors and agents.

To be in a major office like Chicago was to his credit. But why did he want to talk with Eva? Perhaps she'd been named by someone as a personal reference.

Eva phoned Cedric and ended up waiting for his office assistant to connect her with him.

"Hello, Eva Montanna." His melodic voice still sounded the same.

"Cedric, frankly, your message surprises me. I am happy to know you're the ASAC in Chicago."

"Thanks for the return call, Eva. You know how it is, home is wherever the government sends you. For me, home is Chicago."

Eva glimpsed Griff leaving his cubicle for the conference room. "Cedric, I lost track of you since we were on that ill-fated surveillance practicum years ago, back in training."

"You mean the one where Regina Spire's premature arrest assured your place at the top of our class?" he asked with a snort. "She ended up pretty well considering her mediocre beginning. She's risen to our chief headhunter."

"I heard." Eva pressed her lips tightly. "In fact, I saw her recently for the first time since basic training,"

"So, you got yourself in trouble, huh? Must be why you're moving to Chicago."

"What?! No, I'm not going anywhere," Eva protested, frustration rising in her chest.

"Eva, are you sure? That's why I'm calling you."

She bolted from her chair with the phone pressed to her ear and a knot in her throat. "Please tell me what you're talking about."

"You know that besides being the head of internal affairs, Regina is also Chair of the Career Board, which decides where agents are assigned."

"Don't think I knew that. What do you know I don't?"

"Here's the skinny. The short-handed ICE offices get a list of agents due to be reassigned. Here's your name in bold letters on the list available for Chicago. I want you assigned to me and one of my groups."

Eva's mind tumbled out of control. She inhaled sharply to steady her cascading emotions.

"I still don't know why I'm on the list," she managed. "I never requested a transfer."

"Really!" Cedric exclaimed. "Sometimes, our agents find themselves on the list for what I call a 'disciplinary transfer' after getting in trouble with internal affairs. Is your record clean?"

"Absolutely ... well, except I did get summoned by internal affairs recently because of what I thought was an FBI arrest while assigned to an FBI group. I have never been disciplined."

"I see you're back working in DC. Where else have you been assigned?"

"You mentioned it earlier, Cedric. I graduated top of my class and chose to remain in Washington. I never left."

"Oh, oh. Say no more."

"Why?" Eva interrupted.

"You know the agency's policy is for all its agents to be transferred to different parts of the country to broaden their experience. I guess Regina discovered you've never had to experience the disruption of a transfer. I've been transferred four times. She's probably moved at least as many times."

Eva frowned and felt the heat burning her cheeks. "So, it's Regina's revenge."

"Does that mean you're resistant to coming here to Chicago?" Cedric laughed.

"This is all new to me, Cedric. If my only two choices are Anchorage or Chicago, then I'll see you in Chicago. My husband's job is in the Pentagon, so I'll try to stay here."

"Oh, are you married to Scott Montanna, press spokesman for the Secretary of Defense?"

She chuckled. "Yup, he's my hubby."

"Eva, that explains why you've never been transferred. I wish you continued luck."

"Thanks, Cedric."

She'd just hung up when Griff stuck his head around the file cabinet in her cubicle. He lifted up his coffee cup.

"Get yourself a fresh brew. I thought we were meeting about your PC trip."

Eva stared past him, conflicted by all she'd just heard. "I'm sorry, Griff. I got tied up in a most unpleasant conversation."

He started to pull up a chair.

Eva waved him off and stood. "Not here. I'll tell you everything in the conference room, with the door closed."

# Chapter 16

With no time to consider Cedric's news about her looming transfer, Eva sat across the conference table from Griff, a cup brimming with coffee at her elbow.

"What's it going to be, first your unpleasant phone call or the update on your Florida escapades?" Griff asked, swiping a palm across his moustache.

Eva sipped some of the hot brew before saying, "I'm on the transfer list. An old colleague just called, trying to entice me to Chicago."

"Steady on, Eva," Griff barked. "You put in for a transfer?"

Her heart rate skyrocketed. "I'm as shocked as you are! My nemesis is on ICE's career board and put me in for a transfer, which I didn't seek and don't want."

"You have a nemesis within ICE?" he asked, frowning. "That's news to me."

Eva quickly explained, "Regina Spire and I were tied at the top of basic agent's class. She spoiled the training episode by making a premature arrest. As a result, she was assigned to Anchorage, and I stayed in DC. Regina is getting back at me. I'm still processing the hard reality."

"Say no more, partner. I understand completely and am here anytime you want to strategize. Let's talk Florida."

"Assuming you're not interested in our fantastic dolphin cruise or my dad's pine tree farm, I'll get right to the Runner. He is Captain Yang Ming and is a training pilot with Taiwan's Air Force."

She spent the next few minutes describing in detail how she'd shown the surveillance photos to her parents' neighbor, Zion Adelman, and he revealed the Captain's identity.

"Zion did host a bar-b-que for the pilots, which gave me an opportunity to meet Captain Ming to assess his motives for fleeing that day. As you suggested, I engaged him in casual conversation, and Griff, I ended up getting his full cooperation."

Eva transitioned into the sad story of Ming's sister being held captive by the CCP and how the communist agents were using her kidnapping to pressure Ming to spy for China.

"It's overwhelming," Eva admitted. "Too many opportunities. We need to come up with a strategy to help Ming."

Griff raised his outstretched palm. "Whoa, partner. Not so fast."

"What? Am I missing something?"

"Eva, when you called me from Florida, you told me about Danny Boyd. I found out he's working in Atlanta. How does he figure into this caper?"

"Oh yeah." Eva rolled her eyes. "My brain is feeling fried from the long trip. When Zion saw the surveillance photo, he told me that Boyd was the guy following Ming. Have you found out anything else about him?"

Griff stood and shut the door. "Meant to close that when you first came in."

He sat down and, leaning closer to Eva, told her in confidence, "I'm greatly concerned about him. Boyd retired from the FBI in Panama City after twenty-five years. He moved to Atlanta and joined the Lancet Group."

"Who are they?"

Griff kept his voice to a low growl. "A national private investigative firm made up mostly of retired FBI agents."

"So, he moves to a higher cost-of-living city after he retires with less income," Eva observed with a toss of her head. "Makes no sense."

"Lancet pays extremely well. They have global clients who pay them gobs of money for their insider services."

Eva clapped her hands together. "Oh, I nearly forgot. Captain Ming went through the photos in my phone. You know, the ones the Bureau retrieved from the Waldorf and airports at Atlanta and Reagan."

"And?"

Scrolling to the photo in her phone, she said, "These two men claimed to be FBI when grabbing Ming in front of the Waldorf."

"No." Griff was shaking his head. "The Bureau is saying they aren't."

"Exactly. Though their faces are blurry, Ming identified

the man on the right as the same man who tried to coerce him in Arizona to become a spy for China."

"The CCP guy's in Arizona and then goes after Ming in DC. It's a conundrum."

"I agree. Please explain what else you know," Eva probed.

"My buddy Bruce Sterling is on the case at the FBI Washington Field Office. He must have examined these pictures and said nothing to me about any known retired agents or ChiCom intelligence agents assigned to the Chinese embassy."

"Would he tell you, Griff?"

He paused. "Possibly not. Being counterintelligence, he's kinda spooky about things like that. I can't figure why he's not more interested in this whole event. He's gone strangely quiet."

"You've added another layer of mystery to this case." Eva grabbed hold of her cup in two hands. "I should get busy writing it up."

Griff was nodding. "For sure, Eva. They're going to want you to turn the Captain over to them for interrogation."

"No way! He's extremely frightened. He barely trusts me. Handing him over to people I don't know or trust? Not happening."

Griff leaned back in his chair, a quizzical look on his face. "This doesn't have to become adversarial. You always do what's right. I suggest you write up the facts as they have developed, and it will be referred to the FBI Counterintelligence Division."

"Griff, don't you see the conflict here? It's already adversarial."

"I'm listening."

"Here's how I see it," Eva said. "It appears Lancet is working *for* the ChiComs to surveil their targets. We know Danny Boyd from Lancet spied on Ming through Atlanta's airport. Then, the CCP agent who confronted Ming in Arizona just happens to chase after him in DC, yelling he's FBI. It's obvious that on the day I interrupted them, he and the other man were posing as FBI agents and trying to snatch Ming before he could receive help at FBI Headquarters."

Griff studied her face. "Eva, I hear you. Boyd and other Lancet team members are doing the investigative work of corralling the ChiComs' targets and then assisting the ChiComs in harassing or kidnapping them."

"That's how I see it, Griff. I know in the past you've trusted Bruce, but given these facts, if we turn our information over to the CI Division, it permits them to cover up their and Lancet's crimes. Because, the retired CI agents are the agents working for Lancet after retirement."

Griff tented his hands. "Eva, here's what you must do. Write your report as an ICE Report of Investigation, but not on ICE computers. Do it at home. Then, request a private meeting with your ICE Director and give it directly to him. Ask him to give it personally to the FBI Director, who can decide how to handle it within the Bureau. The FBI Director has to do the right thing because either the ICE Director or you can make a referral to the Inspector General for the Department of Justice. I'm sure the FBI Director prefers to clean his own house."

"Oh, I can see another advantage to your plan." Eva smiled. "The ICE Director is going to want to keep me here in DC, for fear I'll go to the IG and claim retaliation if I'm moved to Chicago."

Griff nodded in return. "Eva, we need to brief Sosa. He should have been in here, but I had no idea how complicated things were going to be with your career on the line, as well as the lives of Ming and his sister. You and I can't afford a single misstep."

She agreed, and the two of them went immediately to see Sosa Garcia, the FBI Supervisor of their task force, and fully briefed him.

Sosa sat in silence, stroking his chin for some time. Eva and Griff traded glances and waited.

Finally, Sosa said, "First of all, good work, both of you. Eva, I agree with Griff; this shouldn't be written into the FBI system. At least not in its present state. With my blessing, you write it up and give it to ICE Director Whidbey in person, and to him only. It's much too important to delay."

**THE MEETING WITH SOSA AT AN END,** Eva left Griff to discuss one of his other terrorism cases with their boss and returned to her cubicle. She signed out of her computer and retrieved her service weapon from the desk drawer, which she then locked. Grabbing her purse, she was done for the day and ready to find solace at home with her family.

She arrived home and found the boys working on Dutch's train set in the den. Kaley was busy perusing the FSU website. Satisfied all was well on the home front, Eva brewed a fresh pot of coffee and retreated to her home office.

A few sips of coffee later, she typed furiously on her keyboard, summarizing all the events that had interrupted her vacation. The weight of what Captain Ming was facing fueled her mind and her fingers. If only Director Whidbey would contact the FBI Director in time to help Ming and his sister before it was too late.

Her brain becoming stuck, Eva took time to think. She even drank the coffee without noticing how cold it had become. With no more excuses, she forced herself to finish the factual report, holding nothing back about Danny Boyd, the Lancet Group, and their despicable alliance with the CCP.

As she hit the 'print' button, her favorite Bible verse from the book of Micah bubbled to the surface of her mind: *What does the Lord require of you? To act justly, and to love mercy, and to walk humbly with your God.*

Eva's mission crystallized before her eyes. She had to contact Director Whidbey, get on his calendar for an urgent meeting, and leave the rest to God.

**EVA SPENT THE FIRST HOURS** of the following day in the office answering incoming emails and getting caught up after being gone for a week. By lunchtime, she had little appetite. The turkey sandwich she munched at her desk tasted like dust.

Eva tossed the uneaten half into the trash and headed out to her G-car. When she arrived at ICE Headquarters, Director Whidbey's assistant took a copy of her report, saying the Director would be ready for her once he'd read it. He seemed friendly, even offering Eva bottled water while she waited.

She finished the water, and still no one called her. Eva could only assume Whidbey was reading her work meticulously. Seated on a plush sofa, she started tapping her foot, wondering if she'd have to sit out here all day. Moments later, the assistant ushered her into Whidbey's large executive office.

This was her second time meeting the new director. The first had been at a spring reception honoring two agents who had gotten injured on a case in Florida. Eva had worked on the edges of their case, and so she had shaken Whidbey's hand in April.

She sat before his massive desk, curious if he would remember her.

"Agent Montanna, I just finished reading your report," he intoned, a smile hovering on his lips. "You seem to have a knack for getting yourself involved in sticky cases. It's not every day an agent cracks a spy case on their vacation."

Eva gritted her teeth and replied, "Yes, not only was my vacation interrupted, but as I mention in the report, this all began when lunch with my husband in front of the Waldorf was disrupted by the same man."

"I know your husband is Scott Montanna, the Press Secretary for the SecDef. Now, you may not know it, but Secretary Cortez and I both graduated from the same class at West Point. We are friends to this day. What are the odds of all this happening?"

Eva considered where Whidbey might be going. She had her own idea and plunged ahead.

"I could claim it was a coincidence that I was present with my husband at an attempted Chinese hostage-taking in DC. But then, Sir, for me to be invited to lunch with the same unidentified victim nine hundred miles away is no happenstance. And given my folks just happened to move across the road from the man who knows the pilot and is able to identify the former FBI agent with the Lancet Group must be an act of God. I want to do the right thing in response to what's been handed to us."

Whidbey held up her report. "Agent Montanna, you

surprise me. I thought you'd come here spouting we have to stop the communists, and here you are talking about God."

"Sir, I agree we need to protect our country from dangers from our adversaries, and the CCP is our enemy," she quickly replied. "I also trust in God for everything. I pray He will keep me and our team safe. I know we could never have written an Ops Plan with such success."

"I don't disagree with you," the Director said, narrowing his eyes behind his glasses. "Where is your source today?"

"At Tyndall trying to go on as normal, but he's very concerned for his safety and that of his sister. I've given him a clean phone and told him to stay off his other phone. He understands that I will contact him with instructions in cooperating with our investigation. As you no doubt read in my report, retired FBI agents have joined the Lancet Group and are aiding ChiComs in targeting and monitoring dissidents and potential spies for China within the U.S."

"It's beyond disturbing, Agent Montanna. You leave this with me to contact the FBI Director. I'll ensure your report goes to the correct people."

"Just two things, Sir, if I may?"

The Director nodded. "Go ahead."

"I typed my report at home. There is no copy in the ICE system, and none in the FBI system. If it needs to be activated somewhere, you'll need to let me know."

"Understood, and the other thing?"

"Sir, I have received transfer orders to Chicago, yet I have this matter pending."

The Director smiled. "I assume you'd expect your husband to accompany you if you move. Am I correct?"

"Yes, Sir."

"Well, Agent Montanna, I'm not about to undermine my good friend, Secretary Cortez. Besides, we need you here to help the FBI on this matter."

Eva rose to her feet, thanking the Director. "Sir, I await your further instructions in dealing with Captain Ming."

# Chapter 17

Eva kept busy helping Griff on one of his other cases. Nothing new developed in Ming's case, so by Saturday, she was ready to forget work issues. Giving the house a good cleaning would be the perfect way to clear her head. Donning a pair of old slacks, a comfy tee-shirt, and sneakers, Eva started running a vacuum over the carpet in the front room when she spotted Kaley standing in the driveway, gazing intently down the street.

What was she up to?

Her daughter had been cloistered in her bedroom all morning. Intending to find out, Eva shut off the vacuum and hurried outside.

"Waiting for someone?" Eva asked, coming up behind Kaley.

Kaley whirled around and cried, "Mom, don't sneak up on me like that!"

"It appears I'm not the one sneaking around," Eva replied in a stern tone. "What are you doing out here?"

Before Kaley could answer, Andy hustled toward them, carrying a weed whacker in one hand.

"My sister drives a Slug Bug, and now she's going out on a date with a slug."

"Are you going out with Dylan?" Eva asked. "Why didn't you say anything?"

Kaley acted nervous. "Ah … You were running the vacuum, and I didn't want to disturb you. He called and asked me out to a fair in Leesburg. He's picking me up soon."

"I'd like to know what kind of fair it is," Eva said.

"Yuck," Andy declared, swinging the yard implement in his hands. "I heard her squeal over the phone, saying she'd *love* to go with him to the vegan fair. Nothing but a bunch of booths selling carrots and sandwiches made out of radishes. Maybe even bugs."

Kaley pushed her hands onto her hips. "No, I don't eat bugs, mister smarty pants. And did you hear me tell Dylan that I'll only go with him if he comes to youth group with me tonight?"

"I've heard enough from you two," Eva declared. "Andy, please go find your dad and see where he wants you to use the edger. He's in the basement sorting boxes for me."

"Sure, you can count on me, Mom."

After he darted off, Eva reached for Kaley's hand. "You shouldn't just disappear without telling me or Dad your plans. That's unkind, as we would worry."

"I was going to text you when Dylan picked me up," Kaley remarked.

"That would be okay if we weren't home, but since we are here, I would appreciate my daughter talking to me face-to-face."

"You're right, Mom. I'm sorry." Kaley said, eyeing her shoes.

At the sound of an approaching car, they both turned. Eva spotted Dylan driving toward their house. She squeezed Kaley's hand.

"I want you to have a safe and fun time. I see how you're trying to get Dylan interested in matters of faith. Nothing is impossible with God, but know this. I've rarely seen an unbeliever come to know Jesus in a relationship with a Christ follower. It's usually the other way around."

Kaley dropped her hand, straightening her purse on her shoulder. "You give me more to pray about."

Dylan nosed his car into the driveway.

As Kaley turned toward his car, she told Eva in a gentle voice, "Don't worry about me. I'll text you when we're leaving the fair. Can I pick up any veggies for you?"

"You are thoughtful to ask. Yes, we could use some fresh tomatoes for supper tonight. Dad is grilling turkey burgers. I'll pay you back when you come home."

Kaley waved. "Nope, my treat. See you later!"

Eva watched them drive off with a pain in her middle. She breathed a quiet prayer asking the Lord to keep His protective hand over Kaley and Dylan and bring her to her senses. Then Eva strode into the house to tell Scott of their daughter's whirlwind dating plans.

**ON TUESDAY OF THE FOLLOWING WEEK**, Eva and Griff along with several team members, were conducting surveillance at a restaurant where the director of a nonprofit group in DC was to meet a donor from a foreign terror organization.

Eva noted that Griff had parked his car close to the restaurant. He'd be able to observe any activity in the parking lot. Parked beneath a large elm almost a block away, the shade gave Eva relief from the heat. She found these stakeouts rather relaxing; however, she knew they could turn chaotic in a heartbeat based on the actions of the person being tailed.

Deep in thought about Kaley's recent decision to attend FSU in Panama City, Eva's body jumped when her phone buzzed. Her eyes flew to the screen.

The Runner was calling.

Eva's heart quickened. This was her first contact from Captain Ming since she'd returned from Florida. When she answered, a huge roar emitted from Dutch's old phone.

She shouted above the din, "Hello, this is Eva!"

"Please excuse the aircraft noise overhead. This is Yang Ming. Can you hear me?"

"Yes, I can, but the jet engine noise is very loud. Are you okay?"

"I should ask you. I hear nothing from you. Some FBI agents came here asking for me while I was gone. Did you send them? People say FBI is investigating something."

Eva blinked in disbelief. Could the Bureau truly be so stupid?

Rather than reveal her concerns to the Captain, she simply asked, "Has anything happened since we last talked?"

"No. Nothing."

Eva struggled to calm his fears and hers too. "No, I didn't send anyone to question you. I think your senses are heightened because of recent events. The FBI routinely visits military bases to interview personal references for security clearances required for employees like me or you."

"Oh, I can understand. Is that what happened here?" he asked.

Eva found herself nodding even though Ming couldn't see her. "It is common place. You and I are being more alert and watchful, as we should be."

"Okay, thank you. I must get back inside before I am missed."

Eva quickly added, "Be careful what you do and also what you say on your other phone. I will call you immediately if anything important happens here on my end."

"Okay," came his quick response before he disconnected the call.

Was something going on with Ming that Eva needed to know about? If so, how should she find out?

Eva set down her phone, and just when she decided to call Sosa for his assurance that nothing was happening with Captain Ming without her knowledge, the encrypted radio speaker mounted beneath her dashboard crackled.

Her teammate announced, "Looks like the meet is a no show. We're terminating this. Thanks for your help."

"10-4," Griff's voice crackled.

Eva keyed her microphone and chimed, "10-4."

She wrapped the curled microphone cord around the upright gear selector so it hung down near her right knee. Eva headed back toward the office, intending to corner Sosa about Ming.

As she maneuvered along, her cell phone buzzed again. Picking it up, she noted Zion Adelman was calling. Good thing her surveillance had finished.

"Eva here. What can I do for you, Colonel?"

"Listen," he blurted. "I need to talk with you on a secure line."

Alarm jolted through her. "I'm in my G-car but can be in my office in thirty minutes. Ready to copy a number?"

"Go ahead," Zion said.

After giving him the number, Eva heard the line go dead. *Oh oh.*

There *must* be much more going on than what she just speculated to Captain Ming.

Twenty minutes later, she bolted into the office, her mind pinging with dread. Zion had sounded elusive, panicky even.

What did he know that required such secrecy?

She zoomed straight to the Sensitive Compartmented Information Facility, or skiff, as it was commonly called due to its acronym SCIF. She punched in the combination on the keypad and entered. The room had been left tidy by whomever last used it. In the SCIF, agents viewed highly classified papers or used a secure and encrypted phone to discuss secrets with other officials in distant places.

Eva turned up the ringer on the phone, which controlled the flashing light and alarm above the door just outside the closed SCIF door. Confident she'd be able to see and hear Zion's incoming call from her desk, she returned to her cubicle.

She deposited her gun and purse into her desk, and spinning around to return to the SCIF, she nearly bumped into Griff as he entered the office from their surveillance case.

"If you have time, join me in the SCIF," she said in a rush. "I've had two calls from Panama City. Zion will be calling soon on the secure line."

Griff's eyebrows arched. "That's unexpected. Why?"

"Wish I knew," Eva shot back.

Griff lunged toward his desk. "I'll be right there."

Eva had just stepped into the SCIF when the phone began ringing. She went to shut the door, spotting Griff running toward her. Eva had just reached the phone the moment he entered and pushed the door closed. It latched behind him with a snap. She pointed for him to take a seat before pushing the 'answer' button.

"Eva Montanna here," she said, trying to keep doubts from bombarding her thoughts.

The distinct bass voice of Colonel Zion Adelman boomed, "What in the world have you done, Eva?"

Her eyes widened, and looking in surprise at Griff, she replied, "Zion! I've done nothing. What are you calling about?"

"Recently, some FBI agents came nosing around the base. Rumor is they were interviewing the brass and obtaining data from security cameras on the base."

"That could be related to almost anything, Zion. Do you think it involves you?"

"I didn't, not until this morning that is! Ten FBI agents came banging on my front door while I was still in bed. They had a search warrant for my house. They snatched my computer and downloaded data from my and Noelle's cell phones."

Griff's eyebrows shot straight up. Eva scowled, and her heart rate rose, blood pounding against her ears. She fought for calm.

"Zion, take a deep breath. I will, too," Eva said with feeling.

She paused to stare into Griff's eyes with a laser-like focus. When he shook his head and shrugged his shoulders as if in disbelief, she asked Zion, "Please tell me, did the FBI agents tell you what they're investigating?"

"No!" he barked. "They asked questions about who lived in our house and any visitors we had in the last month. I don't have many visitors, except you and the pilots I train that were there during the time in question. I provided your names, but I don't know what to expect. I hoped you might know more."

Questions assailed Eva. *Why did the FBI raid Colonel Adelman? Did Director Whidbey already give my report to the FBI Director?*

Now the FBI had her name connected to Tyndall Air Force Base!

Eva shot Griff another probing glare, raising her open palms upward. He shrugged his shoulders again, giving her no advice.

"I can think of no explanation," Eva told Zion. "So far, we don't have evidence it's connected to your bar-b-que or my conversation with the Captain. Truthfully, I can't say it isn't either."

The retired colonel groaned into the phone, causing Eva to reflect for a moment.

"Zion, I'm sorry for what you're going through. How is Noelle handling this?"

"She's really frightened by it all. We've been in service to our country forever, it seems. To be treated this way is beyond frustrating."

"Did they force entry or do any damage to your home?" Eva asked sympathetically.

"No. The agent in charge and the others too were polite, but they were here for a long while. It's really creepy having them paw through our underwear drawers and such."

Eva doubted the Bureau could tap the lines between SCIFs. Still, she chose her words with care. "Zion, I'll check on my end. I want to ensure there's not been a comingling of investigations. However, I don't want to interfere with another agency's investigation either. If I learn anything I can share with you, I'll let you know. We can speak again from the SCIF."

Zion responded gruffly, "Roger that, Eva. Thanks."

Instantly, the line went dead.

Griff spoke first, "Eva, we've been involved in many dramas together, but this may turn out to be one of the most peculiar."

"For sure, Griff." Eva nodded, her mind whirling. "What should I do?"

"First and foremost, we need to brief Sosa so there's no appearance of trying to hide anything."

Eva's cheeks burned, and she began to feel like the accused. "What do you mean by *hide anything*?"

"I can't explain what's happening." He ran his hand through his thick hair. "Unless Zion isn't telling you all he knows. Do you trust him with our nation's secrets?"

Eva stared at Griff. "I do, and so does the U.S. military. He's served our country with distinction for longer than you and I have. He's the real deal."

"That's good enough for me. I've learned to trust your incredible instincts."

"Griff, thanks for being in here," she said, "even if you only have questions and no answers."

She headed for the door. It was time Eva told Scott what she could—nothing classified—but that she was under scrutiny at work with a possible transfer dangling over both of their heads.

"I need fresh air and time to think." Eva let out a ragged sigh. "Let's meet with Sosa. Then I'm outta here."

After she and Griff briefed their supervisor of the FBI's

latest concerning actions, she headed for home. The drive was a blur. Her mind became consumed by how her report about the Runner seemed to be snowballing out of her control.

Eva tried convincing herself that Sosa's promise to gain more information would end well. Still, knowing her investigation had already caused harm to Zion and Noelle only stoked the anger boiling within her.

As she turned into her neighborhood, she was startled to see an SUV containing a man and a woman parked in front of a house. It looked like a surveillance team. Rather than turning onto her street, Eva drove right past it. There was no reason for people to be sitting in their cars in this neighborhood.

Was she being watched? Was the FBI coming after her?

She circled around the block, determined to get a better look. Approaching the SUV from behind, it appeared empty. Then she saw the couple enter the front door of the nearest home. With her fears lessened somewhat, Eva continued on home, refusing to become paranoid like some lawbreaker.

Eva hit the garage door opener. What she saw—or rather, who she saw—in the garage startled her. There was Dylan Webb standing next to Kaley's Beetle Bug. Her daughter was nowhere in sight.

She parked her G-car in the driveway and hustled out, asking him, "Young man, what are you doing here, and where is Kaley?"

"Oh, hi, Mrs. Montanna. Kaley said you wouldn't be home from work until six," he replied, kicking at a tire on the Bug.

"You didn't answer my questions."

"Kaley asked me to get her iPad out of her back seat." He held it up. "I'm helping her make connections at FSU for off-campus activities. She's in the house."

Eva exhaled sharply, struggling to sound civil. "Okay, I'll follow you inside, Dylan. It's been a long day."

"At the Census Bureau, right?" he asked.

"You first," was all she said, swinging open the door leading into the back hall.

Having to deal with Dylan at the dinner table was the last thing she needed right now. She wanted a quiet evening to talk with Scott about her possible transfer. If Dylan intended to stay, Eva decided Kaley could prepare the meal, even if all she made was scrambled eggs and toast.

# Chapter 18

Days passed by with Eva hearing nothing about the intelligence report she'd written on Captain Yang Ming. On Friday morning, she dressed for work and then found Scott in the kitchen pouring coffee into his travel mug.

"Hey, sweetie," she chirped. "Want me to toast you a bagel?"

He pressed the lid onto his mug. "I need to head out. Hope I'll be home in time for dinner."

"I've been wanting to tell you something one of the last few evenings," Eva said, lowering her chin. "First, Dylan invited himself to supper, then your sister called the next night, then my parents called, yada yada. Bottom line, you and I need to talk."

A shadow crossed his eyes. "Bad news about Kaley? The boys?"

"No, it's work related. I'll just say, I'm unhappy with what's going down."

He reached out for her, planting a light kiss on her forehead. Then he grabbed her hands and prayed softly for God to protect and help her. The moment they said, "Amen," his cell phone beeped. He snatched it out of his pants pocket.

"It's the Pentagon. I've got to take this."

He answered the call, saying, "I'm leaving now."

Scott hung up. He turned to Eva, and something like sunshine beamed at her from his eyes, "Gotta run, Eva. We will make time for each other tonight, I promise."

She handed him the coffee mug and blew him a kiss. Eva checked on the kids, who were supposed to be working on a project for the youth group at church.

When Kaley came into the kitchen and offered to make her brothers breakfast, Eva replied, "Thank you, that will be a big help. And Kaley, remember what Dad and I said about Dylan not being over when we are not home. Period."

"I promise," Kaley said, sounding chagrined. "I didn't ask him to come over. He showed up with a dietary brochure that some friends had designed, right before you came home. It seemed rude to make him stay outside."

"House rules are not rude. I'd like to see you setting better boundaries for yourself. I need to know I can trust you."

Kaley nodded, then reached in the cupboard for a spray can of olive oil. "I'll fix eggs again. At least, Dutch likes whatever I make."

"Text me later to let me know how things are going."

Eva poured coffee for herself and left the house reluctantly. Once in her G-car, she roared to the office. Her foot pressed hard on the accelerator, which mirrored her mounting tension over her family and work. She decided to ask Scott to speak with Kaley again about their daughter's future. Kaley always seemed to listen to her dad.

Regarding her work issues, Eva couldn't help but wonder if she was being ghosted because either ICE or the FBI, or perhaps even both, doubted her trustworthiness. She gulped down the swirling doubt.

She'd always done her job with the highest ethics and her head held high. Why couldn't she trust more in her own instincts and intuition?

**ONCE IN THE OFFICE,** Eva booted up her computer and immediately checked her recent messages. The top one was from ICE Headquarters. Dread pulsed through her at lightning speed.

The caption screamed: TRANSFER OF POST OF DUTY.

The more Eva read, the more she deflated like a leaking balloon. Somehow, she managed to stay in her chair and read to the end of the message. She stared at the screen, each word parading before her eyes, bruising her heart, and crushing her spirits.

*How can this be?*

Director Whidbey had definitely implied he'd block any such transfer. So much for contacts in high positions. Yet, less than an hour ago, she and Scott prayed for God to protect her from harm. So, was this evidence it was God's plan for them to move?

The words in black and white blazed once more before her eyes.

She, Special Agent Eva Montanna, was being transferred from her assignment in Washington, DC to Chicago, Illinois. She must report to Chicago no later than 120 days from today. Supervisors in Washington and Chicago would determine her exact reporting date.

This was unbelievable! How could things get any worse?

Scott had an important career in Washington. The boys would be forced to change schools. She and Scott would have to move during the next two months, so Andy and Dutch started their new schools this fall.

Eva read further in the email, where she was assured a Mobility Coordinator in ICE HQ would assist them in arranging and paying for a house-hunting trip to Chicago. The government would help with costs related to the sale and purchase of a new home, as well as packing and shipping their household goods.

The truth of her situation weighed upon her, taking the very air from her lungs.

A sense of nausea enveloped Eva. She couldn't even call Scott because he was engrossed in some urgent matter at the Pentagon. She'd have to wait for their promised talk at home later tonight. Her eyes flew to Griff's cubicle, which sat dark and empty. She longed to run this terrible development by him.

Eva turned off her computer. She'd buy a fresh cup of hot java at a local coffee shop. The drive might clear her head. On the way down the elevator, she decided not to even hint to the kids about a possible move. First, she'd exhaust all appeals and efforts to get these orders rescinded.

Meanwhile, she drove from the parking lot, mentally calculating her years of service as Special Agent Montanna. Due to the dangers of her job and the need for agents to be in the best physical condition, Congress had passed legislation allowing them to retire after twenty years.

Eva was beginning her nineteenth year, meaning she'd work in Chicago for two more years before she could retire. This might permit Scott to work on fulfilling his required years until his retirement. His pension would include his years as a Navy pilot plus his current time as a civilian.

At the drive-thru, Eva ordered a large, dark-roasted coffee. Waiting at the closed window, credit card in hand, a thought burned in her mind. Scott's best potential opportunities seemed to be here in DC. He might never find a comparable job in Chicago. Plus, considering good schools for her kids was a must.

Then a clearer thought penetrated through the fog in her mind, which she recognized as pure truth: *Nothing is impossible with God.*

# Chapter 19

Nearly a week had flown by when Eva received a phone call at home from the head of her task force, Supervisory FBI Agent Sosa Garcia.

"I don't want to interrupt your dinner," he said in apology for bothering her at home.

"You're not, Sosa. Dinner is done. The kids are doing KP duty."

It was unusual for anybody from the JTTF to call one's home unless they were needed back at the office. Eva clenched her teeth, waiting for him to lower the boom.

"Eva, the JTTF supervisor in Panama City called. They want to interview you tomorrow."

"Interview me? Do you know why?"

Sosa sounded matter-of-fact as he explained, "Yes. A younger FBI agent from down there wants to interview you in a SCIF conference. My guess is that it's about the Air Force instructor you're acquainted with."

"The one whose house the FBI recently searched," Eva replied. "Sosa, you will recall, the instructor introduced me to the Runner, who we now know as the Captain."

Sosa breathed deeply into the phone. "Eva, I hope the FBI hasn't screwed up the good work you've begun. Let's do this. Come directly to the office in the morning. You and I will review the facts, and I'll sit in on the interview."

"Thank you, Sosa. We should include Griff, too. He knows all about that matter."

"Consider it done. I'll see you in the morning, and don't be worried. We'll get the whole thing untangled, even if we have to elevate certain issues at FBI HQ."

**THE FOLLOWING MORNING,** Eva, Sosa, and Griff were ensconced in their office SCIF, ready for the interview. Their quick morning huddle had eased all of Eva's concerns. When the phone rang, and two images popped onto the screen, Eva was surprised by the extreme youth of the case agent.

The young woman with large glasses said, "I'm Special Agent Crystal Lasher. My supervisor, Doug Montgomery, is here with me."

Both FBI agents nodded to Sosa, and he introduced the two special agents joining him in their SCIF.

"Crystal," Eva's boss said crisply, "The floor is yours. How can we help you?"

The pert mid-twenty-something special agent flicked with one hand her long blond braid draped over her shoulder before hunching closer to the camera. Crystal reminded Eva of the high schoolers Eva had seen expounding on Kaley's chat apps.

"Morning, y'all," Crystal chirped. "This conference call results from our contact with Zion Adelman, who appears to be an acquaintance of yours, Eva."

Sosa slid his chair closer to the camera and suddenly interrupted in a caustic tone, "Excuse me, Agent Lasher. Perhaps you could provide context and explain the predicate for your investigation."

"Um ... " Crystal looked at her supervisor, Doug Montgomery.

After a quick glance at his notes, Sosa interjected, "It appears you're investigating a terrorism matter. We want to make sure you are not working at cross-purposes with us."

FBI Supervisor Montgomery nodded. "Yes, Crystal can provide that for you."

The young agent pushed out her bottom lip and began, "When we executed a federal search warrant at Mr. Adelson's house, he claimed to know Agent Montanna. Moreover, he said she had occasion to be at his home. It's uncommon for us to find subjects of our investigation who are friends with special agents. So, we hope to learn the nature of their acquaintance."

Puzzled, Eva opened her mouth to speak.

Sosa beat her to it. "I'm sorry, Agent Lasher, but you still haven't told us the nature of your investigation. What was the probable cause for your search warrant?"

Here, Sosa waved his hand toward the screen. "Or, the predicate of your investigation, if you will?"

Eva's breathing became shallow. Tension heightened, giving her an ache in the pit of her stomach. She was becoming the subject of the FBI's investigation, and she didn't like that one bit. And why was Griff fidgeting in the chair beside her?

Doug Montgomery spoke up, "Frankly Sosa, what Crystal means to say is we wonder if Agent Montanna was down here in Panama City in hopes of initiating an investigation without our knowledge. Poaching is what I call it."

Eva sensed the two supervisors were getting too involved in protecting their territory.

She leaned in to ask Crystal, "Did you actually interview Zion Adelman?"

"Yes. We aren't sure if we trust what he told us."

Eva quickly asked another question before Doug or Sosa could get involved. "What did he tell you about our acquaintance?"

"Mr. Adelman said your parents live across the road from him, and that's how he met you."

"Did he tell you that I, and my family, traveled down from Virginia to visit *my* family and that he met me as his neighbor's daughter?"

Crystal bobbed her head and, fluttering her braid, said begrudgingly, "Ye-es."

Eva gestured toward the camera with both her hands. "Then he told you the truth. Because that is the truth. We've established his veracity, so we are done here."

"Wait! He said you only visited his home once."

Eva's patience was about exhausted. "If you don't get to the point, this interview is done. It's been established I met my parents' neighbor while on vacation. I wasn't there poaching cases."

Suddenly, Crystal's supervisor took center stage. "We have an open case on a fire at the Grass Fed Beef Processing Plant. It appears to be terrorism. Our leads have taken us to the Adelman residence."

Eva glanced at Griff, who seemed to be nodding like he knew all about Crystal and her bogus case. Wait until Eva could corner him after this call in the SCIF.

"So, now we know what your beef is," Sosa responded with a smirk. "Why did it take so long to determine that?"

Eva jumped in, "We're not investigating any beef cattle terrorism matters. I am familiar with the fire and happened to be talking with Zion Adelman on that day."

Crystal seemed determined to regain control. "Agent Montanna, Mr. Adelman told us you were at a picnic at his home, along with some Chinese pilots."

"Yes, I was."

"On the day of the fire, did you use the Adelman's landline telephone?"

"No," Eva answered, trying to anticipate where Crystal was heading with this interview. "I did not."

"Do you know if any of the Chinese pilots used their phone?"

Eva shook her head. "No. Do you think the pilots might have started the beef plant fire?"

Crystal pulled on the end of her braid. "We are considering all possibilities. Social media is abuzz with theories how the ChiComs are attempting to sabotage our food sources."

Eva nearly laughed aloud, but didn't want to insult Doug Montgomery. Hopefully, he didn't agree with this inexperienced agent.

"The pilots being trained by Adelman are not from Communist China," Eva explained slowly as if to a tenth grader. "They are from Taiwan, the friendly Chinese democracy. Are you claiming our allies are helping the ChiComs?"

"Not really. I'm trying to eliminate them, as well as you, from being possible suspects."

Eva did a slow burn. So now she was a suspect in the Grass Fed Beef fire?

"Then you need to tell us more," she insisted. "Why are you focused on phone calls?"

"We've been tasked by FBI HQ to determine the origins of a phone call placed the day before the fire began. The call was made to a climate activist blogger in Finland, who is at the heart of a movement to destroy animal food sources all around the world. This Finnish blogger is suspected of conspiring with this movement."

At last, Eva thought Crystal was making sense. "And you think the Taiwanese pilots are colluding with the Finn and calling from the Adelman residence?"

"We've searched the Adelman house and reviewed every bit of security video from Tyndall Air Force Base. We determined all the pilots and Zion Adelman were on the base at the time the phone call was made. So, Agent Montanna, if you weren't at his home the day of the phone call, then the logical suspect is Mrs. Adelman."

*Oh, no!* Eva thought. *Poor Noelle.*

Before Eva could respond, Crystal continued, "I'll ask you again, Ms. Montanna. Were you in the Adelman home at 2:28 on the afternoon of Wednesday, June 14?"

"No, I was not," Eva said, noting the time and date on her notepad. Convinced Crystal and her Panama City group had no interest in Captain Ming, Eva toyed with her.

"I'm sorry to complicate your case, but I must inform you that Noelle Adelman, your prime suspect, was serving and eating beef burgers as well as pork on Saturday, June 17."

Crystal's eyes blinked several times behind her glasses. "Why does that disappoint me?"

"I'm sorry." Eva paused for effect. "I thought you had decided she wasn't working for the ChiComs, so therefore, her motive must be she's a vegan."

It was Crystal's turn to educate Eva. "No. We haven't focused on a motive. It could be a disgruntled employee or an international group hoping to reduce global warming from carbon dioxide."

"Or perhaps vegetarians or vegans trying to reduce the availability of animal protein." Eva smiled wryly.

Instantly, Sosa interrupted, "I think we've determined we are not interfering with each other's cases. Eva has told you all she knows about the Adelmans. If you have further questions, you can contact her. I'm sure she will help in those areas where she has knowledge."

Doug nodded and said suddenly, in a friendlier tone, "We thank you for your assistance. I think we're done here."

"Wait." Crystal raised a palm toward the camera. "Can Eva assure us that she will not discuss with the Adelmans what she's learned here today?"

To Eva's curt nod, Sosa responded, "That should *not* be necessary. Eva has many years of flawless service. She knows and honors the safeguards regarding 'need to know.'"

"Understood," Doug said, smiling back. "Thank you."

Instantly, the screen went blank. Sosa stood and reached for the door handle.

"What do you make of it, Eva?" he asked, his brows etched.

Eva shrugged. "It's really strange. The Adelmans both seem as American as apple pie. There must be some other explanation for a phone call to Finland from their home."

"Well, it's not our problem," Sosa concluded. "We have bigger fish to fry."

He walked out of the SCIF. Eva closed the door quietly and sat beside Griff.

"This is really weird, Griff."

"And? I see you are flummoxed."

Eva rubbed her temples, her fingers moving in circles.

"Got a headache?" Griff asked.

"No. I am perplexed. Have you heard of the six degrees of separation theory?"

"I suppose so. Some psychologist back in the sixties experimented and claimed we, as social beings, are all connected to each other through as few as six other people. Right?"

Eva sat staring and shaking her head.

He folded his arms. "What's that got to do with this case?"

"I have this nagging notion. Kaley has met an oddball kid from George Mason University who's been hanging around her."

"So? She's close to the right age for dating. Besides, George Mason is almost in your backyard."

"His name is Dylan Webb. His mother is a defense attorney."

Griff wrinkled his nose. "Oh no, that's almost as bad as being an ambulance chaser."

"It gets worse." Eva folded her arms. "I think Dylan is manipulative and dishonest. Andy doesn't like him because he's seen him using his grandmother's handicap parking permit and juggling several girlfriends at the same time."

Griff crooked his index finger to summon more. "Come on, tell me the worst. His father is a Chinese spy, and he's connected to you by six degrees."

"It's no joking matter," Eva insisted. "Dylan showed up in Panama City and visited Kaley on that Wednesday."

"Eva, he's a normal boy, interested in a pretty and smart girl. When I met Dawn in Panama City, I thought of every excuse I could to fly down there. Today, she's my wife."

Eva waved Griff off. "Bad example. I don't want her marrying a guy like him. You are not getting my point."

"Okay, tell me more."

"He visits Kaley at my folks' house, which is right across the road from the Adelman's home. This is on the very same day the phone call goes to Finland, and after midnight that night, the beef plant burns. Oh, and by the way, Dylan is a vegan."

Griff let out a whistle. "That is within six degrees. Don't you think it's all just a coincidence?"

Eva stood and hastened to the door. "It may be, but Dylan Webb is persona non grata around Kaley from here on out."

# Chapter 20

Eva's drive home morphed into a dark cloud of concern. Her route was so familiar that she had no need to navigate. Instead, her mind chose to wander from the prospects of Scott finding a job he loved in Chicago, to their three kids adjusting to new schools and friends, and how she was going to pry Kaley away from Dylan.

Nearing her favorite coffee place, Eva didn't stop. The heat oppressed her, and even iced coffee held no appeal. She'd enjoyed her fantastic career, finding it fulfilling and successful, until now. Eva sighed, thinking how she'd fallen out of favor and was targeted for transfer by her own headquarters staff. Even worse, a Terrorism Task Force group similar to her own suspected her of misconduct.

"Being emotional won't solve things," Eva said aloud as she stomped on the brakes at the red light.

Eva steeled her mind, forcing herself to contend with the likes of Dylan Webb. She hit a mental rewind to consider anew what she'd learned about Dylan. He claimed to be visiting his uncle in Panama City.

Was that a lie? Who was his uncle?

She couldn't help wondering if Dylan was a terrorist at heart.

A new thought blazed through her mind about the rural phone service near the farm. It was possible Dylan was really an electrical engineering student who tapped into the phone lines near the Vander Goes farm. Perhaps he used this devious means to place a call on Zion's phone.

It was a distinct possibility. Eva doubted he could have been inside Zion's house. Even when Zion was at work, his wife Noelle was home.

Eva pulled into the driveway, ready to call her dad in Florida to learn more about his phone service. The sight of her young son, Dutch, kicking a ball in the yard changed her mind. No need to raise her father's suspicion about Zion. Instead, she had another idea.

**AFTER DINNER THAT NIGHT AND DISHES WERE DONE,** Eva sat in their home office, calculating her next phone call. She really wanted to speak with Zion Adelman, but if she phoned him at the base, he might not be free to talk. Moreover, since JTTF in Panama City had searched his home due to a phone call from his home number, that line most likely had a tap.

Eva made an instant decision to call his cell number.

His warmhearted voice answered, "Good evening, friend."

"To you as well." Eva kept her voice low so she wouldn't be overheard by her family. "Zion, I'm busy thinking about that unknown call allegedly made from your phone."

He barked, "Me too. Can't stop thinking about it."

"Let me run something by you. On the day that call was placed, I encountered a young man on my parent's farm."

"Huh," Zion interrupted. "You seem to attract unexpected encounters."

"Yes, it's like I'm a magnet for the unknown," Eva said. "I wonder if a stranger could have tapped into phone lines in your area. Our neighborhood yards are full of these small green pedestals where utility workers access the phone lines. You know the type; they're on the property line near the road edges."

Zion stayed quiet for a long moment, as if Eva had tossed him a curveball.

Finally, he grunted. "I believe the devices you describe are common for underground utilities. Here in the country, such access requires a worker to climb a pole. That kind of tapping would be harder to do out here."

"You've had no further problems related to that call?" Eva probed.

"We haven't. I've thought about it much. I've even considered if somebody made such a call from my extension phone in the barn."

"You have an extension phone? In your barn?" Eva's mind moved fast and furious.

He chuckled. "Yup. Noelle grew tired of running out to find me in the barn when I had a phone call. Now, she just yells from the back door, and I know the call is for me."

"Zion, that explains how a call was made without Noelle's knowledge."

"True, even though most unlikely. Do you think I should call those agents that came here and tell them a stranger showed up in the area that day?"

Eva was devising a plan of her own. "Let me take care of it. I've spoken to the case agent and will pass along what I know."

"There's no need for me to do anything?" he asked, sounding conflicted.

She understood his reputation at the base was at stake and sought to assuage his concern. "Trust me to handle it, Zion. I do not believe your pilot trainees are connected to the phone call."

He sighed heavily into the phone. "Well, that gives me some relief."

"Good," Eva told him. "Stay tuned. You and Noelle should try to have a peace-filled night."

**THE MOMENT EVA HUNG UP,** she sped from the home office to Kaley's room. Her door was closed. Assuming it was to avoid noise from her brothers, Eva tapped lightly on the door.

"Kaley, it's me. Can I come in?"

The door opened wide with Kaley asking, "What's up?"

Eva closed the door behind her. "I'd like to ask you something about our time in Florida."

Kaley sat on her bed, setting aside a book. Eva perched on the edge beside her.

"Remember when Dylan stopped to visit you at the farm?"

"Of course, Mom." Kaley paused. Doubt edged her voice as she asked, "What of it?"

Eva chose her next words carefully, "Is it possible Dylan might have been at Zion's farm when he visited?"

"Absolutely. We both went over to his farm. Why?"

Not wanting to alarm Kaley or divulge any classified material, Eva fibbed, "Mrs. Adelman looked out her window that day and saw a young man in the yard by the barn."

"Yup." Kaley waved as though swatting a fly. "That was probably when I left Dylan there. That's maybe why she didn't see me."

"What prompted you to go there?" Eva asked, suspicions heightening.

"You and Gram went to make meals for the injured man and his family, remember?"

"I recall being at church with Mom fixing meals. What happened while I was gone?"

Kaley swiped a stray hair from her eyes and then gave Eva a blow-by-blow account of Gramps sending her and Dylan to fetch a trailer from Zion's barn.

Convinced at last that her daughter did nothing wrong, Eva asked Kaley the burning question, "Were either you or Dylan alone in the barn?"

Kaley frowned. "We never found a wrench. Is something missing?"

Eva felt strange interrogating her own daughter about a violation of the law.

"No, I'm just trying to figure out why Mrs. Adelman didn't see you there, too."

"Mom. It's no big deal. When we couldn't find a wrench to unhook the trailer from the tractor, Dylan kept searching the barn while I drove back to get one from Gramps."

Bingo! Eva had her answer. The crazy kid Kaley fancied herself wanting a relationship with had been alone in the barn with Zion's extension phone. He had the means and motive to make the phone call to Finland.

Eva exhaled softly. How to back out of this interrogation without frightening Kaley?

"You're right." Eva rose to her feet. "It's no big deal. Noelle happened to mention it when we were there and I grew curious."

Kaley had more to say. "That's the way you are, Mom. You're always analyzing everything. I think I inherited your same curiosity."

"Oh?" Eva leaned against the door jam. "You still think you'd like to be a special agent?"

Kaley looked quizzically at her mom. "Yeah, sometimes I

do. It's been a nice career for you. You enjoy your job, don't you?"

"Yeah, sometimes I do," Eva replied, echoing Kaley's words back to her. "Remember, you need to maintain a spotless lifestyle to pass a background investigation."

Kaley jumped from her bed. "You don't think I'm capable of that?"

"Sure, I do. My mom, your Grams, cautioned me when I was your age that I would be 'known by the company I kept.' The same applies to you, too."

"Meaning what, Mom?"

"Meaning the likes of Dylan."

"So, you don't like Dylan? Why not?" Kaley spit out.

"Honey, I don't know him. You have to be the judge of Dylan and if he's good for you.  You've been around him enough to form an opinion."

"He seems nice to me."

Eva could have left the subject alone but decided to test Kaley further.

"Is Dylan honest with you about his dating? Are you the only girl he's pursuing, or is he marginal? Is he the kind of guy who would use someone else's handicap parking permit for his convenience and deny the close parking spots to people who truly need them?"

Kaley's bottom lip protruded slightly as she stared at her mother. "Okay, I need to think about that."

Eva had said enough. It was time to check on Scott's schedule for the rest of the week.

Before turning to leave, she said gently, "Pray about it, Kaley. That is certainly what your dad and I are doing for each one of our kids."

# Chapter 21

Early the next morning, Eva sat at her office desk, awaiting Griff's arrival. Since her conversation last evening with Kaley, she'd been thinking about how best to report the new information regarding Dylan. When she heard someone enter the office and head straight to the coffee station, she figured it had to be Griff. He passed her cubicle carrying his travel mug, and she pounced.

"Good morning. I have a new case for you. It's gift-wrapped with a bow. Meet me in the conference room."

Griff stood motionless, eyebrows shooting up. Then he managed, "Count me in."

Eva was seated with her leather folder opened on the table when he hurried in.

Pointing to the door, Eva ordered, "Close it."

After snagging the seat across from her, he took a quick sip from his coffee before setting it on the table.

Then he launched his famous wide smile. "Okay. Amaze me."

"I previously told you of Dylan Webb being near Zion Adelman's house on the day and at the time when a call was made to Finland."

"I recall what you said."

"Since then, I've uncovered evidence proving he was alone in Zion's barn on the day of the phone call. I've uncovered evidence that the barn has a working extension phone. Not only is Dylan Webb the guy who made the phone call, he's the guy who probably torched the beef plant."

Griff slapped the table with an open palm. "For sure!"

"Yes! For sure. You need to write a report identifying him as the suspect."

Griff stared back without flinching. "Nope, I can't do that, Eva. It's your discovery. You need the credit."

"Wrong. I've become a suspect by the misguided FBI. You need to take all the evidence I give you and write it up. After all, he lives near here. It's in your backyard, so to speak."

The two special agents had a friendly discussion about the pros and cons of what Eva had proposed, with much coffee being guzzled by Griff.

He finally set down his empty mug. "Okay, I'm in. Tell me everything you know."

Eva explained how Dylan showed up uninvited in Panama City. "He claimed he wanted to see Kaley. They went over on a quad to Zion's house to retrieve a trailer to haul pine straw for my dad. Kaley happened to divulge to me last night that she left Dylan alone in the barn when she returned on the quad to ask my dad for a wrench. And Zion confirmed to me that he installed an extension phone in his barn a few years ago."

"If Kaley tells me what she told you, then I'll write the report, and you'll no longer be involved." Griff spread his hands on the table. "Right?"

"True, but I don't want Kaley to be identified as the source or a snitch. It makes her sound like a criminal."

"Come on, Eva." Griff waved his hand in the air. "You know lots of respectable people supply information to us, which is why we now refer to them as CHS."

"Griff, I know what a Confidential Human Source is. She can't be a CHS because she's only seventeen. Kaley's still a minor."

"If her guardian agrees, Kaley can be our source," he insisted. "Face it. Her info is critical to stopping a terrorist. We can keep you totally out of the whole process by having Kaley's father be the guardian of record."

"True, but I'm not convinced Kaley should become more deeply involved in this case."

Eva rubbed her neck and lifted up a silent prayer for God's direction. Would Scott even agree?

"Let's do this." She straightened her back in the uncomfortable chair. "If Scott's on board, we'll schedule a time for you both to talk with Kaley. She's admitted she still wants to become a special agent after college. She might agree to this."

"We better act quickly. We don't know what Dylan Webb plans to do next. Warn Zion not to use his phone in the barn again until Crystal's Panama City team processes it for latent prints."

With their plan ready to launch, Eva hurried from the conference room behind Griff. Upon reaching her cubicle, she texted Scott: *We need to have lunch today, if possible.*

Within minutes, he sent his reply: *About to meet SecDef for today's press release. Much happening. See you at Pentagon City café at noon.*

Eva sent Scott a heart emoji in reply. She could hear Griff typing away on his computer keyboard. No doubt he was already preparing the report, which gave her peace of mind about the Adelmans being cleared of any wrongdoing.

If only God would give Eva the same sense of peace about Kaley and her future.

**FORTY-EIGHT HOURS AFTER EVA'S LUNCH WITH SCOTT,** Griff met with Kaley in their home. In her parents' presence, Kaley had repeated what she'd learned about Dylan Webb and his visit to Panama City. Griff was back in the empty office, as everyone else had gone home. He'd eat supper with Dawn after filing his report.

He organized his thoughts and began typing a factual summary. This report would be used to initiate an investigation. An hour later, after reviewing his report, he made a few changes to the synopsis, which now stated:

"A Confidential Human Source (CHS) advised that on June 14, Dylan Webb, a student at George Mason University, a self-professed vegan, and a resident of Fairfax, Virginia, was in Panama City, Florida. He was driving a rented Ford Mustang convertible during the time when fire destroyed the Grass Fed Beef Processing Plant in Panama City. The CHS further advised Webb was at the pine tree farm of Zion Adelman on the afternoon of June 14, and that Webb, who is unacquainted with the Adelman family, entered their barn, which contains an extension telephone, without their knowledge."

Upon further reading, Griff ensured he included all information and physical description available through public records about Dylan and his parents. He added every other detail furnished by the confidential source.

At the conclusion of the report, under the caption

Investigative Leads, he typed the following action items:

*The Panama JTTF is requested to contact local car rental agencies to find corroborating evidence of Dylan Webb's car rental and check local hotels for his presence.*

*The Panama City JTTF is requested to search by consent or search warrant, the Adelman barn and process the barn and any extension phone for latent prints.*

*The Panama City JTTF is requested to examine available security video near the Grass Fed Beef for any evidence of said Ford Mustang Convertible in the area.*

*The Northern Virginia JTTF will apply for a court-ordered monitor on Dylan Webb's cell phone.*

Griff signed off on his report, which he forwarded to Sosa Garcia to approve and disseminate. He remained hopeful that he and Eva could prevent Kaley's identity from becoming known. He called Eva at home and gave her a heads-up.

"I'm at the office and finished my report about the new source's info about DW. I'm concerned PC will want access to the source."

"Griff, I understand," Eva replied. "That's not a problem. They can send you any questions, and you can ask the source. The source insists on not having any other contact but you."

"Okay! That works. Have a good evening."

Griff logged off his computer, ready to have a relaxing meal with his wife. It had been weeks since they had gone on an actual date. He punched in her number.

"Can you meet me at Anthony's, our favorite Italian eatery?" Griff asked when Dawn answered.

"I'd love to, and need a few minutes," she replied, sounding out of breath. "I just got home. It's been a tough drive in the sweltering heat. My car's AC is on the blink again."

"In that case, I'll pick you up, and we'll eat at the bistro around the corner. Their bread pudding slathered with ice cream is calling my name."

Dawn laughed. "You have the greatest ideas, Griff. I'll be ready."

# Chapter 22

On the last Saturday morning in late July, Kaley Montanna sat reading at her bedroom desk. Her dad and brothers were at a men's breakfast at church. Her mom was expecting a visit from Griff Topping, her longtime partner from the FBI. He should arrive pretty soon.

Kaley scrolled through the website for FSU's Panama City campus for her umpteenth time. The more she read, the more comfortable she became about moving to Panama City next month. She'd already been accepted as a commuting student and planned to live in the dormitory above her grandparents' garage.

Pending any changes, she and Mom were driving down in two weeks to their farm. Kaley giggled, thinking about squishing all of her stuff into her lime-green Slug Bug. Mom planned to fly back to DC.

Kaley made a few notes about her fall courses and some campus activities on her notepad when she heard Griff's familiar voice echoing from the kitchen. She closed down her computer and bustled to the kitchen.

Griff stood up from the table and raised his coffee cup in the air. "Kaley, join me for coffee."

She said, "Good morning to you, Mr. Topping," and then poured some of the hot brew into a large cup shaped like an owl.

"You're a young adult and can call me Griff," he replied, grinning.

So far, her mom was strangely quiet. Kaley looked over at her sitting across from Griff.

"Don't you guys see each other enough at the office?" Kaley joked. "What's up today, anyway?"

Her mom slid a plate of blueberry muffins toward Griff and suggested Kaley have one with her coffee. "I told Griff of your possible interest in federal law enforcement, so he thought he'd come and brag to you about the FBI."

Interested in what he might say, Kaley finished adding cream and sugar, stirred her cup, and then sat in a chair at the end of the table.

"How interested are you in a career pursuing justice?" Griff asked.

Kaley nodded vigorously. "Mom's right. I've followed her career and think it's the job for me."

"It may be, but first things first." Griff pointed to her cup. "If you're serious, you've gotta learn to drink your coffee black, like a man."

"What does that mean?" Kaley protested. "It sounds sexist."

"Griff means most cops and we law enforcement types drink our coffee without cream or sugar because many times we're too hurried or the additives just aren't available. Yet, we need caffeine to stay awake."

"Yeah, Mom. You said you used to sweeten yours." Kaley turned to Griff. "I'm not old enough to join the FBI, but am interested in a career with them."

Griff smiled at her again. "Here's a possible idea where you can achieve experience toward being a federal agent. You could use a closely-held program, one that would begin your relationship with the Bureau."

"Really?" Kaley said, widening her eyes at the possibilities.

She gazed at her mom and then back at Griff. Hearing no objection from her mother, Kaley pressed, "How so? Remember, I leave for FSU next month."

When she glanced again at her mother, it was Griff who jumped in to explain, "Certain crimes occur even in Panama City. If you're so inclined, you could assist the Bureau by being alert to those and reporting them to *me*." Griff turned both thumbs toward his chest.

"Oh! That sounds like a snitch," Kaley objected, tossing her head to the side.

"No," Griff countered. "It's the pursuit of justice and what your mom and I do."

Here, her mom intoned, "What Griff says is true. That's what law enforcement is. You can't just overlook crimes. If you've sworn to uphold the law, then you do so even when your friends are involved."

Kaley studied both their faces, trying to understand what

was going on. "What kind of crime are we talking about? Pot smokers?"

"Nope." Griff shook his head. "How about an environmental terrorist?"

"Wow! Terrorists!" Kaley puffed out her cheeks. "Surely not in Panama City. It seems like a safe place to live."

"If I could convince you there are, would you consider it?"

Kaley stared first at Griff and then at her mom. She wrinkled up her nose at what Griff was proposing. Her mom had great respect for him.

*Mom is always super protective of us kids. Yet here she sits, approving and watching.*

Deciding maybe this was a new way of being recruited by the FBI, Kaley gripped her coffee cup and said, "Okay. I'll hear you out."

"Consider this," Griff said. "Somewhere, there's a person or group of people who believe it's dangerous for our society and planet to allow anyone to eat meat or animal products. Let's also say this person or group decides he or they should burn down a beef processing plant in Panama City."

Shock ran through Kaley like a runaway horse. Her hands flew to her cheeks.

With her heart pounding, she cried, "Mom! That happened at Gramps' house when we were in Panama City. Was that by terrorists?"

"We're talking hypothetically here," her mom replied. "If that was true, would that be a crime?"

"Yes!" Kaley said, emphasizing with both hands in the air.

"No humans were killed or injured, but animals were." Griff's voice grew more ominous. "What if someone knew about a similar plan and could prevent the death of a person or the destruction of animals? Should such a person say something?"

"Duh! Of course. Are you saying the people who torched that plant are in Panama City, and you need a freshman at FSU to keep her ears open?"

Kaley looked at her mother, asking further, "Can I help the FBI and get some leverage that way?"

"It's kind of that way," her mom replied, reaching for

Kaley's hand. "Which is why, as your mother, I'm sitting here listening."

For the next thirty minutes, Griff explained to Kaley what would be expected of her. Once she understood she was not an employee of the FBI and must be truthful in everything she reported to Griff, she was also told she'd be reimbursed for all expenses.

"And Kaley," Griff paused. "Most importantly, I insist you tell no one of your cooperation as a confidential human source, not even your brothers. The FBI will do everything in its power to protect your identity and cooperation."

Mom nodded. "Your dad knows, of course."

Griff removed papers from a folder on the table.

"I have a form you need to sign, Kaley." He pointed above the signature line. "It says you understand and agree with all we just talked about. Because you're not yet eighteen, your dad also has to sign it, which he can do later."

He slid the form to Kaley and she read through it.

As she signed her name, she asked, "What you just explained about the beef plant, is it hypothetical?"

"No," he said firmly. "It is an act of terrorism. Meant to frighten the employees and anyone who eats meat."

"It gets worse," her mother interrupted. "Remember when I asked if you had been at Zion's house on the Wednesday before the plant burned?"

"Yes."

"Well, FBI agents have been to Zion's house and searched it. They learned someone at their house was involved in the arson."

"No! That can't be!" Kaley objected. "They're really nice people."

Griff ran his open palm over his moustache, then looked at her so intently that Kaley could feel her cheeks growing hot. She held her breath.

Then he said, "On that Wednesday, the day before the fire, someone made a phone call from Zion's house to a foreign organization known for burning barns with animals and meat processing plants."

"No!" she whispered.

"Yes." Griff gave a nod. "Zion Adelman was at his office at Tyndall, and the only person at the house was his wife, Noelle."

Something terrible nagged at Kaley, and she objected, "It can't be. I know what you're thinking. Dylan was there. But he never went inside the house. Mrs. Adelman knows that."

"Listen, Kaley, he was in the barn, which has a phone extension," Griff countered, his arms folded across his chest. "Was Dylan ever alone in the barn?"

Kaley's hand flew to cover her mouth, and she flashed her eyes at her mother. "Ugh! He was alone in there! It must be him!"

Silence fell in the room like they were all in an elevator going down, down. Kaley dropped her eyes and couldn't stand looking at her mom. Her mind and heart felt like a collision of emotions.

*Why did I ever go out with Dylan? What will Dad say when he finds out?*

Kaley started biting one of her fingernails while her mom drank her coffee and Griff ate a muffin.

She breathed deeply and finally spoke. "Dylan has weird ideas. His friends do, too. I'm used to weirdos from school, but to find out he's a criminal is hard."

The eerie quiet swirled around her like clouds ready to rain. Kaley finally faced her mother. "What will happen to him?"

"It requires more investigating," she said in gentle tones. "Griff will work on it. I'm here to talk with you anytime, honey."

Kaley slumped in her chair. "Griff, maybe you already know this. Dylan texts and calls me. Do you want me to ask him why he did it?"

"I wish it could be that easy and that he'd confess to you," Griff replied. "But, no, it isn't, and he won't. For now, just think of everything he's done or told you. We can talk later to further document his conversations and actions. Meanwhile, I need to take your picture and your fingerprints."

"What? Why? Am I a suspect?"

The way Griff smiled at her just then reminded Kaley of how her dad looked when he beat her at chess. "No, but if we pay your expenses and make a record of the info you furnish, we need evidence that you're really you and also that you're not a felon."

Kaley glanced at her mother and saw she was nodding.

"Okay." Kaley turned to Griff. "When Dylan came to Panama City, he said he was visiting his uncle. We should check for any men named Webb living in that area, or check for Dylan Webb at local hotels in case he was lying to me."

Griff laughed. "See Eva? The apple doesn't fall far from the tree."

He gathered up the forms, leaving the one for Scott to sign. With his cell phone, Griff took her photo.

He gave her a final caution, "Kaley, while that's a good investigative lead, we'll handle such matters. You won't be told of the results. Just remember all you can, and we'll talk again later."

**GRIFF HADN'T BEEN GONE LONG** when Eva again looked over the FBI Confidential Human Source form he'd left for Scott. She was glad when Kaley returned to the kitchen to pour a second cup of coffee and rejoin Eva at the table.

Her daughter held her cup aloft. "See, Mom. I'm trying it black like you said just to see if it improves my career options."

They traded smiles. Eva pushed aside the form. It was time to uncover her daughter's true feelings.

"What do you really think about your conversation with Griff and helping him?" she asked gently.

"I'm not sure," Kaley said. She avoided Eva's eyes by gazing into the owl coffee cup. "Will knowing Dylan have a negative impact on my reputation? I had no idea he was a violent criminal."

Eva patted her hand. "You reacted just as I would want you to. It will be a credit to you that you're recognizing an opportunity to right a wrong."

"Do you think helping Griff as a … What did he call me, a source? Am I wrong to help him that way?"

"First of all, Kaley, you're a witness with valuable information. It's every person's duty to cooperate with authorities in order to maintain order in our society. And consider the opportunity you have to learn what a career in law enforcement is truly like. It's better than spending a semester as an intern. In the end, if you don't like it, you can change your major."

A hush lingered between mother and daughter as Kaley sipped her coffee. Eva tried to imagine all she might be contemplating.

"I have a confession to make, Mom." Kaley thumped down her cup.

Eva sat up straight, questions peppering her mind.

*A confession? Was Kaley somehow involved in the explosion?*

She fought for calm, saying simply, "I'm listening."

Kaley folded her hands on the table, tears hovering on her long eyelashes. "Dylan is not my type. He flattered me when he met me by saying he'd never seen such a beautiful woman as me. I wanted him to like me, even though I spotted some of his strange ways right away, like how he hates people who eat meat. I knew better but encouraged him anyway. From now on, I want to do right, always."

"Kaley." Eva folded her hands around her daughter's trembling hands. "You're a bright young lady with her whole life ahead of her. I'm glad you shared your feelings with me, and I will keep praying for you, asking God to help you. You believe in Him, and He promises to direct our steps when we seek His wisdom. Are you doing that?"

Kaley's sigh was deep and long. "Not as much as last year, when I attended youth group more often. Being a senior, I've forgotten to read my Bible every day or even pray. Sorry, Mom."

"Your dad and I have times when life takes over and we get busy at work," Eva answered carefully. "He and I have learned in our years of marriage that when we put the Lord first in our lives, we're closer to Him and to each other. Would you like to pray with me now?"

When Kaley nodded and chirped a soft "Yes," Eva closed her eyes and prayed over Kaley, asking God to bless her, protect her, and draw her closer to Him.

# Chapter 23

Eva heard Scott and the boys come clamoring in upstairs from their men's day at the church. She was in the basement laundry room, ironing her cotton blouses. It didn't take Scott long to walk down the steps, holding the "source" agreement Kaley had signed for Griff.

He waved it toward Eva. "We need to talk about this form. Kaley said I need to sign it as her legal guardian."

Eva turned the blouse collar and pressed it flat on the ironing board.

"This is a perfect time," she told him.

"For me too." He grabbed a folding chair and sat down. "Do you know she's upstairs trying to create a vegan meal in the kitchen?"

"Yes. She wants to find a recipe to share with Dylan as a way to foster a natural relationship with him."

"Eva," he replied, frustration oozing as he said her name sharply. "This is no good for Kaley. He's not the kind of guy I ever want her to associate with again. You and Griff are encouraging her to become vulnerable to danger and his enticing ways."

Eva unplugged her iron and pulled out another chair. Lowering her voice, she reminded Scott, "You were present in Florida. You know we didn't invite Dylan to come down there or to my folks' home."

"But—" he objected.

"No!" Eva interrupted.

She waved her hand in the air. "Wait. The events that occurred weren't of our making. I've since discovered Dylan was there to commit an act of terrorism. He put all of us at risk. I believe through Divine intervention, Dylan unknowingly blundered into our presence so we could prevent any further such shenanigans."

"Why do we have to involve Kaley?" Scott insisted.

"Scott, we didn't. Dylan did. And he has made Kaley a witness of a federal crime. We can't just ignore that."

"But, do we need this secretive paperwork?"

Eva edged her chair to look directly into his eyes. "No. She can just call the FBI and tell them she was with Dylan at Zion's home, where he phoned his confederate the day before he set fire to the Grass Fed Beef plant. Her name would then be spilled across every report, in search warrants and arrest warrant affidavits."

Scott stared back, his jaw ajar, as if computing the terrible options.

"Then two months from now," Eva continued, "the nightly news will broadcast, 'Kaley Montanna, daughter of the Secretary of Defense's press spokesman, Scott Montanna, is tied to an international terrorism group.' Is that a better option?"

Scott raised both hands, palms out. "No! That's millions of times worse."

"If we permit Kaley to use the cover as 'source' for Griff, the FBI can concentrate on investigating Dylan without knowing anything about Kaley. Kaley also has an opportunity to see the pros and cons of a law enforcement career."

"She will be at some risk," Scott declared.

"Yes, sweetheart, but Dylan already put her at risk. Fortunately, we discovered it in time. So, you and I, along with Griff, are in a position to protect her. And so is God. She and I prayed together after Griff left. She clearly sees the truth of the situation. Scott, she wants to do this."

"I feel better knowing that." He fluttered the source agreement. "As her father, I think I should have done more to protect her, like scaring Dylan off before he got a foothold in our daughter's life. You remind me to pray more about this. Let's you and I do that tonight, okay?"

"Absolutely," Eva said with conviction.

**ON SUNDAY EVENING,** Eva relaxed on the sofa, thumbing through her recipe book to plan a menu for the coming week, when Kaley plunked down beside her. She held up her cell phone to display a cluster of texts.

"Look, I've received four texts from Dylan today."

"Is that normal from him?" Eva snapped shut her recipe book.

"No, and that's my point, Mom. I haven't heard from him in over a week, but earlier I sent him a picture of the spicy rice noodles with coconut that I made and a copy of the recipe. He sent me this text blizzard in response."

Eva raised her eyebrows. "See how easy it is to manipulate a response from him?"

"He even sent me this article from a PhD candidate at Columbia University who claims that by the year 2100, we can reduce heat on our planet by 0.9 degrees Celsius just by reducing our consumption of beef."

"He believes it, I'm sure," Eva answered with a shake of her head. "Meanwhile, he doesn't want people heating or cooling their homes. He's willing to commit acts of violence to force his beliefs on the rest of society."

Excitement rang from Kaley's voice as she continued, "Did you know that beef, goats, and sheep are the greatest sources of methane gas that's nearly eighty percent more potent than carbon dioxide? Harvard Medical School has a model by which they can reduce future global warming by fifty-five percent, which involves a protein-rich diet of bugs that cuts down on saturated fat and cholesterol."

"Stop!" Eva insisted. "What have you done with my Kaley."

Kaley laughed. "Do I sound like one of Dylan's friends?"

"Yes, you do."

"Good. I'm trying to learn how to share his interests, so he confides in me."

Eva felt a need to caution Kaley.

She grabbed her hand. "From now on, you must consider Dylan a criminal. During any contact, whether in person, by text, or by phone, you must carefully weigh in your mind what you're about to say to him. You must always stick to a script so that you won't slip and say something that causes him to see you as a threat to him and his associates."

"Really?" Kaley asked, twisting to look at her mom.

"When I or any other agent or police officer assumes an undercover role, we totally concentrate on remaining in character so that our true identity is never disclosed."

Kaley folded her arms. "How am I doing so far?"

"With these texts, you're off to a fine start. Think through some scenarios, such as when Dylan wants you to do something, which you refuse to do. Then, you must have a ready response for the unexpected, even if it's just a stalling tactic."

"Yikes, Mom." Kaley's face drooped. "Your job is more complex than I ever thought. I better up my game. Can I share my scenarios with you once I come up with them?"

"Yes, I wouldn't have it any other way."

# Chapter 24

It was early in August, when the days were long and hot in the District of Columbia. Eva, along with Griff and Sosa, battled crowds of tourists and commuters on the Metro to FBI Headquarters. As they passed through the security gauntlet, Eva wondered how Captain Ming was doing.

She hadn't heard from him since the FBI had shown up at Tyndall. She hoped the meeting today with the FBI's Assistant Director would provide her with the necessary updates.

The trio rode the elevator to the executive floor. When the doors opened, Eva noted the stark difference between the office space of the work-a-bees and her cramped cubicle at the JTTF and up here, where the executives spent their workdays. While she admired the walnut-paneled walls, thicker carpet, and hushed acoustics, she wouldn't trade her position to be stuck up here, no matter how plush the carpet.

The three agents were ushered into a spacious conference room with a long mahogany table and gathered at one end, near the drinking glasses set beside chrome-insulated water carafes on a silver tray. Griff rolled his eyes at Eva and pointed at the wall behind him.

She turned to see a prominent picture of J. Edgar Hoover hanging on the wall and overlooking the seat at one end of the table, as though he was still in charge.

"Eva, that can be your seat," Griff joked.

"Not on your life," she replied, thinking about the reason for this hurriedly called meeting.

Sosa had explained before they had left their office that they were to confer regarding Captain Yang Ming, but aside from that, he knew nothing.

Sosa was the first to stand abruptly as Assistant Director Kerstin Harvick entered along with an assistant carrying a digital tablet. He silently assumed a chair near the opposite end of the table. Supervisor Sosa snagged the seat closest to Harvick, evidence that he was accustomed to the ranked pecking order of seating.

Harvick stepped directly to Sosa and, towering over him,

extended her hand. "Mr. Garcia, thanks for coming. Please introduce your associates."

"This is FBI Special Agent Griff Topping," Sosa said, turning toward Griff. "And beside him is ICE Special Agent Eva Montanna."

Harvick reached past Sosa with her long arms to shake Eva and Griff's hands.

Gesturing to their seats, she took hers and opened her tablet. Eva and Griff both sat after Sosa did. Eva shot Griff a questioning glance as if he could answer with his eyes how Harvick would proceed.

Eva closed hers for a brief second, feeling like she was being called onto the carpet. Or wasn't she? Fortunately, she didn't have long to wait.

Harvick glowered down at her digital tablet. Eva could only assume she was perusing the summary of investigative facts, which Eva had previously written.

"We are meeting here because Agent Montanna stumbled upon or tackled her way into an unknown foreign attempt at espionage." Harvick smiled at Eva, adding, "Good work, Eva."

Eva's tense neck muscles relaxed; however, she didn't join in the murmured chuckles going around the executive suite.

No one interjected, so Harvick continued, "As Eva and Griff have documented, it appears we have evidence that some of our retired special agents are working for the Lancet Group and quite possibly assisting the ChiComs in recruiting spies."

Harvick turned her eyes upon Eva with a laser-like focus. "This is most embarrassing to me and the Bureau. It's something we must explore. Obviously, we cannot use our OPR investigators or counterintelligence agents to conduct the investigation. Too many of our personnel are working for Lancet or hope to in retirement. I need from each of you an assurance that anything we talk about here or do going forward will remain very confidential and 'need to know' only."

She nodded to Sosa.

He blurted, "Yes."

Harvick continued, "Agent Topping?"

"I'm in. Absolutely."

Next, she sought the same from Eva, who also agreed.

Harvick spent a good thirty minutes explaining what had transpired after she'd met with Director Whidbey of ICE, and then adding, "We agreed ICE will assign a small cadre of its most experienced and trusted special agents to work under the supervision of Trudy Graham, ICE New York. She's on her way to DC as we speak. She will guide the investigation, using Eva's relationship with Captain Yang Ming, and follow all leads arising from further investigation."

"What is the best way to proceed from here?" Sosa asked.

"Great question," the Assistant Director said. "Captain Ming should make a repeated trip from Florida to here in DC. He should contact the FBI field office instead of FBI Headquarters, as he tried on his first attempt when Eva heroically saved him from a kidnapping. All the necessary logistical and financial support will be coordinated between me and Director Whidbey at ICE."

Eva asked her, "Am I to be involved in the investigation going forward?"

"Most certainly," Harvick replied, clenching her jaw as if she personally wanted to go after those retired agents at Lancet.

Sosa raised a few questions before Harvick closed her tablet and stood, signaling the meeting was over. As the group started filing from the conference room, Harvick approached Eva.

"Your idea to scrub your son's cell phone and give it to Captain Ming was pure genius. It will keep the ChiComs from knowing when you have contact with him."

Eva smiled at the rare moment of praise for her work. "Thank you."

"I noticed the unique spelling of your name. Are you related to the press secretary we often see on the news from the Pentagon?"

"Yes, most certainly." Eva's smile grew wider. "Scott Montanna is my husband."

The Assistant Director formed her lips into an exaggerated, "Ohh. I'm told ICE has you on a transfer notice. I'd think that will not sit well with the President's Secretary of Defense."

"You are well informed," Eva replied, straightening her shoulders. "You know from your own experience, home is where the government sends you, although I'd like to remain in DC."

"Well, we can't have you leaving. I think your Director Whidbey and I can stop that transfer cold, before it requires the FBI Director and Secretary of Defense to involve the White House."

"Thank you. I appreciate anything you're willing to do," Eva remarked.

Harvick tossed her a final reassuring nod. "You can count on it. Now, happy hunting."

# Chapter 25

The time for Eva and Kaley to leave for Florida finally arrived. The afternoon before their departure, they were packed, and Eva supervised the loading of Kaley's car. Eva was determined to fit most items into the trunk, so nothing was visible in the hotel parking lot. The trunk was nearly full. Eva rearranged the last bit when Kaley brought one more box.

"What is that? I hadn't seen it," Eva exclaimed.

Kaley set the sealed corrugated box on top of the already overflowing contents.

"It's been in my bedroom. Dylan asked me to take it to his uncle."

Hands on her hips, Eva demanded, "What is it?"

"Dietary brochures."

"Oh no! No, no!" Eva ordered. "He's not using you again. Don't you see what he's doing?"

"Mother, it's no big deal. I'll make room for it."

"No, Kaley. It is a big deal." Eva pointed to the back seat. "Put it in the car. I have an idea."


**TWENTY MINUTES LATER,** they headed out on a strategic mission, with Kaley driving her VW Bug. She slowed at Sully Road, with Eva issuing commands.

"Get in the right lane," she said in clipped tones, "and follow the signs for Dulles International Airport."

Kaley slowed even more, her foot tapping the brake as she entered a sharp curve. "Where to from here?"

"Look for a sign for the air freight or cargo area. We're going to the U.S. Customs receiving center."

Kaley traveled slowly down the winding road with Eva barking orders. A truck behind them beeped its horn.

"He's making me nervous," Kaley said.

Eva urged her to forget him. "You're going the speed limit."

"This place confuses me. I don't see the air freight sign," Kaley lamented.

"Wait!" Eva called. "There it is. The next right. You're doing great, honey."

Kaley turned the Bug into a parking place and parked. Eva opened the rear door and pointed to the label-less corrugated cardboard box.

"We don't need my fingerprints on it, so you carry it," Eva intoned. "Since you received it directly from Dylan, we can account for yours and his. Any others could be his accomplices."

Kaley shook her head, looking dazed. "I'm learning a whole new way to think."

As the duo walked toward the U.S. Customs freight processing center, Eva realized she had more to tell her daughter and didn't hold back in further mentoring her.

"When Dylan asked you to deliver this sealed box of 'dietary brochures' to his uncle, to the same area where an act of terrorism occurred—"

"You mean Panama City, right?" Kaley interrupted.

"Exactly. Given this act of terrorism occurred while Dylan was there, we must be suspicious. I think Dylan's box most likely contains important evidence."

Kaley exhaled in a rush. "Really?"

"Yes, and we're about to find out."

Eva and Kaley entered the bright facility, its polished cement floor shining from the fluorescent lights overhead. Eva strode toward a counter bearing a large U.S. Customs seal. Kaley followed, still clutching the box. They approached a female Customs Inspector who leaned over a computer monitor.

Eva displayed her leather credential case, the one with her gold badge attached to the front. With a flip of her wrist, the case unfolded, showing her picture and title of Special Agent.

"I'm ICE Special Agent Eva Montanna, here for your assistance in scanning this parcel for possible evidence in a case I'm working."

The inspector peered over the top of her half-glasses, first at Eva and then at Kaley. She finally rested her icy gaze upon the carton.

"You could have stopped at TSA in the terminal. They would have scanned it at the pre-boarding area."

Eva flipped open her credential case again and, pointing her finger, said, "It doesn't say here that I'm a Transportation Security Agent; it says I'm an Immigration Customs Agent, and this is a U.S. Customs facility. Why would I expose evidence of a case in the presence of air travelers?"

Without saying a word, the woman turned and disappeared through swinging double doors behind the counter.

Eva turned to Kaley, saying in hushed tones, "Learn from this. I'd bet that woman has fifteen years on the job, and she's spent it all here standing at the counter. She's probably going to get her younger supervisor, who has worked harder and jumped over her on the career ladder."

"Mom," Kaley smirked. "This is fun. We'll see how good you are."

The doors parted. The first inspector returned, and as Eva had predicted, she was followed by a younger, female inspector who looked more professional in her sharply pressed uniform and many brass chevrons on her shoulders.

She approached the counter. "I'm Supervisory Inspector Melissa Dykstra. How can we help you?"

Eva repeated the badge presentation, saying once more, "I am Special Agent Eva Montanna, Immigration Customs Enforcement."

"How can I assist you, Agent Montanna?" Dykstra asked, tenting her fingers.

Nodding at the unhelpful first inspector, Eva explained, "I told your associate I have a carton we believe has suspicious contents. I'd like you to run it through your scanning devices to see if further investigation is needed."

Supervisor Dykstra glanced at Kaley, then at the box. "Certainly. Come around the counter and we'll take a look."

She then walked toward the double doors while Eva and Kaley maneuvered around the counter. They followed her through a large area with high ceilings and cluttered with stacks of shipping cartons. When they reached a conveyor belt that led into a large, enclosed scanning device, the inspector raised her hand to Eva.

"I noticed you aren't carrying the box. Would you like me

to put it into the scanner, or are you concerned about prints?"

"Exactly!" Eva nodded.

Dykstra turned to Kaley. "Miss, just set the box here."

Kaley did so, and then stepped back, her eyes darting to and fro.

The conveyor began to advance, and Eva watched the carton disappear into the scanner. The supervisor typed commands into her keyboard. Instantly, the shape of the box appeared on the computer screen, with its contents outlined in more subdued tones.

Kaley's mouth dropped open, and she uttered, "What is that?"

Inspector Dykstra looked from Kaley to Eva. "Not what you expected?"

"It's supposed to be dietary brochures," Eva answered.

"Thus, the surprise," Dykstra noted. With her pen, she pointed to where the screen revealed dark images and electronic wires. "I believe this box contains two drones. Each is in its own interior box. They are not totally assembled, but here you can see propellers."

She gestured her pen toward a larger dark area. "This could be a camera, but it's bigger and shaped differently than most cameras we see."

Eva removed her phone from her shoulder purse. She stepped up to the screen, snapping photos. After checking to see if she was satisfied with them, she turned to Inspector Dykstra.

"Thanks for your help. Do you have a plastic trash bag to avoid more fingerprints?"

"I do." Dykstra pushed another button, and the box rolled out of the scanner. "Wait here. I'll return with the bag."

As she strode away, Kaley whirled toward Eva. "Can you believe it? I can't trust anything Dylan says!"

Eva pulled Kaley toward her for a side shoulder hug. "You're learning lots today, aren't you?"

Inspector Dykstra returned with a large black plastic bag, which she shook vigorously to open before lowering it over the box. She turned to Eva.

"You may want to take it from here for chain of custody."

"Right." Eva bent to retrieve the box from the conveyor, rolling it over so it was completely enclosed in the plastic bag.

She handed Dykstra her business card. "I've made a note in my phone of your name, the date, and the time. I appreciate your assistance, especially your concise description of the contents."

The moment Eva and Kaley got outside to head for the car, Kaley exploded with questions.

"What did Inspector Dykstra mean by chain of custody? Why didn't she touch the box?"

"Unlock the car, please," Eva said.

She nestled the bag containing the box of drones safely in the back seat. They quickly hopped into the car, where Kaley blasted on the air conditioning.

"Whew, it's boiling out here," Kaley said. "Did you hear what I asked about chain of custody and stuff?"

Eva aimed the vent toward her face. "Inspector Dykstra was younger and knew her job better than the inspector at the counter. Dykstra understands what's needed to secure evidence for a trial. She knows if there is a trial, I will have to testify that the evidence has always been in my custody, or Griff's, or another ICE agent's. She didn't want to possess it for even one minute because she'd have to appear in court as a witness. She's the supervisor because she probably always seeks to learn and excel."

"There's a lot to learn for law enforcement jobs," Kaley said, zooming the VW forward to the highway.

Eva leaned against the seat cushion. "It's fortunate Dylan asked you to make this delivery. We learned the truth about his character. Not only did he lie to you about what's in the box, he once again tried to ensnare you in his devious plans. You drive home while I'm calling Griff."

Kaley turned slowly onto Sully Road while Eva phoned Griff. When he answered, she told him to meet at her house ASAP.

"Sure. What's so urgent?"

"The primary suspect in your new case gave your source a parcel to deliver to PC. He claims its dietary brochures to be delivered to his uncle there. We just took it to Dulles, where

Customs scanned it. The package contains two drones with suspicious-looking attachments."

Griff whistled in her ear. "Amazing. A stroke of luck, or better to say, God is our Supreme Source."

"I agree," Eva replied. "You need to take custody and have your lab do its expert evaluation. If the drones can be made safe, you can have the package flown down to PC in time for the expected delivery by the source. You and the lab will only have about three days to work a miracle because your suspect is pressuring your source to make the delivery."

Griff sighed. "Okay. I guess that cancels my promise to Dawn for dinner out tonight. I'll leave soon, meet at your house, and get the package to the lab yet tonight."

"I'll text you the photos of the contents and see you soon," Eva said before terminating the call.

# Chapter 26

The morning of Eva and Kaley's grand adventure driving to Florida for her freshman year at college dawned bright and blazing hot. Eva filled travel mugs with fresh coffee and shoved a case of water bottles into the back seat of Kaley's Bug. The trunk was jammed full of her clothes, computer, books, and new pillow. Eva slammed the trunk, realizing there wouldn't have been any spare room for Dylan's box.

"Good thing Griff took charge of getting it to PC," she said under her breath.

Scott strolled outside with the boys to send them off with waves and smiles. Dutch rushed up, hugging Eva tightly around her waist. He looked up at her with his large, luminous eyes.

"Mom, don't be gone long," he said. "Dad says you're gonna fly home on a big plane, so that should go fast."

Tears burned Eva's eyes as she hugged him back. "Buddy, I'll miss you too. Remember your treasure hunt. I left you and Andy and Dad fun notes around the house to find while I'm gone."

He nodded and reached into his pocket, pulling out a tiny stone. "Dad helped me find this in the backyard yesterday, so you won't forget us."

"How wonderful. I'm keeping your stone in my pocket all the way to see Gramps and Gram in Florida," she said, forging a smile. She didn't realize how hard it would be to leave some of her family behind. "We'll call tonight from the hotel in Greenville, South Carolina."

Holding something, Andy walked near, and Scott huddled the family together.

"Eva, we have the map book and will follow your route. Andy is using the yellow highlighter, and we'll try to guess where you're stopping for lunch today. Maybe text us a picture of you and Kaley at the restaurant."

Dutch clapped his hands. Eva promised she would, a painful lump sticking in her throat. If she didn't leave soon, she'd dissolve into tears.

Andy handed her a big bag of barbeque potato chips, saying with a lopsided grin, "I know these are your favorites."

"Thanks, sport." She tousled his hair with her free hand.

After Eva and Kaley hugged everyone, Scott walked Eva to the driver's seat. He drew her close and pressed a tender kiss on her lips.

"We'll be fine," he whispered. "So will you. I'm glad we prayed together this morning. I love you, sweet pea."

Eva squeezed herself against him, saying, "I love you too, dear heart."

To Kaley, she asked, "Do you have everything? Go over your list one last time?"

"Yup, over and over again. I'm ready for college!"

Kaley pulled out her cell phone, snapping a few photos of her family. Scott did the same with his, and in another few minutes, Eva backed the Bug out of the driveway, and off they went. Her first child was headed for college in a faraway state. It was hard to believe, and Eva forced her eyes onto the road. She set her mind on enjoying this special time with Kaley.

"You know, this is our first mother-and-daughter road trip," Eva said, trying to sound lighthearted.

"I never thought of that, Mom." Kaley's eyes seemed glued to her cell phone.

Eva chuckled. Some things never changed. She let Kaley be for a few minutes, typing away on her phone. Soon, when they reached the highway, she decided enough was enough.

"Maybe you can put down your phone and see stuff with me," Eva suggested. "This trip of ours for your freshman year at college only happens once. Let's make fun memories."

Kaley let out a tortured sigh. "I know, but Dylan is busy texting me. When am I going to deliver his brochures? How long is it taking me to get to Florida? Am I staying at a hotel? Blah blah blah."

Eva did not like Dylan stalking them. She must put a stop to this.

"Remember, he thinks you're driving alone. You can't text while driving. Tell him you're leaving now and navigating with your phone. You can't deal with distractions. Tell him you're taking your time and will text him when you reach Florida."

"Sounds like a plan," Kaley said, her fingers typing. "How does this sound?"

She read aloud what she'd typed, and Eva approved every word.

"I sent the text, and now I'm turning off my text sounds."

Eva nodded. "And I'll use my phone for the GPS. Use yours for pictures as we drive along. Later, you can make a scrapbook."

They laughed and talked about many things, Eva's fun memories from college days, Kaley's class schedule, and the new Bible devotional her parents had given Kaley to read each day to stay her grounded in her faith. A few hours later, they stopped for gas.

After filling the tank, Eva announced, "I'm hungry. See anything good at this exit for lunch?"

"Hahaha," Kaley laughed, pointing. "See that country restaurant with a yellow Beetle Bug car like mine high up on a pole? We should take our picture and make Dutch laugh."

Eva swung into the lot, and they took a selfie with her phone, making sure to include the yellow VW Bug in the background. Kaley stuffed her phone in her back pocket without looking at the screen, for which Eva was grateful. After washing up, they slid into a booth.

A server took their orders for burgers, fries, and coleslaw, which arrived in a few minutes. Eva was so happy Kaley wasn't really a vegan. That could wait until she cooked for herself.

She prayed a blessing over their food and their trip.

They enjoyed their lunch in silence until Eva said, "Kaley, I am so proud of you as your mother. Your dad is proud, too. You're growing up as a smart and lovely Christian young lady. God is guiding you, and you are seeking Him in your life. You can do anything you put your mind to."

"You and Dad give me great support," Kaley said, dipping a fry into ketchup. "I'm anxious about starting college in Florida. At least I'll be living with Gramps and Gram."

"I'll be coming down to Panama City too," Eva promised.

"Good." Kaley ate a few fries before saying, "I'll be happy when this thing with Dylan is over. He's giving me the creeps by constantly checking on me. If I ever meet another guy I'm interested in, I plan to take things slower to make sure he's not weird or a criminal."

Heartened by Kaley's inner growth, Eva felt the prayers she and Scott were lifting up for Kaley were being answered. After making a mental note to tell Scott later of Kaley's progress, she ate the rest of her meal with a joyful heart.

**EVA RETURNED TO THE CAR,** checking her phone for messages while waiting for Kaley to shop for mementos in the restaurant's gift shop. To Eva's surprise, Griff had messaged her: *Cedric Foster called from Chicago and has news of your transfer.*

Eva found Cedric's cell number in her phone and connected the call.

He was swift to ask, "Eva, you got my message?"

"Yes, and I'm driving toward the Florida Panhandle to enroll my oldest in college."

"As I agreed after our last call," Cedric intoned, "I contacted Regina Spire to request you be transferred to my group if you're coming to Chicago."

Eva couldn't help sighing. "I received my transfer orders for Chicago."

"Well, you did, and you didn't," he replied.

"No, I did."

"Hear me out. Yesterday, Regina Spire phoned me, and I will tell you she was a real spitfire. She turned my ear black and blue because your transfer is being rescinded as the result of orders from on high. She's upset you foiled her plans and is convinced it's all because of your husband's influence."

Eva wanted to shout to Heaven, but said to Cedric, "I know I'd enjoy working with you, but must admit I'm happy to hear that. I also know Scott has nothing to do with it."

Cedric said something to someone else and then told her, "I've got a meeting starting. Just wanted to let you know the competition between you and Regina is heating up. Sorry we won't work together here in Chicago, but I'm glad to know you're still winning."

"Thanks so much for the good news, Cedric," Eva

quipped. "Bye for now."

At that moment, Kaley dashed into the passenger seat, carrying a paper bag. She buckled her seatbelt, and digging into the bag, she pulled out a keychain.

"Look, Mom! It's a green Bug like mine for my keys. And I bought a package of green tea grown here in South Carolina for Gram and Gramps. They like to drink tea on their veranda."

"That's kind of you, Kaley. Are you ready to hit the road, part two of our journey?"

They both giggled.

"Oh, first, I'd better send a photo to our guys at home," Eva said.

She found their lunch photo, which she texted to Scott's number. Eva returned to the highway, switching places with Kaley at the next gas station. They stopped for a quick bite at a taco place, and Kaley pulled into the hotel as the sun was setting, painting the sky with streaks of bright pink and gold.

Eva barely glanced at the beautiful sunset as she dashed inside. After checking in with the clerk, she happily poured herself a cup of coffee from the carafe in the lobby. Meanwhile, Kaley pushed a cart past her mom, piled with her stuff from the car. They took everything down to their room on the first floor. Thankful for the spacious room with two queen beds, Eva set the coffee cup on the small desk.

She fluffed her hair away from her neck. "It's a relief we made it before dark. I'm also glad Griff took Dylan's box. We couldn't fit another thing in your Beetle."

They were getting settled when Eva's cell phone rang. It was Scott.

"All's well here," he said, sounding out of breath. "I worked late and won't say why on the phone. Are you at the hotel?"

"Yes. I was about to text you," Eva replied, pleased to her toes by his sweet voice.

He grunted, "That's great. Turn on the news."

Eva found the remote and navigated to an all-news channel. There before her eyes were aircraft carriers streaming in the ocean, the caption beneath the video proclaiming, *China ups its presence in the Straights of*

*Taiwan.*

Eva unmuted the TV in time to hear a London-based reporter say, "China's ambassador warns the reckless United States not to act, unless they want to receive catastrophic consequences."

"Yikes, I see what has gotten you wound up," she said to Scott in low tones. "Will you be working longer hours? Should we get a sitter?"

"Hmm, it's possible," he said, sounding distracted.

Eva had an idea. "Call Griff. His wife, Dawn, is on vacation this week to redecorate her guest room. He mentioned she's available to help us out in a pinch."

"I'll phone and put them on standby at least."

Eva's mind tumbled. What did heightened tensions with China over Taiwan mean for Captain Ming and his future safety?

"Scott, do me a favor. When you reach Griff, ask him to call me in the morning from the office. I need to ask him something."

"Will do."

He hung up before Eva could say she loved him. Her heart sank, and she sat on her bed. Kaley strode from the bathroom, holding her toothbrush.

"Were you talking on the phone with Griff Topping?" she asked Eva, concern hovering in her eyes. "I heard you say his name. Has something new happened with Dylan?"

Eva shut off the TV. She turned to Kaley, wearing a smile.

"Your dad called and sends his love. He's calling Griff about something, so I asked to have him call me in the morning about one of our other cases."

"Oh good. I hope I can sleep tonight without dreaming of Dylan again."

Her words made Eva pause and made her recall her own upsetting dream about Kaley and Dylan, which she'd finally shared with Scott. Should she ask Kaley for details?

No, she decided she'd let Kaley bring it up tomorrow on their last leg to Panama City.

Eva's phone dinged, alerting her to a new message. She toggled open her screen with her thumb, punched in the passcode, and saw a message from her mother. After scanning the words, she handed her phone to Kaley.

"Read this nice message from Gram before we turn out the lights."

Kaley read it and squealed, "Yay! She and Gramps can't wait for us to come tomorrow. She has a surprise for me and is making my favorite baked chicken with artichokes and mushrooms, and black cows for dessert. She sent like a dozen heart emojis."

"The stuff sweet dreams are made of," Eva said, hoping it would be for her as well.

With her eyes shining, Kaley set down Eva's phone. "Thanks, Mom, for taking this trip with me. I don't think I could have done it without you."

"It's a blessing to be right here with you," Eva said. "Remember though, when talking to Dylan, you did it alone."

Kaley flashed a toothy smile. "I sure did."

# Chapter 27

As it turned out, Eva's sleep was restless. News about increased tensions between China and Taiwan churned through her mind, keeping her awake. She and Kaley hurried down to breakfast at dawn's first light. Amazed by such a wide selection at the buffet, Eva chose creamy oatmeal, fruit with fresh blackberries, and an apple cinnamon muffin. Kaley copied her mom in everything, including hot coffee without cream or sugar.

"Time to hit the road," Eva announced after they'd eaten the last crumb. "First, we fill our travel mugs with hot coffee."

Kaley laughed. "This is the best road trip ever. Let's get a photo of us by the Civil War cannon outside and send it to Dad. He can show it to Andy and Dutch."

"Good idea."

They snapped a selfie and then returned to the room to brush their teeth and collect their luggage. Soon, they were back on the highway, with Kaley driving. Eva inserted her hands-free earpiece to be available when Griff called. And sure enough, forty minutes later, his name flashed on her phone's screen.

Cautioning herself that she was on a cell phone and Kaley could hear Eva's side of the conversation, she said, "Morning, partner. Did Scott remind you to phone me?"

"Yup. How's your trip so far?"

Eva glanced at Kaley, who was concentrating on the road, before telling Griff, "We're having a marvelous time of mother-and-daughter bonding."

With no chitchat, he got right to the point. "I have news. Sosa told me yesterday the top brass met and agreed with Harvick's earlier plan. When you arrive in PC, you are to instruct the Runner to repeat his trip to DC."

"They should have decided while I was still there to have input," she told Griff. "I'll do my best. What's their timetable?"

"Since we control the timing, arrange matters so we all don't have to work through a weekend."

Eva must keep Kaley totally in the dark about Captain Ming, so she thought carefully before replying, "Understood, but that's the best time for the source to travel. The source has weekends off. Should the source travel on a weekday, the source's coworkers will know the source is absent, and regardless of their allegiance, might notify either their superiors or the enemy country in question."

"Right," Griff said. He went silent for a good minute, finally saying, "The source should make travel arrangements on his personal phone so the targets can prepare to stop him again. Phone him on the secure phone you gave him and ask him to make the reservation. If he travels this coming Monday, you should be on the same flight. That way, you can provide surveillance inside the secured areas of both the PC and Atlanta airports."

Eva's mind started spinning. Griff was right. She and Kaley would arrive in Panama City later today, and Eva would normally fly home on Sunday. This way she'd stay an extra day and the government would pay for her flight home.

She agreed, saying crisply, "I like your idea. I'll call the source tonight when the source is off work and provide instructions. I can arrange for a malfunction to enable him … ah … I mean the source to be absent."

"You've come up with a thoughtful plan," Griff interjected. "We'll detain anyone following the source, and we can permit him to escape again, which should enable the source to return to his base Monday night. Instruct him to make his return trip arrangements from the secure phone you gave him."

Eva had her instructions. She could rely on Griff and the ICE team to complete their planning and their job. "I'll speak with the source and arrange to be on the same flight up there. Talk more later."

"Enjoy your trip and be safe."

Instantly, their call ended. Eva returned her attention to Kaley and asked, "How does music sound?"

"Sure, Mom. I'm alert though, in case you're worried."

"You're doing great," Eva replied.

She cast her praise music playlist through the car radio, turning it to a low volume. After driving for some time in solitude, her daughter finally spoke.

"Mom, the form Griff gave me to sign was for a confidential human source. Is that how he refers to me when talking to you?"

"No. Griff's our good friend. He calls you Kaley."

"I know that, Mother, but when he's with others from work, does he call me a source?"

"Yes." Eva patted Kaley's shoulder. "Which he does to protect your identity."

Kaley's eyes never left the road as she continued, "I first wondered if Griff was talking to you about me, and then I heard you call the source, *him*."

"No, I didn't say that," Eva objected.

"Yes, you did. I was listening carefully."

"Well, I was trying not to do that."

"It sounds like you have a source," Kaley insisted. "Just like I'm a source for Griff."

Eva grew more uncomfortable with this conversation by the second. Kaley would not quit digging. Okay, she needed to use this time with Kaley wisely.

In her calmest teaching voice, she began to explain, "Kaley, if you ever get to be a special agent, you'll have to develop skills to establish relationships with people, both good and bad, who you can rely upon to provide you with what we call in the business, intelligence. So, yes, I've had many sources through the years."

"Why have I never known this before?"

"First, because you were a child. Second, because we never disclose the existence or identity of a source for very good reasons. Seldom does anyone have what we call a 'need to know.'"

"So, I won't have to fly back to Washington with you?"

"No, Kaley, you will not. How about if we listen to music, inspiring us to complete our trip."

Eva increased the sound. For her part, Kaley instantly decreased the volume.

"Mom," she chirped, a lilt in her voice. "It's obvious you have a male source in Panama City. You don't know anyone there but Gramps and Gram, and I don't have a need to know. But I assume Gramps is your source, and I can only wonder if he knows it."

Eva marveled at her precocious daughter's tenacity. "Kaley, there's another phrase we government agents use. That is, 'I can neither confirm nor deny' what you've just alleged. Still, I warn you not to mistakenly assume you are correct. There is no more to be said."

Eva sighed inwardly, thankful that when she'd gone to Zion's for bar-b-que, she hadn't taken Kaley with her. Because if she had, her daughter wouldn't be focusing on her grandfather.

Seeking to change the subject, Eva offered, "Let's pull off at the next restroom exit and switch places so you can rest. My turn to drive."

Her tactic must have worked because Kaley nodded before telling her mother, "Okay. When you drive, I'll tell you what I dreamed about Dylan. It still bothers me."

**RAINDROPS SPLATTERED** on the windshield right after Eva started driving. She turned off the music.

"I'm glad you're behind the wheel if it becomes a downpour," Kaley said. "Will it bother you if I talk about Dylan?"

"I'm all ears," Eva swiftly replied.

Kaley downed her coffee and said, "You remember on my school trip to Poland last year, how the ship was overtaken by Russian soldiers, and I hid in the lifeboat?"

"I will never forget how God intervened and protected you!" Eva said with feeling. "My faith in God grew tremendously after you were safe."

"Everything turned out okay, and I put the whole thing out of my mind until recently. I dreamed I was stuck on a ship on the Chesapeake. Dylan is a terrorist, and I hid from him."

Eva exhaled sharply. "I don't like you being afraid of Dylan."

More than anything, Eva didn't want to lecture but rather encourage her daughter to stay strong when facing troubling circumstances.

"Kaley, here's how I see the situation with Dylan. Because God intervened, you realized who he is before you became entangled any further. You won't ever have to see or talk to him again. You can simply text him when you arrive in Florida, telling him where to have his uncle meet you. Someplace public, like the library. You can deliver the box of brochures to his uncle, and as far as you know, that is what the box contains. You walk away. And the entire time, our federal agents will watch over you and protect you. Does that work for you?"

"I'm fine with everything you said," Kaley replied nonchalantly, as if handing over the box was no big deal.

Yet, after glimpsing how tightly Kaley was squeezing her hands together, she probed, "Are you sure? What's really bothering you?"

Kaley coughed out a sigh. "You understand me too well."

"I'm still listening."

"Um," Kaley stopped.

Eva had a growing concern over what Kaley might divulge but didn't want to rush her.

"I'm upset I let Dylan control me, that I ever became involved in his crazy vegan lifestyle. I should have realized he valued his ideas more than he ever did me as a person. I should have sensed he was only pretending to love the Lord. Because I know he doesn't."

Relief cascaded over Eva. This was something she could handle.

"I'm thankful you're comfortable enough to share your innermost feelings with me," she told Kaley. "The important thing is how you live going forward. You've learned much from this dilemma. I'm praying you will bring your cares to God because He cares for you."

"You make all good points, Mom. I know Jesus forgives me, and I am going to stop beating myself up over Dylan."

Eva smiled. "Wonderful! Here's another thought. God is sovereign and knew the people Dylan was working with might kill someone, minus God's intervention. I'm beginning to see God knew your mom would know how to handle the situation when Dylan took advantage of the unknown extension phone in Zion's barn."

"Wow," Kaley said, unclenching her hands. "I see it too!"

"Exactly," Eva replied. "When you deliver the box to his uncle, God will protect you and deliver you from further involvement with Dylan."

# Chapter 28

Eva awoke the next morning in the guest room of her parent's farm near Panama City. She felt refreshed after the two-day trip. When she and Kaley had arrived late yesterday afternoon, Gram and Gramps hugged them tightly. They shared a delicious, welcoming baked salmon dinner with tomatoes and zucchini from their hothouse garden.

While Kaley had gone over to the room above the attached garage to set up housekeeping, Eva lingered with her parents at the dinner table, relishing a cup of freshly brewed dark roast coffee. It felt marvelous to release the pressures, not only from the drive but also from issues that needed resolving. Kaley had bounded into the kitchen just in time to enjoy one of Gram's customary black cows.

Eva's thoughts returned to the present. She rolled out of bed, dressing quickly in beige cotton slacks and a top before checking her phone for messages. Scott had texted a large heart along with: *Miss you much! I'm embroiled at work, so our boys are at Dawn's house, helping her paint. Imagine Dutch wielding a paintbrush. Give Kaley my love too.*

Scott should already be at DOD, so she planned to call him later. She then read Griff's message to phone him at the office. Finding him in her contact list, she pressed his number.

Griff answered as though he'd been waiting. "Eva, good to hear from you."

"Scott said the boys are with Dawn," she replied. "Hope they're not a nuisance."

"Eva, we love having them, and she's grateful for their help. Let me also say we are fortunate to have Kaley's assistance."

Eva inserted her hands-free earpiece into her ear to prevent anyone from overhearing Griff. "And let me say you won't believe how invested Kaley is in this project. I really have to pump the brakes on her."

"She's been invaluable. I just got word the lab is almost finished reassembling the drones. Stay tuned to meet our executive jet in PC this afternoon. The pilots are flying in the box for Kaley's delivery."

"What have they learned?"

He whistled softly. "Each drone contains a canister device with a thermite concoction and an ignitor, just above the camera. The technicians believe one drone can be flown onto the roof of a building, where it lands or crashes and ignites a fire, which burns through the roof and spreads rapidly."

"Yikes! Dylan is not messing around with toy planes." Eva pulled on her tennis shoes and tied them. "I wonder if a similar drone started the fire at Grass Fed Beef here."

Griff answered, "You're spot-on. The agent in charge of the JTTF in Panama City told me the Fire Marshal confirmed that's exactly what happened."

"These people are bent on evil," Eva said, putting it all together. "Someone here is determined to have an encore. Apparently, it's not Dylan Webb, or he would have brought the box here himself."

"I arrived at the same conclusion. The PC agents are eager to discover who receives the box from Kaley."

"Griff, I prefer you be the one to maintain contact with the task force here in PC. Advise them your source will make the drop tomorrow morning. With the lab's delay in processing the drones, Dylan has been bugging Kaley non-stop about the safety of his so-called dietary brochures. I told her to text him and say her car broke down, which she had fixed in South Carolina. Call me when it's a go for us to retrieve the box later today at the airport."

"Wait, don't hang up. We have to talk about the counterintelligence case."

Eva sat back down in the chair. "Last night, I talked with the Captain on his secure phone. He'll use his other phone to make DC flight reservations for Monday morning. I'll make the same flight arrangements once I know his and let you know."

"Then we'll coordinate with the ICE agents assigned to this operation," Griff replied.

"Be sure they're good. It would be terrible if we lost track of the Captain and he got kidnapped."

**THAT AFTERNOON, TEN MINUTES BEFORE THREE O'CLOCK,** Eva and Kaley headed for the Northwest Beaches International Airport, better known as the Panama City Airport. Kaley drove her Slug Bug into the small parking lot at the south end.

Eva hung up from a lengthy call; she'd been on the phone a good hour coordinating between Burt Tripp, the FBI pilot, and Doug Montgomery, the FBI agent she'd previously met from the Panama City JTTF office.

Kaley was poised to collect Dylan's alleged 'dietary brochures' from the FBI pilot. Then she'd promptly deliver them to Dylan's uncle.

As they drew near to a large brick building with an arched roof, Kaley bobbed her head, asking Eva, "Can this be the right place? It's a long way from the main terminal."

"I think this is it." Eva squinted, finally spotting the sign on the side of the hangar.

She gestured toward the tarmac by the front of the small private aviation center, "Yes, this is Sheltair Aviation, where we're to meet the local FBI agent and the plane."

In the same way she'd learned from Eva, Kaley backed into a parking spot against the building. "How's this if we need a quick getaway, Mom?"

"Perfect." Eva gazed around. "I don't see a small jet. He should be landing on that distant runway."

When they both lowered their windows, Kaley turned off the ignition. A blast of hot and humid air assailed Eva's eyes and face.

"You look nice for this meeting," Eva said. "Did you just happen to wear a beige outfit like me?"

Kaley laughed. "Not bad for a rookie, right Mom?"

Before Eva could answer, Agent Doug Montgomery walked up. Eva recognized him from their prior meeting in the SCIF. Who was the younger blonde woman walking with him and wearing clothes suited for the beach—white capris, a lime-green top, and sunglasses?

Spotting the long braid hanging down her back, Eva realized she must be Special Agent Crystal Lasher, who was also at the secure meeting in the SCIF.

"Look, her blouse matches the color of my car," Kaley remarked. "Who are they?"

"Two FBI agents," Eva said, ready to close her window.

Agent Montgomery walked up to her window, saying, "Hi Eva. Nice to see you in person. You should remember Crystal Lasher. She is our newest agent in her first year out of the academy."

He pointed to Kaley's VW, adding, "The lime-green car gave you away."

Eva stepped from the car, relieved that the agents had arrived on time, and shook their hands. She wanted to complete this swap without a hitch, for Kaley's sake and safety. Crystal, who had been looking intently at the car or at Kaley, hung back, saying nothing.

Just then, Doug turned and pointed to the far end of the field. "Our plane is landing."

Eva watched a sleek corporate executive jet touch expertly to the runway and speed toward them.

"We have more agents, but they're in town. One has secured a parking spot in front of Java Central, where we'd like the source to deliver the package," Doug explained.

At Doug's mention of 'the source,' Eva imagined Kaley's mental gears turning. She knew her daughter wanted to complete this mission and be rid of Dylan forever.

Doug nodded toward Kaley. "Griff also explained the unusual circumstances of the source's contact with Dylan Webb, the suspect in this case." He gave a knowing wink to Eva.

"Then you know of our relationship?" Eva asked.

"Which is why I brought Crystal with me. She's been fully briefed. I felt the source might be more comfortable with Crystal."

The small jet rolled to a stop on the tarmac, its engines whining. The strong smell of aviation fuel exhaust enveloped them. Rather than plug her nose, Eva motioned to Crystal.

"Crystal, come and meet Kaley."

The two of them approached the driver's side of the VW, where Eva invited Kaley to join them. She got out, and Eva introduced her to the FBI agents, adding, "Crystal will stay with you while Doug and I speak with the pilot."

Eva strode with Doug to the jet, where the pilot was just lowering the door, which also served as steps to the tarmac. He stepped down onto the tarmac, and with black slacks, a white shirt with captain's epaulets on his shoulders, and aviator sunglasses, he looked every bit a commercial pilot.

He extended his hand. "You must be Eva Montanna. Griff Topping explained you'd be here. I'm Special Agent Alex Tripp, and FBI pilot. Griff and I went through the same FBI training class together."

"Happy to know a pal of Griff's," Eva said.

Meanwhile, Doug pointed toward the cockpit. "Looks like you have a co-pilot."

"Yes, we'll take on fuel, grab a snack, and head back to Joint Base Andrews in time to be home with our families tonight. We're not usually so lucky."

Standing beneath the sweltering sun, Eva was eager to move things along. "I understand you have an urgent passenger aboard. It's a pretty expensive flight for a small box."

Agent Tripp climbed back up the steps into the plane, returning with the same box Dylan had given to Kaley. He started to give the box to Eva, but she held up her palm.

"No. Please hand it to Agent Montgomery."

Doug nodded, accepting the box, while Eva explained, "From here on, I won't be in the evidentiary chain of custody. Besides, Doug doesn't mind being summoned to DC for trial, right?"

"No problem." Doug tucked the box under his arm. "Still, the trial could be held here in Panama City."

The pilot handed Doug a clipboard. "Sign the custody receipt. I'll tear off a copy for you to keep with the evidence. If we've no further business, we'll prepare the plane to fly back."

Eva and Doug hurried to rejoin Crystal and Kaley. At Doug's instructions, Kaley popped open the Bug's trunk, where Doug inserted the package. He surveyed the trunk for other contents and then closed it. Next, he motioned for them to join him in his government car.

Eva and Kaley climbed into the back seat, with Crystal

sitting in the front passenger seat.

Doug started the engine, and turning on the air conditioning, he asked Kaley, "Did you contact Dylan and tell him to get his uncle ready to receive the package today?"

"I did." She nodded curtly. "I said I was in Panama City with the brochures and could give them to his uncle this afternoon. His uncle Norm will be ready."

"Good. I noticed you and your mother cleaned out the trunk, so there's nothing personal of yours."

Eva interrupted, "We also tidied the interior, so there's no info about Kaley in case he examines it."

"Excellent." Doug reached over his shoulder to hand Kaley a slip of paper. "Text Dylan with this address to Java Central, where his uncle can meet you in town. Crystal will be driving her G-car, leading you. Enter the address into your GPS just in case. You will never be alone. Other agents will be near you always."

He twisted further to look at Eva, who sat behind him. "Mom, you ride with me. I'll drop you a block from Java Central. You walk in from there. Crystal should already be inside by the time you arrive. Eva, go right in and join her."

"Understood," Eva replied.

"Good." Doug instructed Kaley to drive into the front parking lot. "We're reserving a spot for you. When you enter the lot, our agent, who is backed in a spot by the windows, will pull out. That's your reserved spot."

"So, I will park there?" Kaley asked, creasing her brows.

Doug looked over at her. "Yes, but back in as you did here. We don't want your license plate to be exposed to Uncle Norm when he drives in. And we want Crystal to get a close-up picture of him from inside the coffee shop. Okay, so far?"

"Ye-es." She pressed her lips together.

Eva patted her hand. "Don't forget, I'll be walking into the coffee shop then. Mom has done this type of thing for years, Kaley. You will be fine."

"Keep your doors locked and let him approach your window," Doug explained in serious tones. "At this point, you're in charge. If you don't like his looks or attitude, you say his package is in the trunk and hit the trunk release. He can remove the box and close the trunk. You drive away."

Kaley nodded as if she agreed and would do everything he said. Eva had confidence her daughter could and would handle this situation with pluck.

Doug rubbed the back of his neck, no doubt aching from craning his head so far to talk with Eva and Kaley in the back seat.

"On the other hand," he intoned. "If you're comfortable, talk to him through an open window, but remain in your car. Say nothing about yourself. He may already know you're in town as an FSU student. If he wants to talk about Dylan, dietary issues, or global warming issues, it's totally up to you. If you get uncomfortable, say good-bye, raise your window, and drive off."

"That's cool. I can do that," Kaley said, sounding confident.

Doug had more advice. "Remember, if he says something you don't like, tell him you're only doing Dylan a favor, and you've done it. End of story."

"If Crystal can do it, be an FBI agent, I mean, then I can do all this so I can also be an agent one day," Kaley quipped.

Eva noticed her daughter was no longer clutching her hands together, and she smiled at her warmly. Doug asked Eva if she had any final instructions or questions.

"Where is Kaley to drive after she leaves Java Central?" Eva asked.

Doug turned to the new agent. "Crystal, you and Eva should leave Java Central right after the uncle does. Once our surveillance team knows where he's going with the package, and we've confirmed there's no counter-surveillance on Kaley, Crystal and Eva should drive by Kaley and beep the horn."

"I understand," Crystal said with a brisk nod.

Doug continued, "Kaley, you'll follow them somewhere nearby. Eva can get a ride from there with Kaley. How about it, Mom? Does this plan work?"

"First, let me check my cell phone to see what is nearby," Eva answered, putting the address into her phone. Some moments later, she said, "Okay, there's an ice cream shop just down the street. Crystal, do you know the place?"

The rookie FBI agent glanced at Eva's phone and replied, "Sure do. Other agents took me there for a great sundae for my birthday. They make their own ice cream."

"Sounds good to me," Doug grinned. "After driving around in this heat, I'll be ready for a deluxe hot fudge sundae."

Everyone chuckled, lightening the tension.

Doug veered back to telling Kaley, "As soon as it's convenient afterward, call Griff and tell him everything the uncle says and does. Time to text Dylan with the address. Tell him thirty minutes."

# Chapter 29

Twenty minutes later, after being dropped off by Agent Montgomery, Eva hurried along the remaining block to Java Central. She felt totally out of control. Had she knowingly inserted her soon-to-be-adult daughter into a risky situation? What was she thinking?

Usually, Eva put her life on the line for people she did not, nor ever would, know. But the tables had turned, and today, instead of protecting her daughter, she was forced to watch Kaley fend for herself. Eva reminded herself of every argument she'd given Scott: that Kaley's cooperation as an FBI source was necessary to keep her identity from being heralded in the media and to keep Kaley from being deemed an accessory to a federal crime.

Turning the corner, relief washed over Eva. There was Kaley driving her lime-green VW toward Java Central. Eva hastened her pace and almost ran. The instant Kaley pulled into the lot, just as Agent Montgomery had scripted, a car pulled from a parking spot in front of the coffee shop.

Eva swung open the door to the café, watching Kaley back into the empty spot. Eva didn't see Crystal, but she did observe an empty table at the front window facing the rear of Kaley's car. Eva grabbed the table, and Crystal hurried inside. The young FBI agent slid into the seat across from Eva and grinned, showing her perfect white teeth.

"Excellent timing," she told Eva. "Kaley just pulled in."

Eva stood. "I'll get us each a black coffee and a muffin."

Soon, Eva carried their order to the table, saying to Crystal, "I'm not used to being on the outside, so to speak. She's acting as the gladiator. Here I am on the sidelines watching."

Crystal started fidgeting with her cell phone, saying nothing.

"She's still my baby," Eva protested softly, but Crystal seemed oblivious.

*Is she even aware of what's going on? Is she making a date with her boyfriend on her phone?* Eva wondered.

Crystal kept working with her phone. Then, Eva noticed

the special agent had set her cell phone to shoot video. She propped her camera on its edge behind her coffee cup so only the camera lens faced toward the parking lot. A mother and her teenaged son left the café, and after getting into a car parked next to Kaley, they drove off.

Their empty place stayed that way for mere seconds. A newer Land Rover swung right into the spot. When the male driver, who appeared to be in his thirties, remained in the car, neither Eva nor Crystal paid him much attention. But then suddenly, Crystal activated the shutter and began shooting video.

"His window is down, and so is Kaley's," she hissed. "They're talking to each other."

Eva's pulse quickened. There was nothing she could do but sip her coffee, eat her muffin, and pretend she and Crystal were two friends catching up. She sure didn't want to become a witness in the case against Dylan.

This thought led her to pray silently with her eyes open for God to protect Kaley and use this situation to deepen her faith.

With a flutter of action just outside the window, Eva saw the man swing his legs from the Rover, his long brown hair touching his shoulders. As he did so, the trunk lid on Kaley's car popped open. Eva could see the box. She could see the long-haired dude walking to the VW's trunk.

*Would Kaley stay in her Beetle Bug?*

Eva hoped so. She prayed so!

Eva realized this guy was much too young to be Dylan's uncle. He reached down into Kaley's trunk, retrieved the corrugated box, and slammed her trunk. Next, he opened his rear door and set the box most carefully in his back seat. After closing his rear door, he spoke to Kaley before shaking her hand.

As Kaley closed her driver's window, Eva knew she was done.

The moment the guy slid into the Rover and shut his door, Crystal deactivated her video. He backed out and disappeared from the lot. Eva collected her coffee cup.

Crystal prepared to leave. "The exchange went well. Our

surveillance team is following the target and will sweep Kaley for surveillance."

"I made mental notes, but trust that because of your efforts, I won't need them," Eva said.

She followed Crystal to her car in the lot, where the special agent walked in front of Kaley's car, gesturing for her to stay put. Eva slid into Crystal's rather worn Chevy Impala, reminding Eva of that junky car she'd been assigned as the office rookie.

The instant Crystal started the engine, the FBI two-way radio became alive with chatter from Crystal's colleagues reporting their progress in tailing the Rover.

An agent barked, "He's turning east on Fifteenth Street."

"This is good," Crystal observed aloud to Eva.

Unfamiliar with the area, Eva had to take her word for it. She immediately phoned Kaley and put her on speaker. Kaley answered on the first ring.

"Good job, honey. Did the man say where he's going now?"

"No, Mom."

"Okay, hold on for a moment," Eva cautioned. "Stay where you are."

A surveillance agent reported over the FBI radio, "Subject is pulling into a shopping center on Tyndall Parkway, south of Seventh Street."

The other agent quickly responded, "Drive past him. I've got the point."

"Kaley," Crystal said, her voice loud enough for Kaley to hear, "Here's what we'll do. Watch me as I pull in front of you, and then follow me to the ice cream shop we discussed."

She looked over at Eva. "As agreed, Mom?"

Eva nodded, her body tense, her mind alert.

Crystal pointed at her radio microphone, saying quietly, "No need for her to listen to this chatter."

"Right." Eva spoke into her phone, "Follow us, Kaley. I'm hanging up."

As Eva held her now-silent phone, she appreciated the wisdom Crystal had shown already. Because Kaley had no 'need to know' what the FBI surveillance reported, she had

Eva end the call.

Kaley pulled out behind the Impala, and Crystal drove in a circuitous route for a good mile, checking after each turn to see if anyone other than Kaley was following her. She drove into the ice cream shop parking lot, stopped to let Kaley back in, and then parked next to her. Eva wanted to hoot but instead simply grabbed her coffee from the cup holder.

Crystal lowered the window on Eva's side and, leaning over, said to Kaley, "Good job. You and your mom are free to get the ice cream you wanted."

Eva shook Crystal's hand. "Great working with you. Tell Doug that Kaley will be in touch with her controlling agent, soon. Doug can check with him for updates."

"My pleasure, Agent Montanna. Enjoy the rest of your time in Florida."

Eva hopped out. As Crystal drove away, Eva knew she was off to join surveillance of the Rover, and who Eva concluded was Dylan's supposed uncle.

**FINALLY, EVA WAS BACK IN CHARGE.** Kaley was no longer taking orders from the local FBI agents. Eva had her daughter back. She opened the passenger door and stepped around to the driver's side.

She leaned down, telling Kaley, "We're switching drivers. You should call Griff."

Kaley complied, but when she was barely in the passenger seat, she exclaimed, "Mom, Crystal isn't much older than me. Did you see she talks to other agents without using her cell phone? They have special radios. That's cool."

"Okay." Eva shifted in the driver's seat. "Kaley, we need to finish your job. Griff needs to know what happened. Doug and Crystal are following an unknown man. You know more about him than anyone, and Griff must notify Doug."

"Okay," Kaley said, sitting and looking down at her phone.

Eva raised her cell phone. "Please focus your thoughts. Griff will want your observations about the guy. His name, description, accent, and anything he said about himself. The other agents saw him, but only you spoke to him. Ready?"

"Yup," Kaley mumbled.

Eva punched Griff's office phone number, and he barked, "Eva, what action to report?"

"She just made the delivery. The local JTTF is following the subject. Doug will want to know what you're about to learn from your protégé. Here she is."

Eva handed her phone to Kaley, who chirped, "Hey, Griff."

"Thanks, Kaley, for doing this. Everything go okay?"

"Yeah. These agents are so cool. Crystal is just a little older—"

Eva interrupted, "Focus, Kaley."

"Tell me what happened, Kaley," Griff said in a calm voice.

"I was parked at Java Central. This guy pulled in next to me, lowered his window, and asked if I was Kaley."

"Did he introduce himself? What did he look like?"

"He didn't say his name. He's a white guy with long, brown, wavy hair. He combs it back behind his ears, and it hangs down to his shoulders. He has a moustache. No accent."

"How old is he?"

"Oh, that's interesting," Kaley said excitedly. "He's not Dylan's uncle. I'm guessing he's in his thirties. I told him that he's younger than I expected because Dylan said he was his uncle."

"And you don't think he is?"

Kaley giggled. "No, because the guy shook his head and said he doesn't know Dylan well. He must have talked to Dylan, though, because he knew my first name and that I'll be attending FSU."

"Were you surprised Dylan told him so much?" Griff probed.

Kaley quieted for a moment before answering, "Maybe not. I think Dylan had to say enough to get him to agree to meet me. Obviously the guy wanted the box."

"Did he say what was in it or why he wanted it?"

"No." Kaley glanced at Eva. "He might think Dylan and I share the same interest in ecology."

"Why is that?" Griff asked, a questioning note in his voice.

"Because he asked if my major is environmental and science policy. Could he be a teacher at FSU, I wonder?"

Griff said, "Really!"

"Yup. He was quite friendly. He said I could take prerequisite classes here at the PC

campus, but that I'll have to *come* to Tallahassee to take any of the major classes."

Eva noted Kaley emphasized the word 'come.'

"Did you sense he knew what was in the box, Kaley?" Griff asked.

"I can't be sure. He acted like he was in a rush. He stopped talking to look toward my rear seat. I explained his box was in the trunk. When he turned toward the back, I popped the trunk. He grabbed his box. He said good-bye and left."

Griff paused for a moment. "Eva, is there anything else I need to know?"

"I think you have a good start, Griff," she replied.

"Bye for now. I'll get back with any questions."

Eva hung up and gazed over at Kaley, who had her eyes closed.

"Honey, is everything okay?" Eva softly touched her forearm.

Kaley sighed. "It feels like I lived an entire month of my life in one day. I had no idea the kind of pressure you face on your job. Probably Dad, too. You guys always put us kids first when you're home, providing for us and involving us in church and with friends who share our values. Mom, you're always encouraging me to have a strong faith in God."

"I hope so and can see you're growing into a fine young lady. Would you like to go inside and order ice cream?"

"That sounds great." Kaley said, seeming to sag. "First, tell me the truth. Do I have the stuff to be a federal agent?"

Eva smiled at her daughter. "I couldn't be more proud of you and how you handled this mission to right a wrong. You have a solid core, Kaley, to ensure justice is done. A strawberry sundae sounds good to me. How about you?"

"I'm all in, Mom," Kaley said.

# Chapter 30

Eva awoke in her parents' home early the next morning to the sounds of a rooster crowing noisily. So much for sleeping late. Still, she couldn't help chuckling at the idea of her mother and father becoming true farmers. Since the price of eggs had soared sky-high with shortages across the country, her dad and Zion had each built chicken coops on the property behind their homes, stocking them with laying hens and a rooster.

After changing into jeans and a tee-shirt, Eva readied herself for the day. She sent a text to Scott saying: *All is well here, my love. You are in my heart and prayers. Call anytime.* She signed off with two red heart emojis.

Last night, Kaley had offered to feed the chickens and check for eggs, so she was probably up already. Eva went to the kitchen, where her mother, Marcia, was stirring a big bowl.

"I love being with you and Dad again," Eva said cheerily. "What are you making?"

"Blueberry pancakes with maple syrup. Hard-boiled eggs, too. If you set the table, I'll make the pancakes, so we can eat pretty soon. Oh, and Eva, coffee is made. Pour yourself a cup."

Eva reached into the cupboard, taking down a big cup with an etching on the side: *Believe in Jesus*. She filled her cup to the rim. As she sipped the hot brew, Eva and her mom talked heart-to-heart about their move.

"You and Dad seem happier here than in Virginia," Eva suggested.

Her mom stirred fresh blueberries into the bowl. "We love the space, living among the green pine trees, and being part of our church. Zion and Noelle are wonderful neighbors, including us in their lives."

"I have no doubt Kaley will thrive here among you both. Makes me wish we lived closer."

"You could one day," her mom said with a tender smile. "Give it to God, as we did."

Eva finished her coffee, sensing this sweet moment with her mom was about to end. "I'd like to take Kaley to FSU and drive around the campus again."

Which is exactly what they did after breakfast. They visited the bookstore, where Eva bought Kaley an FSU ball cap and a license plate bracket. She selected a refrigerator magnet with swimming dolphins to take home. Eva and her mom then took Kaley shopping for a few essentials: a new dress and jeans. At the local Western shop, Gram insisted her granddaughter try on a pair of cowboy boots.

"I love them!" Kaley squealed.

Eva found a pretty plaid shirt for Kaley to wear with her jeans and her boots. She also bought her mom light blue slacks and a blouse, which matched her eyes. When they returned to the farm, Gramps put the FSU license on the Beetle Bug, and they took a group selfie on the veranda, which she texted to Scott.

Later, as she read her Bible app on her phone, a message from Scott scrolled across: *Great photo! We miss you and Kaley. When are you coming home?*

Eva enjoyed finally hearing from Scott, so she texted him right away. *Missing you greatly. Sorry, I forgot to tell you. I fly to DC on Monday and will assist on a case. Texting details next. Hopefully home for dinner Monday. Love and kisses.*

She kept her phone on for a few more minutes in case her hubby wrote back. He did, sending her beautiful red heart emojis. For the first time in as many weeks, Eva slept soundly.

**EVA'S SWEET DREAMS WERE RUDELY** interrupted Saturday morning by the rascally rooster crowing before dawn. Her eyes flew open. It took a moment for her to realize she was in her parents' farmhouse. She hurried to dress and get to the kitchen before her mom, wanting to treat her parents and Kaley to scrambled eggs. Eva fixed them special with diced tomatoes and chopped spinach.

She found her father adding water to the coffee carafe. Eva came up alongside him, joy filling her heart.

"I'm just like you, Dad. Nothing like the aroma of fresh coffee to wake me up in the mornings."

"Ha, I like knowing we're alike," he said. "I'll pour you a large cup when it's brewed."

Eva set a cup by the coffee maker, telling him, "I'm making breakfast this morning. It's the least I can do with all you and Mom are doing for Kaley."

"Ha, it's our greatest pleasure, Eva, to have our granddaughter staying with us here. She's out gathering eggs."

"I'll run out and help. Have Mom relax. I'll be back in a flash."

After helping Kaley collect eggs, Eva enjoyed making breakfast with Kaley. It was her way of making a lasting memory. Sounds of a noisy quad echoed outside just after Gramps said grace.

Moments later, Zion hollered, "Hello," as he knocked on the front door.

Clifford got up from the table to let in his friend and neighbor. Eva wondered if there would be an awkward moment given everything that had happened with Dylan. But no. Zion grinned with his whole face.

"Happy to see y'all. Stop by this morning. I'm working on something I'd like to show everyone."

"We'll come over after breakfast," Clifford promised.

Zion fired off a salute. "Cheerio."

With that, he hopped onto his quad and zipped back to his farm across the road.

Puzzled, Eva asked her dad, "What's that all about?"

She hoped it had nothing to do with Dylan.

"We'll just have to go over and see," Clifford said, his eyes sparkling.

To Eva, that was a 'tell,' meaning it must be a good surprise. They finished their eggs and toast, and Kaley cleared the table. Soon, Gramps rode over with Gram on his quad. Eva and Kaley followed in the Bug.

About to enter Zion's pole building, Eva pictured it dusty and covered with spider webs. Her dad called it a barn; however, Eva considered it a pole barn, with its large timbers forming a structure over the metal sheeting of the exterior walls. Zion had put in a wide sliding door to accommodate his tractor, and a service door through which Eva, Kaley, Marcia, and Clifford now entered.

She instantly changed her mind. What a neat and clean man cave Zion had made for himself. Panels of fluorescent lights hung from the ceiling on long chains.

Zion greeted them with a "Howdy," and then gestured below the lights toward a wooden workbench. Eva was amazed by the various vices and tools of all shapes and sizes set along panels of pegboard. Eva inhaled deeply, enjoying the aroma of hay and alfalfa.

Did she also detect the scent of cedar wood? She vividly recalled her grandmother's clothes closet lined with cedar, which Eva had enjoyed exploring as a child.

"Meet my sanctuary," Zion said to the group, his eyes shining. "When I first retired, I had this place built and spent most of my time out here repairing equipment I found for cheap on the Internet."

"Were you retired long before being called back to help the Air Force?" Eva asked.

"Just long enough to sharpen the woodworking tools I inherited from my dad. He taught me the little I know."

Zion walked over to a pile of lumber. "I'd just gotten my barn set up and collected this here wood when I bumped into a guy at the Base Exchange. Wouldn't you know, we got talking, and he found out about my flight experience and knowledge of simulators, so he asked me to speak with his CO about their needs at Tyndall."

"Ha, I can attest that Zion is handy with every one of these tools, including drywall taping," Eva's dad remarked with a smile. "He helped me build the garage bathroom for the barracks."

"I'm glad I have what was supposed to be a part-time job," Zion said, selecting a chunk of cedar wood. "It probably keeps me from getting bored, but unfortunately it cuts into my wood carving time."

Thinking Scott would be interested in Zion's wood carving, she asked, "What are you making today?"

Zion bounced the piece of wood in both hands, saying, "This piece of cedar will be a small lamb for this year's Christmas crèche. Carving Joseph and Mary will be my biggest task."

"Your carving is exquisite." Eva picked up and admired a small wooden infant. "I see you're nearly done with baby Jesus. I can't imagine how to even begin such a project."

Clifford began lobbing questions at Zion about painting the wooden figurines, distracting him. This gave Eva time to nose around. Then she spotted it, the extension phone attached to the wall beside Zion's tools.

She motioned with her eyes and whispered to Kaley, "Look, the scene of the crime."

"Huh," Kaley grunted, her eyes wide. "I never noticed that telephone on the wall when we were in here before."

Just then, Zion strode up to Eva. "Well, what do you think? Can I get Mary and Joseph, plus some more lambs done in time for the Christmas cantata in early December?"

"Maybe you should get my dad over here to help you," Eva suggested with a grin.

"Good idea, Eva. He seems mighty interested."

# Chapter 31

Eva looked out her bedroom window on Sunday morning and saw dark clouds threatening to rain. After getting dressed in a flowered cotton skirt and blouse for church, she peered out again at nothing but blue skies. She grinned at how unpredictable Florida's weather could be, hoping she'd have clear flying for her flights tomorrow through Atlanta and on to DC.

When she went downstairs, her smile traveled all the way to her toes. There was Kaley looking happy and laughing as she drank a cup of coffee with Gram.

"Kaley, you look so pretty in your new dress," Eva said. "And the cowboy boots are a fun touch."

After a quick breakfast of toast and fruit, they all went to church, with Clifford driving their SUV. Eva entered the building behind Kaley, once again noting the vast differences from what she experienced at her megachurch back home. The small country church had gorgeous stained-glass windows depicting the life of Jesus Christ on every wall rather than stark, large plate-glass windows. Wooden pews lined the sanctuary instead of the individual cushioned seats Eva was used to.

More importantly to Eva, everyone in the church seemed to know one another. She met many of her parents' new friends and could see that when they worshipped together on Sundays, it was like they were with family they had missed during the week. Gladness and well-being enveloped Eva.

"Pastor Dobson has preached here for two decades," her mom said quietly before the music started. "He and his wife have been so welcoming to your dad and me."

Someone tapped Eva's shoulder. She twisted her head to see Noelle Adelman standing behind her and beaming a smile.

"Zion and I hope you and Kaley and your folks will join us today for Sunday lunch," Noelle said. "A nice beef roast is simmering in one slow cooker and a whole chicken in the other. Another family will also join us. We'd like you and Kaley to meet them before she starts school."

Eva's mom replied, "Kaley helped me bake an apple pie last night. We'll bring that with ice cream for dessert."

A tall lady wearing a long print dress, her hair swept up atop her head, sat down at the piano and began playing a medley of hymns, some of which Eva recognized. She saw Kaley tucking her arms beside her and looking around, moistening her lips.

Sensing her soon-to-start-college daughter might be feeling a bit lost, Eva patted her hand. "You're going to excel here, Kaley. I just know it."

Her daughter simply shrugged. Pastor Dobson invited everyone to stand and sing. Eva recognized the praise song as one they often sang as a family, heralding the beautiful name of Jesus. Kaley started singing with gusto, as then did Eva. And so, she and Kaley shared a precious time of worship.

After the message about Jesus being the Good Shepherd and not wanting even one sheep to be lost, they all sang "Amazing Grace." Pastor Dobson asked people to come forward to pray.

"This altar is God's office," he beckoned, spreading his arms out wide. "You just come on down here and do business with Him. If you want someone to pray with you, I'm here."

Moments later, Kaley leaned over, saying in a low voice, "Mom, I want to go pray about starting on the right track at school. Will you go with me?"

A man in overalls walked down the aisle ahead of them to talk with the pastor. Eva and Kaley went forward and kneeled down by the altar.

Eva prayed quietly over her daughter, "Heavenly Father, bless Kaley and keep her safe. Draw a hedge of protection over her all her days, and give her much wisdom in her classes and in finding new friends. Thank you for all Your care, in Jesus' Name, Amen."

They hugged, and when they returned to their row, Gram and Gramps were ready to give more hugs. Eva felt so loved by God and her parents in this moment.

An hour later, at the Adelman farm, everyone sat around the several round tables on the spacious screened porch out back. They introduced Eva and Kaley to their veterinarian, his wife, and their son, Stephen Wilson. Eva was pleasantly surprised to learn Stephen was Kaley's age and also enrolled at FSU. And he was studying biological science. His family attended a Baptist church in town.

"I want to be a vet like my dad," he declared. "I've already signed up for the pre-vet club. It's good for anyone who likes animals, even if they don't want to be a vet. Kaley, you could come to the first meeting and see what you think."

Kaley nodded shyly. "I just might."

**EVA'S MONDAY MORNING BEGAN WITH A START.** Her phone alarm buzzed her awake at four a.m. before the rooster was up. She figured she'd have enough time to make her six o'clock flight at the PC airport. She checked if any text messages had arrived during the night.

Finding none, Eva forced her mind to focus on her other major case. She must ignore concerns over last Friday's FBI terrorism case involving Dylan and turn her full attention to working on the Runner's case.

Recalling the planning meeting with Kerstin Harvick, Eva prepared herself for her flight from PC to Washington. She would change planes in Atlanta. The mission ahead was to discover if retired FBI agents working for the Lancet Group were helping the ChiComs harass their perceived enemies in the U.S., including Eva's source, the Runner.

Within the hour, Eva would hug good-bye to her firstborn child, for she didn't know how long. She hoped to do so without shedding too many tears.

Eva showered and then hurried to finish packing. She checked the time. Though Kaley had agreed to take Eva to the airport, her daughter was no early riser. Eva phoned her at the new digs above the garage. She surprisingly answered right away.

"Are you up? We leave in twenty minutes."

"Mom, of course I'm up! I was just getting in the shower."

"Okay, honey. Be quiet so we don't wake Gram and Gramps."

Eva placed her bag at the side entrance by the garage

before making coffee and toasting bagels for the two of them.

"Ha, trying to sneak out." Gramps came shuffling into the kitchen in his slippers.

"Oh, Dad," Eva lamented. "We were trying to be super quiet. Is Mom still asleep?"

He reached up into the cupboard, taking down two cups. "Nope, she's putting on the new outfit you bought her."

"In that case, I'll drop more bagels into the toaster," Eva said with a smile.

Wearing the new matching slacks and top from Eva, Gram wanted to make fried eggs, so she sizzled them in the pan. After eating a nice but hurried breakfast with her folks and Kaley, Eva grabbed her carry-on suitcase and joined her parents on the front porch. Kaley had already backed the Slug Bug out of the garage and was ready to take Eva to the airport.

Mom and Dad each hugged their daughter Eva tightly.

"Be safe, and know we're praying for you each day," Mom whispered in her ear. "I'll be missing you!"

"Me too," Dad croaked, wiping his eyes.

Tears stung Eva's eyes, and she tried laughing off her surging emotions. "Scott and I will be talking about spending our Christmas vacation with you."

Eva blew her folks a kiss and dashed to the car, tossing her bag in the back seat. With Kaley behind the wheel, she slid into the front passenger seat. They each lowered the windows and waved as they drove off. Kaley seemed quite comfortable navigating the roads toward the airport as she followed prompts from her cell phone hanging on a holder from her rearview mirror.

They hadn't driven far when Kaley said, "Dad and my brothers are waiting for you back home. I know I don't have to say it, but don't forget me."

"Never!" Eva promised. "You'll soon be very busy enjoying your new college and friends. Dad and I will stay in touch as much as you want us to."

Kaley nodded as she turned at the light. "Sounds perfect, Mom. Will you be working on the flight home today?"

Eva suspected Kaley had reverted back to her mystery mode. "Yes, I'll be going directly to the office when I land."

"No, I mean will you be tailing a suspect? I heard you talking last week about a source in Florida."

"Do you want to know because of your new curiosity about everything FBI, or do you have a 'need to know'?"

Kaley passed a slower-moving truck and slid back into the right lane. She glanced at Eva. "You know I don't 'need to know,' but I have my reason for being curious."

Eva laughed at her daughter's new understanding of the importance of secrecy regarding investigations. "There's nothing I can tell you. You'll just have to resume the innocence of your youth and believe your mother is simply going to work as usual."

"Okay, Mom. I think I've figured out who your source is. Zion Adelman, right?"

Eva laughed out loud. "Kaley, the same 'need to know' applies. Let me ask, why did you make such an assumption."

"Ah hah, I think I'm right because you're avoiding answering me. I've been with you all weekend. The only man you've talked to besides Gramps is Mr. Adelman."

"I'm glad to see how stimulated you are by the excitement of last week. Yet, you have much to learn before you'll figure it out," Eva wanted to end Kaley's line of questioning.

There was something else she needed to discuss before they arrived at the airport. "Kaley, have you heard any more from Dylan after delivering his brochures to his fake uncle?"

"Not a word. Or in his case, a text," Kaley replied. "I'll be sure to let you and Griff know if I do."

She slowed the Bug as she entered the airport departure area. Eva knew there might be agents on surveillance watching their arrival. She glanced around, thinking Kaley was clueless because she had no 'need to know.' Eva intended to keep it that way, so she didn't caution her daughter to be extra careful.

After pulling to the curb, Kaley jumped from the car and removed her mom's suitcase from the back seat. Eva collected her tote and gave Kaley a heartfelt hug.

"Remember to call me and let me know how things are going."

"I will, Mom."

Eva gave her a second bear hug. "Notice, I said to call me. A text isn't enough. I want to hear your beautiful voice."

"Hahaha! You'll be hearing from me!"

Kaley returned to the driver's seat in the Slug Bug. Fresh tears pricked Eva's blue eyes. She dashed them away as she watched her wonderful daughter drive off, her arm waving out the window.

At least Eva had work to occupy her mind. She scrutinized the milling passengers in the airport as she entered through the automatic sliding doors. Seeing no one or anything she considered suspicious, she checked in and hurried to the gate.

Captain Yang Ming was also scheduled to be on the same plane. She'd spoken again with him briefly yesterday to let him know she'd be on his flight, departing the PC airport at 6:00 a.m. this morning.

But where was he?

Eva's eyes scanned the several dozen passengers in the waiting area. She didn't spot Ming anywhere. Eva expected she'd be on the lookout during the layover in Atlanta for Danny Boyd and his other retired FBI cronies who might be trailing Captain Ming.

Were other agents here also watching for him? Eva couldn't be sure and remained watchful for anyone trying to prevent his arrival at the FBI's Field Office in DC.

Captain Ming planned to use the ride-share app on his personal cell phone to get to this airport. Thus, Eva presumed the ChiComs knew all about his ride and ultimate destination. She stayed alert to spot any other agents from the local ICE office who might be at this airport assisting Eva to ensure Ming made his DC flight with no trouble.

Still, he was nowhere in sight. Did something or someone scare Ming off?

# Chapter 32

Fortunately, the Panama City airport terminal was small and pretty much what Eva had expected. The good thing was she cleared the TSA passenger screening and check-in process in ten minutes, though she'd arrived nearly one hour early. The downside was she had forty-five minutes until departure and Captain Ming still hadn't appeared.

Perusing the gate area, Eva didn't spot any kind of surveillance by ChiComs, their hired U.S. counterparts, or even the FBI or ICE. She leaned against a wall. Truth be told, she hadn't expected any. Who would spend money for a ticket just to get through TSA and watch people board a flight?

Assuming ChiComs were indeed monitoring Captain Ming's smartphone, as Eva and Griff suspected, then they'd be expecting him to change planes in Atlanta, as his reservations reflected. Eva reminded herself that Zion had identified Danny Boyd, the retired FBI agent, as following Ming when he'd changed flights inside the Atlanta terminal on his earlier trip to DC.

It was in Atlanta where Eva fully expected more action.

She checked the time on her phone, noting it was 5:40 a.m. She walked toward screening, checking out approaching passengers.

*Come on, Ming. Show your face!*

Boarding would begin soon. She wondered if he'd failed to find a ride-share.

A gate attendant, lifting up a microphone, announced, "Flight 486 to Atlanta is ready for boarding. We invite priority passengers needing assistance or those with children at this time."

Eva blinked. Did she really see him? Or a look-alike?

Yes! There was Captain Ming walking into the boarding area.

He took a seat in the back corner, giving him a broad view of the room. Dressed in beige slacks and a navy-blue buttoned and collared shirt, he had no carry-on luggage. Eva surmised he intended to fly back to Tyndall this evening.

She watched as his eyes scanned the room, and passing by Eva, he quickly gazed back. He gave her an ever-so-slight nod. She wondered if perhaps he'd stayed in the bathroom as a safety measure.

Eva made her way into the plane, taking her seat in the second row of the coach section. She fully intended to rush off the plane in Atlanta before Captain Ming did to discover if Danny Boyd or any Lancet employees were hovering around the secured area of the terminal.

Ming was one of the last persons to board. He walked slowly by Eva and went on back to the rear of the plane. As she expected, Eva detected no evidence he was being followed.

Before switching her cell phone to airplane mode, Eva texted Griff: *Captain and I are aboard, ready to depart. Captain in navy button-up collared shirt. Beige slacks. No baggage. No sign of trouble. Advise the others. Will report more after connecting in Atlanta.*

**EVA WAS THANKFUL HER FLIGHT SAFELY ARRIVED IN ATLANTA.** As the jetway moved into place, Eva reached for her tote beneath the seat and prepared to depart. She checked the time on her phone. Oh oh. She and Ming had very little time to make their next flight. They would have to hurry. She grabbed her carry-on from the overhead and headed for the exit.

Moments later, Eva emerged from the jetway into the terminal, wheeling her carry-on. She lingered momentarily to allow Ming to hurry past her. Keeping close behind him, she strode with purpose to the new gate. Her eyes skimmed across the area, which was mostly empty.

Relief filled her. She grabbed a seat near the gate, pretending to look at her phone as she waited for the Captain to emerge from the restroom. And then, across the walkway at the other gate area, she saw someone she recognized. Her pulse elevated.

Danny Boyd was sitting arrogantly with a jacket on his lap. He wore business casual dress, his arm resting atop his carry-on bag. He seemed to be watching intently. Another man holding a magazine, who sat facing Boyd, also seemed to be observing passengers from Eva's flight.

From her seat, Eva casually raised her phone, enlarged the image, and photographed both men. She changed the setting to video and held her phone at the ready. Then she rose, switching to a seat in the next gate area so disembarking passengers wouldn't block her view of Boyd and her other target. She'd barely aimed her camera when the Captain came out of the restroom and headed for their next gate.

With her video rolling, Eva saw Boyd stand and start following Captain Ming. She filmed Boyd abandoning his carry-on bag. In mere seconds, Mr. Magazine Man stood, retrieved Boyd's bag, and took off following Ming, too.

*Ah-ha* Eva thought. Her craft of reading people had only gotten better.

She jumped to her feet, shut off the video, and hurried down the corridor. She didn't look at all unusual as others were passing by her, also walking fast. Eva succeeded in reaching their gate ahead of Captain Ming and his adversaries. She sat in an empty gate area across from hers, where she took close-up photos of Boyd and his accomplice, who wore cargo shorts, a striped golf shirt, short socks, and white running shoes.

The accomplice's combed-back pewter-colored hair confirmed for Eva that he was probably a retired FBI agent employed by Lancet. She continued looking about for others but doubted Lancet had budgeted for more than two members to tail the Captain. Eva observed both men take seats and surreptitiously begin taking photos of Yang Ming.

While still alone in the empty gate area, Eva sent pictures to Griff of Boyd and the other Lancet thug. Then she texted him: *Boarding soon for DC. Danny B. and partner in striped golf shirt, both tailing and taking pics of source.*

Boarding began. This time Captain Ming boarded first, giving Eva an opportunity to observe Danny Boyd and associate remain in the area and seeming less attentive with Ming on the plane.

Good! They obviously had no interest in her.

Eva boarded, spotting Ming in the first row of the cabin.

She found her seat behind him on the opposite side, which provided her with a good view to ensure his safety. He waved off any refreshment and simply held his phone.

In the quiet time on the plane, she reminisced about the marvelous days she'd just spent with her parents and Kaley. She scrolled through fun photos, especially enjoying the carvings Zion was creating for this year's Christmas nativity. Would Scott agree to spend two weeks in Florida over Christmas?

Eva hoped so and cast her mind to already making plans. She was determined not to become consumed by Captain Ming's case until reaching Reagan International Airport in DC, where, if Boyd and his crony were any indication, the action would most certainly be heating up.

# Chapter 33

Eva's plane landed at Reagan. She gave God thanks for being safely on the ground before hurrying from the plane on the heels of Captain Ming. She slung the tote over her shoulder, and wheeling her carry-on, she briskly followed him from the airport to the Metro station.

Her hubby Scott had amazingly found Ming's Metro Smart Trip card after Eva tackled him during his first DC visit, so she expected Ming would choose the same mode to travel into Washington again. And he did.

After watching him buy a Smart Trip card at the vending kiosk, Eva retrieved her card from her wallet, which she always carried with thirty dollars on it. She readied herself to ride whichever Metro car he hopped onto. The Captain waited on the platform for the Blue Line into DC, shuffling his feet. He looked nervous. Eva stepped beside him, not only to assuage his fears, but to also scrutinize the nearby passengers.

Who were innocent travelers?

Who were private detectives from the Lancet Group?

Who were other ICE agents sworn to secrecy and looking for evidence of crimes committed by the Lancet Group?

Eva ruled out families with kids and luggage. Next, she crossed off her mental list anyone who appeared they couldn't pass the grueling physical requirements for becoming a federal agent. Just then, the Metro train bound for DC pulled into the platform.

Eva watched Ming step into the second car. Two men and one woman walked up beside Eva, and they hopped on the same car. She followed them aboard.

Just as overhead speakers announced, "The doors are about to close; please step back," two additional men hurried to enter the car, one at the front and one at the rear doors. Both were professional-looking, as if they could be with Lancet or other players in the operation at hand. Everyone found seats, including Eva, which was a plus as she texted Griff a brief update.

The train pulled smoothly away from the station. Eva stayed on alert at each stop, watching for any of the five she suspected could be players to exit the train. Metro Center was the next station in the heart of Washington, and it was where Captain Ming had to change trains to get to Judiciary Square, the closest station to the FBI's Washington Field Office.

The speakers announced, "Metro Center."

Hordes of passengers crowded toward the doors. When the last suspected player remained seated after Eva and Ming got off the train, she assumed that man was going elsewhere on the Blue Line and not involved.

Captain Ming was in no hurry to venture toward the escalator rising toward the upper platform for the Red Line. Interestingly, each one of the remaining four suspected players slowly ascended the escalator and stayed behind the Captain; not one hurried past him like typical DC commuters rushing to their destination. Eva stayed behind them all, and being the last on the steps going up the escalator, she kept her eyes open to what happened ahead of her.

Once upon the Red Line platform, one of the first men Eva suspected of tailing Ming dashed across the platform and jumped on a train going in the opposite direction. So, he was off her list of potential enemies. The Red Line train for Judiciary Square swooped in, stopping at the platform. The doors swished open. The three remaining suspected players—two men and a woman—all hopped aboard the same car as Captain Ming. So did Eva.

The train pulled away, announcing, "Next stop, Judiciary Square."

Eva was able to snap pictures of one man and also one of the woman; however, the other man stayed well behind her, so any attempt to photograph him would be too conspicuous.

She texted the two photos to Griff with a hurried message: *These two, and one additional man, appear to be following the Captain. JS next stop.*

Eva gazed up and saw Captain Ming was studying his phone. No doubt he relied on his GPS to show him the route to the FBI field office. After it was announced, "Judiciary Square. Stand clear of the doors," the Captain stood. He approached the sliding doors, but Eva stayed seated, gripping her carry-on bag for a fast exit.

Glancing at the three persons she expected were tailing Ming, she realized they were very sly at disguising their intent. None of them even looked toward him.

The doors slid open. Captain Ming stepped onto the platform behind three women. Eva noticed the women proceeded right to the escalator, whereas Ming stepped to the middle of the platform, his eyes glued to his phone. Eva waited for the first announcement that the doors would be closing to see if any other passengers left the train. She stalled in her seat another moment.

When the second and final warning came, "Doors closing. Step back from the doors," Eva bolted through the opening just as the doors closed behind her. On the platform, she stood in shock. Where was the surveillance team to ensure Ming's safety?

The three she'd thought were ICE agents had stayed on the train and were now en route to the suburbs.

Eva observed further down the platform an Asian-looking woman with a ponytail studying her phone and also several men ascending the escalator. Even though there was a chance the Captain might board the next train heading in the opposite direction, Eva walked toward the escalator, hoping he'd take the hint and follow her.

She reached the top of the escalator and looked back to see Captain Ming riding up. The Asian woman was coming up below him. Eva stepped off the escalator, noticing numerous people heading for the down escalator. Also, two men were purchasing tickets at the Metro kiosk.

Eva looked around in frustration.

Were those guys on the ICE team? If not, where were they hiding?

She stepped away from the Metro entrance into the middle of Judiciary Square and into bright sunshine. She shielded her eyes and blinked. Beyond her stood the historic National Building Museum. It had been renamed from the Civil War era Pension Building, and with its huge interior columns, was a popular venue for presidential inaugural festivities.

She expected Ming would walk toward it and then turn right for the remaining one-block walk to the FBI field office on

Fourth Street. To get behind Captain Ming, Eva pivoted to walk briefly in the direction of the Law Enforcement Memorial. She looked over her shoulder.

Ming was indeed walking toward the Building Museum and 'F' Street. Concerned that no agents appeared to be watching out for Ming, Eva turned to follow him. At 'F' Street, Ming turned right toward the FBI office. Without warning, two Asian-looking men jumped from a car at the curb and grabbed for the Captain.

It was déjà vu all over again!

Eva sprang forward. Ming bolted and ran toward the FBI office. He collided with two men, who looked to Eva like FBI agents. They seized Ming and, spinning him around, dragged him toward Eva and the two Asian men.

Suddenly, Eva was surrounded.

Men and women were shouting, "Federal Agent!"

Others yelled, "FBI!"

Guns were drawn. Gold badges were displayed.

Eva whirled around. A man and woman she recognized as ICE agents leapt from a car on 'F' Street. They instantly began struggling to handcuff the two Asian men who had grabbed for Ming.

Tourists screamed at the sight of guns and the hand-to-hand tussles on the street in the nation's capital. Eva yanked on the shirt of the bewildered Captain Ming and hustled him away from the chaos. Griff's car screeched to a halt next to her on 'F' Street. She opened his rear door and shoved the Captain inside along with her carry-on bag.

As Eva swung open Griff's front passenger door, she recognized the Asian-looking woman from the Metro platform. The ponytailed woman was being put into handcuffs and stuffed into the back seat of what Eva assumed was an ICE car by a man, who she assumed was an ICE agent.

If only she knew who out here besides Griff was the real deal. But she didn't, so she slammed the door shut, thankful Ming was safe for now.

**AS FAST AS IT BEGAN,** the chaos ended. Anyone suspected of tailing Captain Ming to kidnap him had been scooped up and thrown into government cars, which roared away from the scene. Eva looked out the window of Griff's G-car to see if any other agents needed help. All evidence of the arrests had vanished, except for several blue and white Metropolitan Police cars converging onto the scene, lights flashing and sirens blaring.

"Captain, it's good to see you unharmed." Eva turned to him. "We've arrested several people. By way of introduction, the driver is my partner, FBI Special Agent Griff Topping."

Griff looked into his rearview mirror and waved. "Pleasure meeting you, Captain."

"You need to know." Captain Ming paused to look out the rear window as Griff started driving away. "The same man tried taking me again—the man from Arizona and my last DC trip."

"I saw him being arrested," Eva replied. "He will be charged in our federal courts."

Trusting this was so, she glanced out the window, seeing no other arrest team members on the street. Local police just arriving would encounter tourists who claimed to have witnessed a crime, yet there was no evidence of any such event. Recalling incidents where witnesses claimed to have seen flying saucers, Eva chuckled.

What would the MPD officers report back to dispatch?

She was mindful of how Zion had faked an equipment failure on the Tyndall Base simulator so the Taiwanese pilots could have this Monday off. Therefore, Captain Ming had flown to DC without his associates being none the wiser.

Determined to comfort Captain Ming, Eva told him, "If we hurry, we'll get you back to the airport and on a return flight to Panama City. In the future, I and possibly Griff, will fly to meet with you in Panama City. First, we need to chat a bit and show you some pictures."

Ming nodded, staring out the window.

*He's probably watching the monuments we're driving by,* Eva thought. *Or he's worried for his sister and not seeing a thing.*

Griff drove across Memorial Bridge into the grounds of Arlington National Cemetery, and after winding around the streets to the U.S. Marine Corps National Memorial, he found a parking spot. The trio walked in blazing sunshine to a nearby park bench beneath a shade tree.

Griff handed Ming a bottled water, saying, "Please take a seat and be comfortable. We're close enough to the Reagan Airport that we can get you there for your flight in just ten minutes."

Eva sat beside Ming, where she quickly scrolled through her cell phone photos.

Handing him the phone, she explained, "I took these four pictures today on the train. Do you recognize anyone as having followed or assaulted you on your previous trip here?"

He studied each face before saying, "I saw these two men on the train today, but never before. I did not see them after I leave the train. I never saw the others."

Eva took back her phone and scrolled to show him additional photos. "This picture shows the two men who assaulted you on your first trip to Washington."

"You showed me this one before," Ming replied after glancing at the picture. Then he looked at Griff, who was sitting on the lush green lawn, adding, "I saw one of these men that first day in DC. This man."

He pointed to an Asian-looking man with cropped black hair and wearing glasses. "This same man cornered me before I leave Luke Air Force Base in Arizona. I was eating alone at a Chinese restaurant. He sat down at my table."

"Had you ever seen him before that?" Griff asked.

"Never!" Captain Ming insisted.

Eva leaned a bit closer to ask, "What did he say?"

"That my sister, who disappeared in Hong Kong, was in a Chinese prison, a very dangerous prison, for crimes she committed in Hong Kong. That her life was at risk every day."

He gazed at Eva, his eyes bright with unshed tears. "Remember at bar-b-que, I told you a different ChiCom came to me in Taiwan to say my sister was kidnapped in Hong Kong?"

"Why was he the one telling you these things?" Griff demanded.

"The man in Taiwan knew I am pilot for Taiwan's military."

Ming stopped to drink some water. After composing himself, he continued, "He demanded I provide information to him so my sister could be transferred to a safer prison."

Eva pointed to the man in the picture wearing glasses. "Are you sure the man in this picture is *not* the same ChiCom you saw in Taiwan?"

"Yes, Agent Montanna. No doubt. I do not forget such a man who keep threatening me."

Griff asked, "How did it happen that this man in the picture knew you were in Arizona, that he found you in the restaurant, and then shows up here again each time you are in DC?"

Ming looked from Griff to Eva and shrugged. "I do not know. I and some of our other pilots were in Arizona training on F-16 fighter aircraft. I believe he is spy for ChiComs. This spy assaulted me last time in Washington and again today. I believe they listen to my phone."

"But Eva gave you another phone for getting in touch with her," Griff said. "Correct?"

"Yes, but I have many questions about my future with my unit and how to deal with this man," he said, his voice rising and his finger jabbing at the picture.

Griff answered, "Agent Montanna said she saw the ChiCom spy being arrested. After today, it's possible his network will be disrupted. Meanwhile, we will be investigating. The time may come when we will confer at a higher level with your military command. Eva will contact you before that would happen."

"Would that be helpful?" Eva asked.

Captain Ming appeared somewhat relieved when he said softly, "I am hopeful."

# Chapter 34

I n the front seat of Griff's G-car, Eva peered over her shoulder to be sure Captain Ming was getting safely on his way to Panama City. Griff consulted his phone before pulling away from Reagan's departure area. For her part, Eva couldn't shake the feeling she should accompany Ming to Florida and told Griff so.

"Should I drop you off, so you can buy a ticket?" he said, snickering. "Don't forget your carry-on's in the back seat."

"Oh, I get your point," she huffed. "I know those who meant him harm have all been arrested. What if there's another communist thug out there ready to pounce on him?"

With a jerk to the wheel, Griff merged with traffic heading toward DC. "You're a dedicated agent, Eva, but you can't protect everyone from everything."

"And I can't be in two places at one time." Eva knew she needed to let go for now. "Okay, I'm trusting in God to answer my prayers and get Ming to Florida intact."

"Sounds wise," he said.

Suddenly, Griff floored the accelerator, forcing Eva's head to bob against the seatback.

"Watch out!" she grumbled. "It's been quite a day so far, and it's barely beginning. I'd really like to make it home for dinner."

Griff glanced her way. "Right before we left the airport, I got a text saying we're being summoned to the Triple Nickel for a meeting. It's urgent."

Eva recognized the Triple Nickel as the nickname for the U.S. Attorney's Office (USAO) at 555 Fourth Street, Washington, DC. It was located directly across the street from the very spot where Griff and Eva had rescued Captain Ming from being stuffed into a ChiCom's car an hour ago.

"Great," Eva replied, blinking her drying eyes and doing her best to ignore the need for caffeine. "What's up at the USAO?"

Griff cranked the wheel at the corner. "For this morning's operation, a bevy of ICE agents set up makeshift operations in the basement at Triple Nickel. They've arrested six here and identified two others to arrest in Atlanta."

"Not bad for a day's work," Eva said with a grimace. "Are we being summoned because Ming's still in danger, as I thought?"

"They need our help because they've arrested more suspects than they expected."

Eva checked her cell phone for any texts but had none. "I'm still trying to sort out what happened at Judiciary Square as I followed Ming before the chaotic arrest scene. I identified several people I thought could be tailing him, but when he exited the Metro at Judiciary, three of them stayed on."

"Right. You texted some photos to me," Griff reminded her.

"I wonder if they were even involved. The other ICE agents on the team must have done an excellent job because I never spotted any of them."

"We'll find out."

Griff headed down the street adjacent to the Triple Nickel and fortunately found a car just leaving a parking spot. They took its place and hurried into the large building that housed the prosecutorial nerve center for DC's Federal Court system. After identifying themselves to the screening officers, Eva and Griff found their way down a stairway leading to holding cells, a conference room, and small offices.

The place was abuzz with many agents talking on phones and to each other. Eva traded astonished looks with Griff. He gazed around the noisy room and simply shrugged off the chaos. Eva felt odd recognizing no one.

A female agent wearing a brown shirt and slacks with a badge showing on her belt stepped forward, asking, "Are you Agent Eva Montanna?"

"I am," Eva answered with a curt nod.

The professional-looking agent, her graying hair pulled into a bun, reached out her hand. "I'm Trudy Graham, ICE Supervisory Special Agent for the New York City office, and am temporarily supervising this group."

"Agent Graham, I assume you've already met FBI Special Agent Griff Topping." Eva turned to Griff. "We're partners on the FBI Joint Terrorism Task Force. We also stumbled into this strange case requiring your special team."

"Call me Trudy," she replied, nodding. "And yes, I met Griff during a planning session for today's operation. As I told Griff earlier, it's more like you tackled your way into this case."

The trio chuckled.

Trudy's facial expression turned serious. "Eva, I was disheartened to read how you tried to help the two men claiming to be FBI agents when you tackled their target, only to have them and the target vanish before your eyes."

"It's a mystery I'd still like to solve," Eva replied.

Her eyes flickered around the room. With agents working and talking around various folding tables, she felt more like an interloper than an integral part of the operation.

"Listen, Trudy," she said. "I've been in Florida and don't know what to expect here. Will you bring me up to speed?"

Trudy led them to a quieter corner, where she explained, "ICE Headquarters summoned ten of us from offices around the country, but each of us had been previously stationed here in DC."

"Good idea to bring in some who know the area," Griff said, pocketing his cell phone.

"We've arrested six suspects and are sorting out their roles in assaulting the pilot," Trudy said. "In the mix of arrestees are one or two spies for the Communist Party of China and perhaps three retired FBI agents."

Puzzled, Eva drew her brows together. "I count five. You said six. Who's the remaining person?"

"Ah, yes." Trudy tented her hands. "That's most interesting and the reason we've waited for you and Griff to arrive."

Before Eva could question her further, Trudy turned to Griff. "The top FBI officials wanted us ICE agents brought in because evidence suggests several retired FBI agents are suspects. The FBI Director wants to avoid *any* appearance of impropriety."

"I agree." Griff glanced at Eva.

She understood the FBI's precarious position and wondered if Griff's look suggested he was concerned he knew the retired FBI agents. This could get sticky.

Trudy mentioned ICE, so Eva forced herself to focus on what the supervisor was saying, "We arrested a retired ICE agent who also works for Lancet. We'd like you, Griff, to interview him and follow-up because your being an FBI agent lessens the possibility of bias or a conflict."

"The net is widening," Eva exclaimed.

Trudy beckoned them toward a table. "I'll brief you on what else we've found."

As Eva observed the color mug shots spread across the table, each having a stack of papers beside them, she said, "Looks like these are our six suspects with the surveillance notes and reports written thus far."

"This man and this one woman work for Lancet and are retired FBI," Trudy said in disgust. "This third guy is the retired ICE agent. All three tailed the pilot through the Reagan Airport and on the Metro coming here today. This Asian man is a ChiCom agent who was in the front passenger seat of the rental car."

Eva interjected, "Plus, I photographed Danny Boyd and another of his colleagues in the Atlanta airport this morning who were following the pilot."

"We need to decide quickly if we want to arrest Boyd and his colleague before they beat feet and disappear." Trudy crossed her arms as if deep in thought.

Eva agreed to their arrest, then asked about the two photos on the table of the remaining suspects. "What's their story?"

"I saved the best for last." Trudy picked up the two photos. "This man is Kim Wu, who is a ChiCom operative. The female with the ponytail is Nelly Jin. She's the same. Both have green cards and immigration documents and insist they work for a large Chinese corporation, which has a small lobbying office in DC, not far from here."

Eva snatched up Kim Wu's photo, and with excitement rising in her voice, she told Griff, "I believe he's the same guy who yelled FBI when they tried grabbing the pilot on his first trip to DC."

"I understand the pilot you mean," he said in low tones. "We won't say his name in here."

"Exactly." Eva looked over at Trudy and said, "This pilot, who I call the Runner, identified Wu as the communist operative who threatened him in Arizona and warned that the pilot's sister would die in a Chinese Communist prison if said pilot refused to spy for China."

With both hands, Eva fluttered Nelly Jin's photo. "I saw this very woman standing on the platform when I and the pilot exited the Metro car."

"That's excellent to know," Trudy declared. "When the pilot arrived near the curb on 'F' Street, Nelly and the retired ICE agent tried wrestling the pilot into a rental car. And who was driving that rental? None other than her comrade, Kim Wu."

"Where do I and Griff begin?" Eva asked, eager to get in the mix.

Trudy lifted her hands, palms up. "Griff, you were in the planning meeting where it was agreed FBI counterintelligence agents will take custody of any foreign operatives, so they will arrive soon to take Kim Wu and Nelly Jin. These agents did quick checking and discovered Wu and Jin entered the U.S. in Seattle three years ago. While their green cards appear legitimate, their means for obtaining the cards seems suspect. I believe someone within Immigration pulled some pretty long strings."

Eva didn't like the idea of the FBI being involved with this operation, given their retired colleagues played a dirty part in trying to kidnap Captain Ming. But the counterintelligence group did have jurisdiction over foreign spies working in the States. If only Eva could call on Bo Rider, her friend and agent at the CIA, for help. All of this flashed through her mind in seconds.

She was about to object when the ICE supervisor lifted up the picture of the third male, his salt and pepper hair styled in a buzz cut.

Trudy handed the photo to Griff. "This is Jordan Clouse, the retired ICE special agent who was arrested as he and Nelly tried to push the pilot into the car. And here's a photocopy of a business card found in Clouse's wallet for Gregory Feng, partner at the Lancet Group."

Eva studied the writing on the card when Trudy drew their attention to another image beneath it. "This is the card's reverse side, which contains the name Regina Spire and her cell phone number."

Eva's eyes widened, and Trudy didn't miss it. "Oh. Eva, do you know her?"

"Yes." Adrenaline pumped through Eva as she considered the implications. "Regina and I went through rookie school together. Griff has heard me speak of her. She's now the head of ICE Office of Professional Responsibility."

"I know of Regina but have never met her," Trudy said with her lips in a fine line.

Griff whistled, then smoothed an open palm slowly over his moustache. "This is beginning to look like a can of worms. Do we think Regina might be the insider at Immigration who's been getting these green cards?"

"Griff, this is why you're leading the investigation of Jordan Clouse," Trudy declared. "Copy these papers so you have a place to begin. Your suspect's in a holding cell down the hall."

**AS THEY HEADED TOWARD** the cell holding Clouse, Griff whispered to Eva, "Let me begin the questioning."

She gave him a thumbs-up as they approached a locked steel door. Griff leaned down to gaze into the cell through a peephole.

He turned his head, saying to Eva, "This is him."

She twisted a large steel key to unlock the door. As she swung it open, Griff greeted Clouse with a come-hither motion with one hand.

"Jordan Clouse, please come with us," Griff stated with firmness.

Eva led Clouse, followed by Griff, down the corridor to a sparse office containing only a small desk and three chairs. She motioned for Clouse to take the chair in the corner, while Griff snagged the chair behind the desk.

After Eva shut the door, she adjusted the remaining chair so she could sit in front of the closed door to prevent Clouse from escaping or anyone from disturbing their interrogation.

She hung the tote bag over the back of the chair, Regina's name peppering through her mind.

Eva grit her teeth, thinking, *What will Clouse divulge about my nemesis? What will I do about it if he does?*

Clouse's beady eyes swept the room, pausing for a moment on Eva before focusing on Griff. He shifted on the chair as if nervous, unused to being in the hot seat.

Griff removed his FBI credential case and badge from his trouser pocket and handed these across the desk to Clouse. "I'm Griff Topping. As you see, I'm with the FBI."

Like a pressure cooker ready to explode, Clouse let loose. "I can see how it's going to be. Because I'm a low-level cog in the Lancet Group, you've left me for last to be interviewed."

He gestured dramatically toward the hallway beyond the door. "I already heard agents escorting my colleagues down this hall for the past hour to cut their deals with the government. Here I sit, and finally, you get around to me."

Surprised briefly by the prisoner's outburst, Eva quickly perceived he was atypical. As a retired ICE agent, he knew the law as well as she and Griff, so he was cutting right to the chase.

"Sorry you feel neglected." Griff leaned toward Clouse and proclaimed in a calm voice, "A conscious decision was made to conduct this investigation using highly trusted ICE agents because the Lancet Group was founded by retired FBI agents. When you, as a retired ICE agent, were arrested, I had to be summoned to talk with you to avoid any conflicts."

"Stop." Clouse raised both hands. "Let me just say, I know the ropes. Everyone at Lancet is retired law enforcement. We all know how to save ourselves. I can help the government more than the others, so let's get down to business."

Griff interrupted, "No, you stop. I must first advise that you've been arrested for violations of federal laws, including conspiracy to commit kidnapping and most likely espionage and treason, which you must know carry very heavy penalties up to and including death. You can remain silent and do not have to answer any questions. If you choose to talk or make statements, anything you say can and will be used against you in court. You have a right to have an attorney and to have an attorney present with you. If you cannot afford an attorney, the court will appoint one for you."

Clouse continuously bobbed his head up and down.

"Do you understand?" Griff said. "Answer me with more than a nod."

"I do," Clouse hissed. "And, yes, I still want to tell you everything. I know the U.S. Attorney won't accept cooperation from every defendant, so the defendant who helps the most will probably be the only defendant to get a good deal."

Eva could remain quiet no longer. "You do realize such cooperation doesn't mean dismissal of all charges. A deal may only result in a lesser prison term, which is up to the judge."

"Yes." Clouse spun in his seat to face Eva. "I do know that."

Griff interrupted, "I'm sorry. In your haste to make a deal, I failed to introduce my partner. She and I are assigned to a special FBI task force here in DC. This is ICE Special Agent Eva Montanna."

"Wonder Woman!" Clouse gasped. "As I live and breathe, we finally meet."

He managed to startle both Eva and Griff this time. They sat staring at each other.

Griff recovered first. "You and Eva are from the same agency, but I assumed you didn't know each other."

Both Eva and Jordan Clouse shook their heads.

"I feel like I do know Eva," Clouse explained. "You're married to Scott Montanna, Press Secretary for the Defense Department, correct?"

When Eva and Griff nodded, Clouse chortled. "Every time I see him on TV, I'm reminded he's married to Wonder Woman."

"Okay," Griff objected. "Tell us more."

"I was an ICE special agent in Seattle. My group supervisor was Greg Feng, and his boss was Assistant Special Agent in Charge, Regina Spire."

Griff waved the copy of the business card in the air. "Both are mentioned on this card we found in your wallet."

"Yeah," Clouse confirmed with a shrug. "One night after work, we're at a local bar celebrating an agent's promotion when Scott Montanna appears on the muted lounge TV. Regina points him out to everyone and begins a tirade about his wife, who she calls 'Wonder Woman.'"

Their suspect narrowed his eyes at Eva. "Don't mean to insult you in any way. This may be material to my cooperation here."

"Keep talking," Griff insisted. "We'll decide what's material."

"Yeah, and Regina Spire doesn't like Eva one iota. That night, she told us all how you graduated top of your rookie agent class and that you're some kind of hero for all your spectacular cases. You caused her to be sent to Anchorage early on before she ever managed to be transferred to Seattle. As she tells it, she blames Wonder Woman for her career slide, and because of Wonder Woman's successes and her husband's clout, she's never had to leave Washington, DC."

Griff jumped in to defend his partner. "Sounds like sour grapes to me. While I agree Eva is somewhat of a Wonder Woman, she's intentionally declined promotions to remain in DC to support her husband, while Regina has climbed the command ladder. What's her job today?"

"She's number five in ICE's leadership and heads the Office of Professional Responsibility, or the headhunters as they're known," Eva said evenly.

She refused to let Regina's grudges rattle her or impede this investigation.

Clouse raised a finger as though he had a question. "So, can I assume you aren't working under Regina's command?"

"Correct." Eva smiled. "What's more, she's still trying to get me transferred."

"Okay, now we're talking." Clouse broke out in laughter. "Then I have much to tell you both, but first, I need to use a bathroom."

Griff stood, calling for a break. "You can use the facilities, and maybe Wonder Woman here can find us coffee or water. Which do you want, Jordan?"

"Water's good for me," Clouse replied, standing to his full height and smacking his lips.

# Chapter 35

Eva and Griff continued to interrogate Jordan Clouse in the basement of the U.S. Attorney's Office in DC. Their suspect quickly demonstrated his knowledge of investigations and the federal system.

He'd barely retaken his seat after the break when he began ranting, "I must tell you this immediately. Today, you've arrested Kim Wu and Nelly Jin. I suspect they'll be turned over to the FBI Counterintelligence Division, but that's the last thing you should do."

Griff's expression remained unchanged. He looked at Clouse with steady eyes, then wriggled both index fingers, coaxing Clouse to say more.

"Wu and Jin are ChiCom nationals and spies. They were provided with green cards with the help of Regina, Lancet, and the FBI. They work for China, but they're also confidential human sources for the FBI's Counterintelligence Division. If you release them to the FBI, they will disappear, and the FBI will claim they can't be found."

Eva couldn't believe how, in mere seconds, Clouse was peeling back the layers of corruption! It was worse than she thought!

Griff didn't even blink. Instead, he stood.

"Excuse us just for a moment. Eva, come with me."

He opened the door and waited for Eva to leave before he turned to Clouse, warning him to stay there. "We'll be right outside the door."

In the hall, Griff whispered, "Go find Trudy and bring her here ASAP. I'll keep an eye on our prisoner."

Eva soon returned with Trudy, where Griff had remained in the narrow hallway.

Standing about four feet from the interview room, he quietly told Trudy, "This retired ICE agent is a gold mine of info and has diarrhea of the mouth. Are the two Chinese prisoners still here?"

"The Counterintelligence Division is sending agents here to take them into their custody. Why?"

"We can't let them do that," Griff demanded.

Trudy acted unconvinced. "How can we not? They are ChiCom spies."

"Because they'll be released by the CI division to advance a cover-up within the FBI," Eva said, her voice hushed. "They received their green cards with the assistance of Regina Spire and retired agents at Lancet."

It was Trudy's turn to profess shock. "Oh! We can't have a guns-drawn confrontation with the FBI here in the basement of the U.S. Attorney's office."

It was Eva's turn to speak up. "Look, even though Wu and Ji have green cards, we suspect these are fraudulent. Wu and Jin are foreign spies under investigation by ICE, so I propose that two ICE special agents immediately transport them to a confidential ICE detention facility. Let the FBI and ICE directors fight later about who gets to keep them."

"I agree," Griff said, sounding confident in Eva's plan.

Trudy nodded sharply. "Okay. I need to move quickly, and I'll deal with the heat."

Griff and Eva returned for more grilling of Jordan Clouse, this time armed with pens and paper. The moment Griff picked up a pen, Clouse began talking again.

"I assume you conferred about how to handle Kim Wu and Nelly Jin. I don't need to know but do need to explain why I can help you more than your other arrestees. I need to talk fast before you decide to go home for the day."

Eva heard the sounds of holding cell doors banging shut. She assumed Trudy was being true to her word and getting the two ChiComs out of the building.

"You talk, and we'll take notes," Griff said. "We'll also try to hold clarifying questions so you can finish. We can always talk again tomorrow."

"Eva, you will remember some of what I'm about to say. Griff, you may not know it, but you'll understand how it all relates." Clouse stopped to rub his temples.

Eva and Griff waited, pens poised.

Clouse guzzled water, then wiped his sleeve across his mouth. "A few years back, Regina Spire was the ASAC in Seattle."

Eva wrote with interest that Regina was the Assistant

Special Agent in Charge for Seattle, making a note to verify which years. Meanwhile, Clouse kept weaving his tale.

"Regina was quietly dating Greg Feng, who is Chinese American and a group supervisor in the Seattle office at the time," he said. "And lucky me, I got to be an ICE special agent in his group. Because a large population of Chinese people live around Seattle, the FBI staffs a bigger CI group there with a greater number of Chinese American agents. Keep in mind, a retired Chinese American FBI agent from the Seattle office is the founder of Lancet."

Clouse fixed his bloodshot eyes upon Eva. "You might remember that five years ago, a broad investigation ensued after a bunch of U.S. Citizenship and Immigration Service (CIS) employees were arrested for taking bribes and for expediting citizen applications. In some cases, they issued fraudulent Certificates of Naturalization."

"I remember it well." Eva pursed her lips, recalling the far-reaching CIS conspiracy to break U.S. immigration laws.

"That investigation began and centered in Seattle. It spread to CIS headquarters in DC, but really focused on two of its clerks in Seattle. Greg Feng and two FBI agents in Seattle were deeply involved, along with the same retired FBI agent who founded the Lancet Group."

When Clouse stopped to take a swig from the bottle of water, Eva quickly wrote what he'd just said.

She stopped writing to listen as he continued, "Most folks in our ICE office didn't know it, but Regina was secretly dating Greg Feng, her subordinate. Shortly after the investigation began of the two clerks, Regina somehow got herself transferred to ICE Headquarters in DC. Unbelievably, she was put in charge of all investigations of misconduct by ICE employees, including my supervisor and her boyfriend, Greg Feng. The two of them married, though he remained in Seattle."

Clouse fixed an icy glare at Griff. "I always wondered if they married so they couldn't be compelled to testify against each other. What do you think?"

"I don't want to get you sidetracked," Griff replied. "I'll give you an opinion when we've heard your whole story."

Eva's stomach burned, as she'd eaten nothing since that early breakfast at her folks in Panama City. How long ago that seemed. Well, she'd have to forget about getting any food because what Clouse knew was too explosive to interrupt.

"You have more to tell us, right? Eva asked, hoping he'd expound.

"Sure I do," he shot back. "I know what I know for a good reason. Before Greg Feng was promoted to group supervisor, he was my partner during the time he dated Regina. He was instrumental in helping certain corrupt FBI agents sneak information from immigration files. Feng also worked with those two clerks I mentioned who received money for their misdeeds. When Regina arrived to head ICE's internal felony squad in DC, she began working with the FBI's Office of Professional Responsibility. Guess what their OPR discovered?"

When Eva and Griff remained silent, pens in hand, he grinned. "Here's where things get messy. FBI agents in Seattle were violating federal laws to facilitate their confidential human sources, or let's call them what they are, 'snitches.'"

Griff and Eva wrote rapidly.

Clouse tipped his chair back on two legs, and as if enjoying the attention, he asked, "Should I slow down a bit?"

"We're keeping up," Eva stated.

"I'll just keep keeping on, then," he said, with the same grin plastered on his thin face. "The Bureau got real concerned for their reputation. Some FBI executives didn't have clean hands, so to speak, with regard to the Seattle affair. So, both the FBI OPR and ICE OPR under Regina's command put the brakes on any further investigation of Greg Feng and other FBI agents. The whole matter died. But, don't you know it, Greg still knew some CIS clerks who were willing to help him. He had eighteen months to go to retirement, so he managed to coast into a cushy retirement with a promised job here in Washington."

"Tell us how it all relates to what happened here today," Griff said.

Before Clouse could respond, loud voices erupted in the

room outside the door. A man was yelling, "How could they be gone? Who took them, and where did they go?"

Eva assumed the FBI counterintelligence agents had arrived and were unhappy that Wu and Jin had been whisked away. She rose with flair, stuck her head out the door, and pressing her finger to her lips, made an exaggerated, "Shhhh."

Four persons surrounding Trudy gaped at Eva. Things instantly became quiet.

Eva closed the door behind her, returning in time to see Clouse swinging his head toward Griff and opening his mouth wide.

"You ask how it relates to today. Because she derailed the investigation, Regina was given a one-third partnership interest in Lancet. However, it was actually done in Greg's name. When you do a record check, you'll find he's one-third owner of Lancet. Because I knew so much about Greg's illicit contacts and bribery within the CIS, I was offered what I thought was a swell retirement job with Lancet. They even paid for my move here to Washington, where they have so much work."

He stopped to rub his temples again, and Eva caught up on her notes. While Griff was writing, she dug in her tote bag, finding a tin of peppermints. She took one for herself and offered one to the others, which they gladly accepted.

"Today was a typical case for Lancet." Clouse bit his peppermint before adding, "Wu and Jin are Chinese Communist Intelligence Officers. They're not attached to their embassy with diplomatic immunity but work at the headquarters of Conepatus Corporation, a Chinese company with plants throughout the U.S. They built a large battery plant in western Michigan, which manufactures batteries for electric vehicles, and have other facilities scattered around America. They are wholly owned by Communist China and staffed at the highest levels with Communist Party members."

"Can you prove this?" Eva interrupted.

"Yes, ma'am, every word. You and Griff here can do some digging and unearth a stinking cabal of corruption and treason, all paid for by the U.S. taxpayer. The local Conepatus office is ostensibly a lobbying office to ensure favorable legislation, but many of its staff are really Chinese government operatives working throughout the U.S. Today, they were attempting to contact a Chinese dissident who flew in from Florida. They hired Lancet to surveil the dissident until their own operatives, Wu and Jin, intercepted him."

Eva shook her head, interrupting, "No, he wasn't a Chinese dissident. He was a military pilot from the democratic nation of Taiwan."

Clouse looked at Eva in shock, his eyes wide. "That's not what Wu told us."

"Is it possible you've been used by the ChiComs to investigate others from Taiwan or even Americans?" Griff demanded to know.

"Is it possible the ChiComs lie to us?" Clouse asked with a shrug. "I suppose you have to assume they do, but Regina Spire, Greg Feng, and even I have been well paid."

**AFTER THEIR LENGTHY DEBRIEFING** of Jordan Clouse, Eva and Griff spoke with Trudy Graham in a hurried strategy meeting.

Eva held up her notes. "You're welcome to read these, which document his many condemning statements."

"Thank you, perhaps later," Trudy answered as if stalling.

Griff tried another tact. "What will happen to those retired special agents with Lancet? You can't lodge them in local jails to be victimized by criminals just because they were law enforcement."

"While you were questioning Clouse, we've been handling demands from the FBI, the U.S. Attorney's Office upstairs, and the media." Trudy fanned herself with the papers she was holding. "The media is reporting that according to eyewitnesses, a group of Asians got into a skirmish with each other and dispersed before Metropolitan Police arrived. It's not far from Chinatown, so the media are speculating they were tourists."

Eva shook her head. "What do the FBI and U.S. Attorney's Office say? It happened on the street right outside their buildings."

"They are denying any knowledge of the incident," Trudy

said. "Meanwhile, the three retired FBI agents and Clouse, the retired ICE agent, are being charged with simple assault cases with no mention of their prior employment. They will be released on low bonds."

"No fear of them fleeing?" Griff lifted his eyebrows.

Trudy pushed out her lower lip. "They all have federal pensions. I think they'll be negotiating to save their pensions and cooperating."

"I agree." Eva nodded. "What about Wu and Jin?"

"Of course, they assert they're U.S. citizens who did nothing wrong, simply hailed a cab when some other Asian man tried to jump into it, and an altercation ensued. They refuse to talk further. We're holding them for the night. There'll be a major conference at the highest levels yet tonight to decide on how to charge them and how much to release to the press."

Eva flicked through her notes. "Based on Clouse's statement, Wu and Jin might have papers showing they're citizens."

"Right." Trudy waved off more papers from Eva. "I'm needed in a meeting, and you two need to head to your office. Use your notes to write a detailed report on everything you learned from Jordan Clouse."

She handed her business card to Eva. "Once it's complete, send me a copy on the ICE internal email system. At least for a while, for security reasons, it will be the only copy. I'll distribute it on a 'need to know' basis."

As she turned to leave, Griff gave Trudy his business card. "This has my cell number. Let us know what else you need from us. Until then, we'll be writing our sizzling report on Clouse."

# Chapter 36

While Griff drove to Fairfax, Eva texted Scott: *Honey, I've landed safely. On my way to the office. Call anytime you're free.* Her rumbling stomach gave her an idea.

"Griff, I'm starving. Please stop for take-out," she implored. "Burgers, tacos, pizza, any or all."

He pumped the brakes. "Perfect timing. Here's a chicken place. After all, we'll be working late typing our lengthy report."

Two chicken sandwiches and a large chocolate shake later, Eva walked down to the break room to brew a fresh pot of coffee. Sosa was on vacation, so she and Griff spent many quiet hours putting the final touches on their interrogation report of Jordan Clouse.

Long after five o'clock, Eva prepared an email to Trudy Graham and sent their report as an attachment. Then she locked her desk. Eva put the tote bag over her shoulder and gripped the carry-on handle.

She walked over to Griff's cubicle. "Are you ever going home?"

"Let's beat it," he quipped, covering a yawn with his hand. "I've had enough of this place and enough of corrupt agents. You know your boys are painting at our house, so Dawn is fixing supper for us all. What about Scott?"

"I haven't heard from him. I suspect he's knee-deep in some diplomatic kerfuffle with China. I'll text and invite him."

Eva rode with Griff to his house. She remained in the car long enough to phone Kaley. There was no answer, so she left a message that she'd arrived home okay. She'd just hung up when Scott called.

"It's wonderful to hear your voice," Eva purred, picturing his beautiful smile.

He chuckled. "And it makes my day to talk with you. Have you reached Griff's house yet?"

"Just pulled in. Can you join us for supper? I have no car here to get me and the boys home."

"I'll head your way the minute I clear off my desk. I love you."

"Love you back!" Eva said.

**SEVERAL DAYS PASSED BY IN A WHIRLWIND.** Eva shopped for a week's worth of groceries on her way home from work, then laundered hampers full of clothes. Scott had to stay longer hours at the Pentagon due to military escalations by China near Japan and Taiwan. They barely had time to catch up with each other.

With all the drama she'd endured, Eva felt the need to check on Kaley. She appreciated the daily texts from her mom, with assurances that Kaley was being cared for. Still, Eva longed to speak with Kaley herself. So, at seven a.m. on Thursday morning, she placed a call to Kaley's cell phone.

She heard a groan and a muffled-sounding, "Mom?"

Eva detected Kaley's effort to hide the fact she'd been asleep. "Good morning to you, sunshine. How are you doing?"

"Fine … is everything okay?" Kaley mumbled.

"Of course. Why?"

"Because you're calling so early."

Realizing Kaley was in vacation mode, Eva chuckled into the phone. "If you were here, you'd be hustling around as we get ready for work. Your brothers are already up and have eaten their breakfast."

"Then everything is okay," Kaley said, sounding relieved.

"I'm missing you and wanted to hear your voice before I leave for work. What's planned for today?"

"Gramps and I are helping Zion with his wood carvings. Gram is excited to show me how to bake bread in her machine. My classes begin next week."

"Did you get to relax yesterday?" Eva asked warmly, wanting to know how Kaley was doing living so far away.

"I drove to the campus to better learn my way around. The coffee shop where students hang out is interesting. Notes are posted on a corkboard, so I can read what others are doing. I may try out the vet club with Stephen."

Eva imagined her daughter driving about campus in the Slug Bug and tried to remember her own actions at that age.

"Mom, guess what? I discovered who picked up Dylan's box."

Concern swept over Eva. "Really! How did you manage that?"

"I was searching the Internet for bloggers and meetings in the Florida Panhandle about climate change. Can you believe it? I stumbled across a picture of the same guy at a lecture at FSU in Tallahassee."

"I'm glad he's at least far away from you."

"Tally is only two hours from here," Kaley piped.

Again, Eva was reminded of Kaley's continued exposure to terrorists. She tried to put on the brakes. "You need to prepare for your college studies. Sherlock Holmes would advise you to concentrate on getting good grades."

"Should I tell Griff what I found? Remember, I am his source."

"Yes. Text and ask him to call you when it's convenient for him. It's best to avoid details in texts because they can be subpoenaed by defense attorneys."

"Oh, right. I must learn to be more careful. I'll text him to call me."

"You're in our hearts and prayers. I have to run. Be sure Gramps and Gram always know where you are, and remember to abide by their curfew. Love you."

Eva ended the call, realizing Kaley had the bit in her teeth and she wouldn't be easily refocused. Wasn't Eva just like her as she began college?

*But I had safer friends,* she reminded herself.

She let out a sigh, searching for a foothold. Scott left hours ago to prepare for the Pentagon's Thursday press conference. He'd slept very little as he'd tossed and turned. As a result, Eva had been awake most of the night. The boys had already started arguing this morning about Dutch misplacing Andy's cell phone.

It was an abrupt reminder. She hadn't replaced Dutch's cell phone after giving his other one to Captain Yang Ming. Well, she'd rectify that today.

Work issues and pressures Eva handled with more ease. But when her family faced difficulties that were beyond her control, she required help from above. Eva slipped to her knees at her bedside, taking her internal battle to the Lord.

She prayed for the ones she loved: *Heavenly Father, lead us all beside still waters and guide us. We need Your help! In Jesus' Name, Amen.*

She rose, determined to leave her anxiety over her family with God and not take it back again. Her dad had once shared how, after Eva's sister Jillie had died in the Pentagon on September 11, he sometimes gave his grief hourly to the Lord.

After straightening up the kitchen, she assigned Andy and Dutch their chores for the day, telling them, "I'll stop on the way home from work and buy a new cell phone for Dutch. Try and get along today. What should we have for dinner? I'll pick up something special."

"Pizza!" they both chimed.

"Pizza sounds great."

Eva departed for the task force, flipping her mind from family to what she might learn today about Captain Yang Ming or Jordan Clouse. She reached for her coffee mug, and it wasn't there. She'd left it at home. So, when she reached the office, she walked straight to the coffee kiosk. She passed Griff, sitting in the conference room with stacks of papers before him.

"Howdy," Eva waved. "Let me grab a coffee and join you."

"I hoped you would. We have important matters to consider."

After first securing her Glock pistol in her locked desk drawer, Eva grabbed her pen and leather folder with her digital tablet. She joined Griff in the conference room, her foam cup full of hot coffee.

"You look like a man on a mission." Eva gestured at his papers.

"I am. I spoke with my Panama City source this morning."

Eva nodded. "I told her to contact you."

"The girl amazes me, and reminds me of you, Eva. She's identified the guy she met on the parcel delivery."

Eva sat across from her partner and opened her tablet. "She mentioned it to me, but I thought maybe you already knew his name."

"No. Because he drove a dealership loaner, the license plate told us nothing. Rather than tip our hat by contacting the dealership and asking who drove their car, I asked Adam to do some research to identify him, but still no answers."

While Eva knew their intelligence analyst was loaded with requests to assist other agents, she also realized Adam lacked initiative.

"In Adam's defense," she offered. "Kaley had seen the man driving the Rover and looked for pictures of his likeness on the Internet by perusing blogs that posted about climate change."

Griff pounded his coffee cup down onto the table. "Look, Eva, we have pictures copied from the video Agent Crystal Lasher took at the coffee shop in PC. Adam has a picture of the guy Kaley says is Jesse Kingsley, a doctoral student at FSU in Tallahassee. Adam's paid good money to do the type of search Kaley did, he just doesn't share the same ambition as Kaley, who's just graduated from high school."

Eva tapped her fingertips on her tablet. "I don't disagree. As her mother, I think Kaley is exceptional, but I also am concerned we've created a monster. She's beginning her college experience and thinks she's already an investigator."

"Just consider, Eva." Griff burst out laughing. "If she becomes a special agent, she'll enter the academy with so much more knowledge than you did. Look how well you've done. Kaley will be a monster agent."

Eva grinned. "Oh right, another Wonder Woman. Are we now transitioning away from the Chinese espionage case to Dylan Webb and vegan terrorists?"

"We should be, but there's a pending lead from the arrest of Wu and Jin."

"I'm listening."

Griff lifted a sheet of paper from his pile. "This lead from Trudy Graham is addressed to you and copied to me. She's asking you to contact your source and get as much info as you can about Captain Ming's missing sister from Hong Kong."

"I'm thinking ahead, and of course I will," Eva replied. "How is this a lead in Wu and Jin's case?"

"I've been thinking about it. Don't lose sight of the fact that Lancet's people were working for the ChiComs. Most of

Lancet is retired FBI, except for Regina Spire, her husband Greg Feng, and Jordan Clouse, the guy we interviewed."

"Regina is still with ICE, and her husband and Clouse were with ICE. So?" Eva coaxed.

"The FBI Director, working with ICE Director Whidbey, knows they can't trust most of the FBI Counterintelligence Division because of their close working relationship with Lancet and, thereby, the ChiComs. So, they have Trudy Graham and her ICE team doing all the work. I think they've already determined Wu and Jin are stone-cold spies. Our government sometimes swaps spies with our enemies. I think they're going to try to get China to produce Captain Ming's missing sister in a swap for Nelly Jin."

Eva leapt from her chair. "You've nailed it! A swap! Having his sister returned would indeed make a happy ending for Captain Ming."

"My only hope is someone has squeezed Wu and Jin enough to learn how many other spies they've recruited here in the States."

Eva walked to the doorway. "He already gave me a picture of his sister. I'll reach out to Ming on my young son's old phone and see what other information I can get."

Griff straightened one pile of papers before picking up the other.

"Once you make your call, we need to discuss Dylan Webb's case and consider a trip to Panama City. I'll freshen my coffee and meet you back in here in five minutes. I have much to tell you."

**WITH FRESH COFFEE IN HER CUP** and the call made to Captain Ming, Eva returned to the conference room. Griff drank his coffee, waiting. She closed the door.

Griff leaned forward after Eva took her seat across from him and quietly said, "Since Kaley began providing info about Dylan, this investigation has really taken off."

"Because of her information?" Eva asked.

"Partly. Apparently, the Bureau and EU authorities knew there was a cell of committed activists in Finland, but we didn't know how many radical sympathizers they had in the U.S."

Griff patted the second stack of papers. "Since Kaley helped us figure out the connection between Dylan and the phone call to Finland, it's opened up our knowledge of a whole new terror system. By the way, I understand Dylan had invited Kaley to go on the family yacht, but you were already on your way to Florida."

"How do you know that?" Eva sputtered. "Did Kaley tell you?"

"No. Thanks to Kaley's help as my CHS, an application was made for a wiretap under the Foreign Intelligence Surveillance Act. Since Kaley moved to Florida, there's been a secret FISA tap on Dylan's cell phone. They have received all his texts for the last six months, including texts to Jesse Kingsley in Tallahassee. He's the man with long brown hair who got the box from Kaley."

"So, he's the same man Kaley found and told you about," Eva repeated, shaking her head in amazement. "And now his conversations with Dylan will be monitored and recorded."

"Great! Right, Mom. You'll know if she's misbehaving."

Eva took an exaggerated swipe at Griff's arm. "Stop it. This is serious."

"What's funny, Eva," Griff smiled, "is how an intelligence analyst sends me an investigative lead to investigate Kaley Montanna to see if she's a sympathizer with Dylan Webb and accomplices."

Eva slapped the table. "This isn't good, Griff. I don't want my child being in FBI records as a suspect."

"Consider the irony, Eva. Kaley is the source of the invaluable information, which enables the analyst to get the tap and inquire about her. But, because of the very secretive records protecting Kaley, the analyst has no idea that thanks for the lead, in fact goes to Kaley."

Eva pressed her open palm against her forehead. "Please, I'm praying this all works out for Kaley. And, if she ever applies to become a special agent, this case with Dylan won't be held against her."

"Don't worry, Eva, she'll become famous within the Bureau. The Philadelphia JTTF is already investigating the guy in their suburbs who provided the two drones you and

Kaley drove to Florida."

Eva sat with her mouth ajar. "Really?"

"Yes. According to Dylan's text records, just before giving the box to Kaley, he texted this guy in Philly and immediately received the address where to meet him. Our team is now watching that guy's home."

Griff stopped. "Do you want me to continue?"

"Why wouldn't I?" She did wonder what possibly could come next.

"Remember, I told you the drones were modified with a thermite concoction to start fires? Well, our lab also installed a court-ordered tracking device."

Eva sipped her coffee before saying, "Tell me what we learned from the court order."

"You're familiar with an 'air tag,' right? The kind you can buy online to track your suitcase if it's stolen."

"I've never used one, have you?"

"No. The device our lab installed is like a more sophisticated air tag and is always transmitting its location. Right now, the box of drones is in Jesse's garage. If he puts them back into his Rover, we'll know. It takes the pressure off us because we'll know if and when Jesse tries to use them. The drones will tell us whenever they're moved again."

Eva studied Griff's serious-looking face. "Is the tap telling us when that might be?"

Griff consulted his notes. "After Jesse picked up the drones from Kaley in PC, he drove to a shopping center, where he then met another man who is an instructor in PC. It's not known if he's involved because, after their meal, Jesse drove a couple of hours to a Land Rover dealership in Tallahassee. Surveillance watched him exchange the loaner for his own Rover. He transferred the cardboard box to his vehicle and then drove it to his Tallahassee house. Jesse's name is registered to the second Rover and to the same phone Dylan was texting about the box Kaley brought to Florida."

"And Kaley has confirmed it by identifying his online photo," Eva replied.

Griff's expression sobered. "Dylan and Jesse are sending

cryptic texts about Dylan returning to Florida. We're thinking Dylan is the person who flies the drones. He had Kaley drive them down to PC so he could fly commercially without bringing the drones through TSA screening."

"Yes! We know the drones are disabled, but Dylan does not," Eva added, her voice rising. "We must follow him to prove his intent and shut him down before he can enact any more violence and someone is hurt. I will protect Kaley at all costs."

"Right. We need to be ready to fly to PC on short notice so we can be in touch with our two sources there and assist the JTTF—"

"However, and whenever we can, Griff," Eva interrupted. "Scott and I will keep praying for God's help and protection."

"As will Dawn and I," he said.

# Chapter 37

t was Kaley's third day on campus. So far, her confidence hadn't been shaken. After attending each of her classes, she felt equal to the other students. Kaley swung by the Student Affairs Office before going to her last class of the day, where she pondered a large bulletin board overflowing with invitations for special interest clubs.

Additional posters were taped along the walls and doors. Kaley strolled past the many offerings. She read about the various ministry groups, hoping to find a familiar one, but didn't.

One advertisement caught her attention.

A picture showed students in brightly colored garb surrounding the Florida State Capitol and waving signs demanding 'Climate Awareness.' This invite urged students concerned for the future environment to sign up and join in picketing to support a legislative bill. Examining the fine print, Kaley noted the group involved students from the Tallahassee campus.

*If I go, I might learn something to help Griff,* she thought. *But maybe not.*

She was about to forget it and head to class when she spotted an index card stapled to the bottom of the poster, which stated: *Contact me if interested in travel to Tally for this event.*

Beneath it, a guy named Larry had posted his phone number. Kaley pulled out her phone, snapping a picture of the poster and Larry's number. On a whim, with twenty minutes before her class, she phoned him.

Surprised when he answered, she said, "Ah … is this Larry?"

"It is. Who's this?"

"Kaley, and I'm a new student here at FSU in PC. I saw your number on a poster for a demonstration in Tally to protect our environment."

"Cool. That's an old poster. I forgot to pull it down."

"Yeah, I noticed that, but I'm wondering if there are other interested students here. I just moved from Virginia."

"There's a few of us," Larry replied. "Not as many as I would like. I'm trying to find a professor to sponsor a group. So far, no luck, but let me keep your number and call if we get another chance to support a bill in the legislature."

"Okay, I'd like that. Bye, until then."

**LATER THAT EVENING,** Kaley turned into the long drive through the straight rows of pine trees leading to her grandparents. They reminded her of the perfect rows of crosses in the Arlington National Cemetery back home in Virginia.

It was a strange thought, and Kaley forced her mind to think of something more positive. She was glad her grandparents' home was now her home during the school year. Kaley punched the garage door opener Gramps gave her and maneuvered the Slug Bug into its new home. She grabbed her backpack and headed to her room over the garage, entering the only two-star feature of her new college experience.

Gramps had built a downstairs bathroom in the garage for the barracks quarters upstairs. It was clean and adequate, but she did wonder if the small electric heater would give her enough heat during winter's colder days.

Recently, Gram had offered with a smile and a plate of cookies, "Kaley, you should stay in the guest room in the house."

"Thanks, Gram," Kaley had told her, "I'd like to try the barracks for now."

Her grandmother sure baked delicious cookies and pies. While Kaley valued her independence, right about now, she'd sure love one of Gram's black cows. After washing her hands in the downstairs bathroom, she bounded up the open stairway to the entry door, where she stopped to remove a decal from her backpack.

She held up the decal next to her new door sign. Where the 'Barracks' sign had been, the decal would now adorn her new 'Girls Dorm' sign.

Hurrying into her dorm room, Kaley looked around at all the changes Gramps had made since her brothers stayed up here at the beginning of summer. Gramps created more space for the twin bed he'd brought in for Kaley's dorm experience by pushing the two double bunks to the far side of the end dormer.

She sat on the edge of the twin bed, with its pretty quilt Gram had sewn, and admired her additions of bookshelves, a small desk and lamp, and the wooden floor lamp Zion had carved.

And then Kaley giggled. There was her pride and joy— the giant flag of the FSU Seminole Indian Head hanging beneath a wall lamp between the dormers.

"Time to do some homework," she muttered to herself.

When no one answered, she realized the quiet seemed a little lonely. Her brothers were nowhere around.

"Oh well, this is me!"

Kaley pulled the digital tablet from her bag, wondering how her grandparents felt about her not eating with them tonight. Her agreement with Gram was if she wasn't having supper with them, she should text by three in the afternoon.

Today she'd done so, and she took time to explore the campus as evening students arrived. She'd walked to her favorite place for a chicken sandwich and waffle fries.

She walked over to the desk and logged onto the Internet, thankful for the better service Gramps had ordered. Instead of starting her studies, she instead navigated to the blog where she'd found Jesse Kingsley's writings. Jesse was the guy who accepted the two drones she delivered to Florida. He was really a PhD candidate at FSU and not Dylan's uncle. Another lie Dylan told her.

Since reading Jesse's blog, Kaley realized that Dylan's buddy was really a terrorist with an interest in changing environmental policy by way of violence and fear. She again wondered if she could help Griff by getting to know Jesse better. He posted on his blog as much as twice a day. Some of his writings were informative and reasonable, but some were more radical.

Kaley read his latest posting and had a sudden epiphany. He was cunning enough to hide the depth of his convictions.

"You are a sly one, Jesse," she said softly, as if to remind herself to proceed carefully.

Much to her surprise, she found a brand-new posting from Jesse: *Students! Come assist me at a meeting with legislators to support the important new bill requiring the Florida State government to contract only with vendors who avoid the use of fossil fuels.*

After reading every detail, Kaley took a screenshot with her phone. It definitely sounded like Jesse planned to attend the rally. She wondered if Larry was going. If he was, and if she met Jesse in Tally along with him and other students, it wouldn't appear she was investigating Jesse.

Could she trust Larry?

Kaley decided there was only one way to find out, so she texted him the screenshot of Jesse's writing: *This might be interesting. Should we meet for coffee on campus to discuss?*

Satisfied she'd done the right thing, Kaley opened her backpack and finally began studying.

**JUST TWO WEEKS** after Kaley began FSU, she was already skipping classes. Her contact with Larry had paid off. He'd introduced Kaley to a sophomore girl and a freshman girl, who, like Larry, were totally concerned about saving the Earth's future ecosystem.

Today, Kaley drove her fully loaded, bright green Slug Bug onto the FSU campus at Tallahassee. She felt really pumped up, and she couldn't help but wonder if her mom would approve of her creative investigative techniques.

Kaley and her new friends were ready to hear a doctoral student share how they could best influence lawmakers to pass unpopular laws for the good of mankind. Kaley always believed she cared about the planet and for people, but the conversation on the way to Tally opened her eyes. No way was she as radical as her three new friends.

She hurried with her friends to find a good place to listen in the lecture hall, eager to discover what she could learn. After all, didn't she have to use the right jargon to better relate with Jesse?

They joined a larger group to hear the guest speaker. Instead of listening, Kaley started searching the crowd for

Jesse, Dylan's fake uncle. Her new friends seemed energized by the speaker and couldn't wait to rush over to the State Capitol with the speaker. He intended to show them how to influence the legislature by using their voices to demand action.

As the students hurried to the back of the lecture hall, they started yelling and acting rowdy. Kaley thought it smarter to keep her distance. The others gathered around tables and provided their names and contact data in hopes of picketing. They might even be asked to collect signatures for petitions or be nominated to hold office. Kaley didn't sign up for anything.

The students combed through a bunch of posters attached to sticks.

Larry handed her a sign, saying, "Here's a good one for you."

"Yeah, it's great," Kaley replied, taking the sign with a polar bear cub that declared: *Avoiding Meat Isn't Enough!*

"Come on!" Larry urged with a wave of his arm. "We're off to the Capitol!"

She and her friends ran to the parking lot, where Kaley soon discovered her Bug was too small to hold all their signage. Larry scrunched in the front seat, his arm out the window. The girls tucked their signs under their arms and against the side doors.

Kaley walked around to the driver's side. Just then, a man with long brown hair stopped to point at her.

He stammered, "Um, I met you at ..."

"Yes," Kaley quickly replied. She would recognize Jesse Kingsley anywhere.

She added with a smile, "I'm Kaley. We met at Java Central in Panama City."

"Weren't you starting at the PC campus?" he asked with a quizzical stare.

Kaley tightened her grip on the Beetle key chain. "Right. My friends and I drove over. It's a great opportunity for our future lives, and we have nothing like this on our campus."

"I hope you're headed to the Capitol with us." Jesse flashed a lopsided grin.

Kaley slid behind the seat and, with a wave, said, "See you there."

Soon, she and her new friends joined the massive gathering outside the Capitol building, holding and waving their signs. They chanted in response to commands shouted by their guest speaker and walked in repeating circles.

Kaley could barely stomach the scene. These kids were bizarre. Florida's Legislature was not even in session, yet plenty of media milled around, filming their demonstration. She wondered if they'd be on the evening news or if the film was just stored for background footage for future news stories. After thirty minutes of practicing their demonstration skills, volunteers collected the rather worn signs.

Kaley found Larry and the other girls, telling them, "I'm ready to leave. It's a long drive back."

They had reached her car when Jesse Kingsley again walked up to her.

"Sorry to hear there's no active group of environmentalists on your campus. I have a friend in PC with a PhD in the program I'm in. I can contact him and see if he'd help sponsor your group."

"Fantastic," Kaley fibbed.

A sudden shadow passed across Jesse's eyes. "The University might not approve of him, though. He's now working for the military. I could come over to Panama City and help your group get started."

"Even better." Kaley pulled out her phone. "Give me your number, and I'll text mine."

Obediently, Jesse provided his cell number, which Kaley punched into her phone.

She texted her number, reminding him, "My name is Kaley."

"I remember, and I'm Jesse Kingsley."

Kaley wasn't done. "Let us know of more events. We'll drive over from PC."

He agreed to stay in touch. Kaley headed for home, listening to Larry and the girls bragging about raising interest in the environment with Jesse's help. Though nodding her head, Kaley was busy planning her next move.

**ON THE BRIGHT SUNDAY MORNING,** Kaley drove into town to Bay View Chapel, her inner spirit sagging and no match for the sunshine beaming in her car windows. She struggled with Gram's disappointment at supper last night.

"Oh, Kaley," Gram had sputtered by the sink, "are you sure we can't convince you to attend church with us tomorrow? You said you really enjoyed going with us."

Kaley had given her a side hug. "Don't worry, I am going to church."

Gram seemed happier after Kaley had explained, "Ashley invited me to go with her to Bay View Chapel. She's nice and says they have a great Bible study for college students."

As she pulled into the Bay View's lot just two blocks from campus, Kaley tried to kickstart her morning with a new thought—her mom would approve because Kaley was fulfilling her promise to find a church where her faith could grow. She hoped so!

She spotted other cars in the lot with FSU decals, which already made her feel welcome. Collecting her Bible, she locked her car. Walking up to the chapel's front entrance, Kaley suddenly felt shy, like an outsider. What if Ashley didn't show up?

For a fleeting second, Kaley thought about heading back to her grandparents' church. But she steeled herself, pulled open the door, and lo and behold, she spotted a young woman with red hair. Was that her friend? Kaley walked closer to the coffee kiosk and saw it was Ashley mingling with other students.

Her friend squealed, "Kaley, you made it! Grab a latte and meet our Bible class members."

Ashley grabbed a good-looking guy as he passed by. "Hey, Stephen, meet Kaley. She's started classes at FSU."

"Hi, Kaley." Stephen peered at her more closely. "Did we meet before?"

"Yes, at the Adelmans," she said. "They live across the road from my grandparents."

"I recall telling you about the vet club."

Kaley liked his warm, brown eyes. She held out her hand to shake his. "If I remember right, you're Stephen Wilson.

"Your memory is great," he said, smiling and grasping her hand.

Kaley's smile grew wider. "It's nice seeing you again. I didn't realize your family attended church here."

"Oh, they don't. I come here because my friends from FSU are here."

They finally dropped their hands. Kaley felt an instant connection bubbling within her.

She turned to Ashley, "I'm so glad you invited me today. I was afraid I wouldn't find other Christians at school, and yet here you all are."

"You'll like Tim, our Bible teacher," Stephen told her.

Ashley nodded. "He teaches math at FSU. He and his wife, Katherine, are like parents away from home. It's time for class to start. We're studying the book of John. Follow me."

As they made their way toward the classroom, Ashley stopped abruptly to introduce Kaley to a tall man.

"Tim, meet my new friend, Kaley, from school," Ashley said in a chirpy voice. "She moved here from Virginia. And Kaley, through Tim's teaching, I've learned so much about God and His Son Jesus in the Bible."

Stephen stood beside Kaley, nodding. Tim seemed even taller than Kaley's dad.

And he sounded nice, saying, "Thanks for trying us out, Kaley. Are you a freshman?"

"I am. My grandparents moved here, so I'm living with them and commuting."

"It's good your family is close by. Students can be intimidated when some professors challenge them about everything, especially Christians and their faith. Are your grandparents Christians?"

"Yes, and so are my parents."

"Excellent. Share with them when you have doubts. Remember, when professors attack your faith, consider the evidence you've seen of God's faithfulness in your personal life. And you can always come to me and my wife, Katherine, with questions."

Kaley lifted her Bible and smiled. "I'm striving to read this every day, which helps me remember God has a plan for me and that Jesus loves me. I think I'll be back."

As she followed Stephen and Ashley into the classroom, Kaley knew deep in her heart this Sunday would be the first of many good weeks for her first year in college.

229

# Chapter 38

Eva read the latest intelligence bulletins at her desk early Monday morning. These important updates were distributed to all FBI agents and task force officers from other agencies. Most of these gave security alerts from highly classified operations and wiretaps.

She sipped the last of her coffee, thinking about how, a few months ago, she'd read warnings about eco-terrorists intent on destroying food producers. Eva suddenly recalled the acrid smell of the burning Grass Fed Beef plant when she and her family visited Florida.

Since then, Griff had become the case agent on a related case, resulting from the confidential human source, who was very familiar to Eva. As things happen sometimes, there was Griff standing at the entrance to her cubicle.

"I was just thinking of your source and your terrorism case," Eva said.

His face looked grim. "Eva, I don't believe in coincidences. We have a new development with Dylan. Meet me and Sosa in the conference room. ASAP."

"Sounds urgent." She signed out of her computer. "I'll refresh my coffee and join you."

A filled thermal cup in hand, Eva took a seat at the table. Sosa was already talking with Griff about getting flights into Tallahassee.

"What? Is someone traveling?" she asked, wanting to get up to speed.

Sosa looked up from the papers in his hand. "You and Griff are."

"When?"

"We'll get to that," he told her, adding in an ominous tone, "Griff, tell us the latest about her daughter."

Eva's heart missed a beat. "What about my daughter? Is Kaley in danger?"

Raising his hands, Griff protested, "If that were the case, I would have told you at your desk. It's just one of those serendipitous benefits of having a daughter who is a CHS."

"Okay," Eva breathed out a sigh. "I'm very interested, but

please don't keep me waiting."

Griff walked around the table to sit beside Eva. "If it weren't for the fact the wiretap is classified, you could tell Kaley you already know she was with Jesse Kingsley at a climate change demonstration in Tallahassee. Wouldn't she be surprised you can see what she's doing from Virginia?"

"Is that why we're going to Tally, so I can reprimand my daughter? Tell me everything," Eva insisted.

Sosa plunked on his half-glasses, and picked up his papers as if prepared to read from them. "We've just learned from a conversation between Dylan Webb here in Virginia and Jesse Kingsley in Tallahassee on the tap, Dylan is headed to Tallahassee. Kaley's name came up."

Sosa gave an exaggerated clearing of his throat before beginning to read:

*Kingsley: "Dude, maybe you can see your girlfriend while you're here."*

*Webb:"Girlfriend? What girlfriend?"*

*Kingsley:"Kaley. Just saw the little fox on Friday."*

*Webb:"She ain't my girlfriend."*

*Kingsley:"Maybe she should be. She's very helpful to us."*

*Webb:"Did you see her in Tally?"*

*Kingsley:"Yeah. She was here demonstrating at the Capitol."*

*Webb:"She shouldn't know about our bird hunting. I won't be in touch with her."*

Sosa laid the paper on the table and glared at Eva.

For her part, Eva sat in shock. Her mind replayed the words she'd just heard.

She growled, "Little fox! How dare that creep call my daughter a little fox. What kind of pervert—"

Sosa cut her off and said as if to be reassuring, "Eva, you should take comfort in the fact the creep is totally unaware your beautiful daughter is smart enough to endear herself to him and Dylan in the pursuit of justice."

"Yes, apparently so," Eva agreed, but found no consolation in his words. "What's the bird hunting all about, it's not even hunting season."

Griff answered, "Jesse phoned Dylan and invited him

down to Tally for their bird hunting. Sosa and I think 'birds' is code talk for the drones."

"Dylan then asks if they have a place to hunt, and Jesse said they do, which is available this week," Sosa said, swiping off his glasses. "Based on their monitored phone calls, we have gotten quite a collection of accomplices. It's a perfect time for our roundup."

Griff laid both hands on the table. "Eva, the top brass want you and me in Tally to arrest anyone we can catch in the act. The others will be arrested throughout the country."

"I have questions, but when do we leave?" Eva again asked.

Sosa replaced his glasses. "You and Griff make your arrangements, and then fly to Tallahassee as soon as possible, where you will arrest Dylan Webb and his co-conspirators. When he's secured and behind bars, you two head to Panama City, where you will assist Captain Ming to close down his contaminated cell phone. Reset it to factory settings and throw it away. If he even tries to transfer one photo, the ChiComs may get access to his new phone. Buy him a new one with a new number to replace your son's phone. He can switch over to a new local number back in Taiwan."

"I feel sorry for him," Eva replied. "He's helpful to our government, and I wish we could do more."

Sosa flashed a rare smile. "Here's what else we know. Nelly Jin, the ChiCom spy we arrested, has identified the employee at CIS who was instrumental in getting green cards for her and Kim Wu, as well as other ChiCom spies. While you're in Panama City, it's highly likely a swap with China will occur. Nelly Jin will be traded for Captain Ming's sister as well as an American businessman held in China on phony charges."

Eva clapped her hands. "Terrific! I hope we can at least keep Kim Wu in prison for claiming to be FBI."

"Okay, you two." Sosa collected his papers and stood. "Make your flights. I want to be advised of your successes down there. You'll be working with the JTTF teams from both Panama City and Tallahassee."

Eva was first to leave the conference room with Griff right behind her when she heard Sosa say, "Griff, regarding that other matter, the answer is yes. And for the amount we discussed."

Eva whirled around, demanding to know, "Griff, what was Sosa just saying?"

"Nothing to do with Dylan or associates," came his swift reply.

Too abrupt for Eva's liking, but perhaps this was one of those times when she didn't have a 'need to know.'

"Should I make flight arrangements?" she offered.

Heading for his cubicle, he said over his shoulder, "Please do. Remember, it's one-way into Tally. We can delay our reservations out of PC. And reserve a rental car."

**EVA AND GRIFF FLEW INTO TALLAHASSEE** on Wednesday afternoon. After renting a black SUV, Griff went directly to the Tally JTTF office for a meeting with their agents and officers. Eva greeted FBI agents Doug Montgomery and Crystal Lasher, who had driven in from Panama City.

In the hurried meeting, Doug took the lead and advised, "Dylan Webb arrived on a flight from DC. He was followed driving a red Jeep rental to Jesse Kingsley's condo near the main FSU campus here in Tallahassee."

"Are they still at his condo?" Eva asked.

"Yes," Doug replied. "We prepared an ops plan to surveil the actions of Dylan and Jesse in hopes of arresting them should they attempt to destroy any persons or property with the drones. Crystal will distribute our plan."

"Thank you," Eva told Crystal, and after a quick perusal, she felt compelled to recap, "Doug, this states the FBI's Technology Operations office in DC is in constant contact with the tracking devices installed in the drones. So, we on the surveillance teams can remain further away from Dylan and Jesse. What is the status of the drones?"

"Good question," Doug replied. "The two drones have been stored in Jesse's garage since the day they arrived after Griff's CHS delivered them to Jesse."

"Looks like all is in place," Griff observed. "Now, we wait."

After a lively discussion of possible scenarios, Griff and Eva left the meeting, stopped for a bite to eat, and then checked into the hotel, getting rooms across the hall from each other.

Eva settled in her room and prepared to call Scott, thinking tomorrow Dylan would make his move. With no warning, a knock sounded on her hotel door. She walked to the door and looked out the peephole.

Whoever was standing there was too close to make out, so she asked, "Who is it?"

"It's me, Griff. Are you still up?"

Eva released the bolt and opened the door. "Come in. What's up?"

Griff stepped in. "Sorry. I would have texted but thought you might already be asleep. I just got a call. The package is moving."

Eva was glad she was still dressed in her travel clothes: a black blouse, black cargo slacks, and sneakers. "Is the package on the street or just moving at his house?"

"TechOps in Washington phoned me, saying it's been moved several feet but may still be in the garage. The beef plant fire happened at night, so it's possible Dylan and Jessie are getting ready to leave the house."

Eva snapped her hair back into a ponytail, which she flipped through the opening at the rear of the FSU ball cap.

"Have you called for help?"

"Yup. Doug and Crystal and their other two officers are here in the hotel. Two Tally task force officers are on their way here. Doug will take one with him, and Crystal will take the other. Crystal is ready to drive to Jesse's condo, so we'll have eyes on the package."

Eva pocketed her cell phone and grabbed her shoulder tote containing her Glock pistol. She prayed she wouldn't need to use it.

"This could be an all-nighter," she said. "Just like old times, right?"

Griff nodded. Then he turned toward the door, saying before he opened it, "Meet us in the parking lot. Doug has a portable radio for us."

# Chapter 39

Twenty-five minutes later, as Eva and the team waited in the hotel parking lot, the portable radio crackled in her hand.

She recognized Crystal, saying, "We just passed the target's condo. Garage door is open. Two men are getting into the target's Land Rover."

Instantly, the other team members headed to their cars, as did Eva and Griff. He started the SUV, cranked up the AC, and answered a call on his cell phone. His conversation was brief. After ending the call, Griff reached for the portable radio.

He broadcast to the other team members, "TechOps advises the package is moving eastbound on St. Augustine Street nearing the Capitol."

"That's a 10-4," Crystal replied. "We're giving him lots of room. No chance of losing him."

Eva turned to Griff. "Hope we're not dealing with another Oklahoma City bombing here. They aren't stupid enough to attack the Capitol building, are they?"

Griff simply drummed his fingers on the steering wheel, as if waiting for the order to head out. Moments passed in silence before the next report came, "Package is eastbound on Highway 90."

Doug Montgomery walked up to Griff, prompting him to lower his window.

"Griff, since you're getting reports from Washington about the movements, let's both drive east on I-10. Crystal can remain loosely on the package on Highway 90. They intersect just east of here."

"Good plan," Griff responded. "We'll follow you."

After the highways merged minutes later, the three cars from the hotel and Crystal all proceeded eastbound on I-10 through northern Florida. Jesse's Land Rover led the way. Eva stared out the front window, fixing her eyes on Doug's taillights in the dark.

They continued east just over the speed limit. Griff received periodic text messages on his phone, alerting him to the location of the package.

"One advantage of the darkness is that it's cooler and there's less traffic," Eva observed.

"Right, but less traffic means our surveillance is more obvious."

"Yeah, I thought of that. From what I can tell, Doug's hanging back a good distance from the Rover."

More than an hour later, Crystal announced, "Target signaling to exit I-10 at Live Oak."

Team members pressed the transmit key on their microphone buttons all at once. There was no need for everyone to respond. Each knew what to do.

Griff slowed down, as did the others, so they wouldn't congeal at the bottom of the exit ramp. Then, about a half-mile before reaching the exit ramp, Griff sped up.

"Target turned right, now left into a gas station," Crystal broadcast on the radio.

"Great, I see a burger place across from the gas station," Eva quipped. "I need to stop."

Griff swung into the parking lot. "No problem. We shouldn't all be too close to the package. We'll make a quick pitstop and get coffee."

Eva jumped from the car, saying over her shoulder, "Whoever's out first, order coffees."

Minutes later, with fresh coffee in hand, Eva and Griff returned to the SUV.

Griff started the engine, telling Eva, "Washington TechOps texted. The package is stopped at the gas station and still in the Rover."

"It's amazing what they can know from the transmitter in the drones," Eva said, then tried some of the delicious coffee.

Griff took time to drink his. "They watch their high-tech maps and know exactly what's at these locations."

He'd just returned his cup to the holder when Crystal broadcast, "Target moving! Going south on Route 129."

"There he goes." Griff nodded slightly toward his window. "No need for us to hurry."

Eva enjoyed her coffee, relishing the dark roast taste. Griff pulled slowly from the lot and headed south. Traffic was so light the team had to lag further behind to avoid spooking

Jesse and Dylan.

Griff handed his phone to Eva. "Since I'm driving, go into my contacts and push TechOps. It should be on the screen. Talk with whoever answers and maintain voice contact."

They were continuing south when another surveillance car reported, "Target still heading southbound, approaching city of Live Oak."

Eva phoned TechOps, telling the technician who answered, "We're the team surveilling the package in northern Florida."

"Yes, ma'am. You're the action we are monitoring here."

"We'd like to keep this call open so you can talk to us," Eva told him. "This late at night, there's almost no traffic, and we have to permit the package to get so far ahead of us it's sometimes out of sight. Can you help us this way?"

"Our pleasure."

Eva had just put Griff's phone on speaker when the DC technician reported, "Your package has crossed the railroad tracks and continues south."

*Train tracks? Would they be stopped by a moving train?*
Eva hoped not.

*Oh no!*

Up ahead, the railroad crossing signals began flashing. The gates began to drop. She saw Crystal jam on her brakes.

Crystal reported excitedly, "The gates are down! We're stuck. We have the point. Can anybody get by?"

Other reports flooded in, "We're stuck, too. Can't back up. Traffic behind us."

As Griff approached Duval Street, Eva cried, "Turn right here. Train's coming from the east. It's a freight with two engines."

Griff cranked the wheel to the right and hit the gas. They shot forward. After a few blocks, Eva spotted a crossing without gates.

"Turn left," she yelled.

Griff turned left against a red light. They approached the crossing.

"Oh no!" Eva cried. "They're flashing red! Step on it!"

He sped toward the tracks and glanced to the left. Eva

spotted the train about half a block away.

"Gun it, Griff! You can make it!"

He floored it, and the SUV cleared the tracks in time. He forced his foot on the brake at a traffic light that suddenly changed to red. He cranked the wheel left, speeding through the red light. He roared east on Route 90.

"Tech lab, can we have the status?" Eva barked into the phone. "Is the package southbound on 129?"

"Affirmative. Through town and out in the countryside."

With the portable radio, Eva quickly broadcast, "We're past the train but don't yet have point. Eye in the sky advises target still heading south on 129."

Static clicking in her speaker indicated the team heard her message.

Someone answered, "We're held up by the train. Can't say how long."

Eva thought the deep voice belonged to Doug Montgomery.

Griff didn't respond. Rather, he sped through town, rushing by a brightly lit courthouse with brick columns. They blew by small shops and merchants and darkened fast-food restaurants. Once they cleared the last traffic light on 129, Griff accelerated to eighty.

He pointed ahead, saying, "It's the elusive Land Rover," and slacked off.

Eva broadcast, "All is well. We have the point again, about four miles south of town."

She dipped her head to look out both the front and side windows. "Griff, it's so dark you can't tell, but the satellite view on my phone map shows farms and crop circles on both sides."

"Where are they going?" he grunted. "It can't really be to a firing range. It's too dark to shoot."

Eva widened the map with her fingers, seeing nothing but farms. "It appears we're paralleling the Suwannee River, which runs a few miles to our west."

She broadcast again, "Passing through the one flashing light in the town of McAlpin."

"We're finally leaving Live Oak," came a response.

Suddenly, the tech op announced over Griff's phone, "Here at the lab, we've enlarged the area on our equipment and observed a possible destination for your package."

"Great. Let's have it," Griff commanded.

"O'Brien is the next small town you'll come to. It's even smaller than McAlpin. To the southwest of O'Brien, close to the Suwannee River, is a chicken processing plant. It's very large and surrounded by nothing but farmland. It's labeled here as 'Chicken Little Farms.'"

"Oh boy. That sounds about right for their hunting birds," Griff replied.

"At least we have a destination," Eva intoned. "It's spooky chasing these guys out here in the dark, not knowing where they are going. I don't want us being ambushed."

They zoomed through the intersection with a flashing yellow light. Eva reported on the radio, "Southbound through flasher at O'Brien."

She expanded the map on her phone, searching to the southwest of their present location, telling Griff, "I have pulled up the chicken processing plant. It's huge and must be where they're going."

When he asked her to update the others, Eva spoke into the microphone, "A large plant is showing on our map. Chicken Little Farms could be the destination, southwest near the river."

Doug Montgomery's deep voice boomed over the radio, "I'll call Suwannee County Sheriff Department (SCSD) and ask a deputy to meet me at the small office building here in McAlpin."

"Excellent," Griff responded. "A deputy will know the area well."

Then he pointed ahead, telling Eva, "Target is turning. I'll keep going. Notify the others."

Keying the microphone on the portable radio, Eva said, "Target's turning west on County Road 248. The large chicken processing plant is down that road. It's pretty rural, so we won't chance following the target just yet."

Griff turned on his high-beam lights and slowed abruptly. He wheeled down a dirt, two-track road running between pine trees. After driving about fifty yards, he backed between some trees and turned around. Shutting off his lights, he and Eva were plunged into total darkness.

And they sat in total silence until Crystal chirped, "We're nearing 248. Where should we meet you?"

"Slow down," Eva said. "We're on the right, parked on a two-track road in the pine trees just south of 248. We'll turn on our lights so you'll see us."

Eva pointed through the rows of trees, telling Griff, "Headlights approaching on Highway 129."

Griff turned on his lights.

"I see you," Crystal said over the radio.

As she turned into the pines, Griff flipped his light to the parking feature. Soon, Crystal was turned around and parked next to them with her lights off. All lights and engines off and windows down, the agents and officers waited in both cars, prepared to act.

Griff's phone on Eva's lap sprung to life with TechOps in Washington advising, "Your package drove beyond the entrance to Chicken Little and just stopped at a park along the river at the end of road 248."

Griff picked up his phone and said, "Thanks. Will you stay on the line and advise us of other developments? We need to know if and when the package leaves the vehicle."

"Sir, we will," the technician replied.

Eva heard Doug's voice crackling on the portable radio, "Suwannee County deputy is here. I'm briefing him now. We'll head your way. Griff, I'd like you to ride with him in his vehicle."

Griff turned to Eva. "Since the package went beyond the chicken plant and down to the river, I think it's safe for us to head to the plant. Before I meet Doug, let's check that out."

Griff motioned out the window to Crystal and her partner. "You both stay here. We'll advise what we find at the chicken plant."

Pulling the gear selector into drive, Griff rolled slowly down the two-track toward the highway. He switched on his lights and swung to the left before making another left onto County Road 248. There was total darkness so he drove with his high-beam lights on. After about two miles, they saw the large sign for Little Chicken Farms.

"Eva, look way down the road," he said. "See reflectors and a sign? That could be the park entrance."

Griff turned into the large parking lot at Little Chicken. Parking lot lights were ablaze, but the plant looked quiet. "Doesn't look like there's a night shift working."

"What about those three cars?" Eva gestured toward the plant. "Maybe it's a crew cleaning equipment during the night."

"Hmmm … you might be right." Griff then backed their SUV next to a storage shed and shut off the lights. "We look like part of the cleaning crew."

Eva swiftly calculated. "I just realized something. Dylan probably intends to launch his drone by the river and land it on the roof here. The others should join us here quickly."

"Partner, you're right on."

He grabbed the microphone and broadcast, "We're in the parking lot of the chicken plant. Three cars here, a possible cleaning crew. Suggest you all get here ASAP. Targets may be launching from the river."

"10-4," Crystal quipped.

Doug came next. "10-4. The deputy and I are heading your way."

Eva was still holding onto Griff's phone when the TechOps reported, "Package is out of the vehicle. It's moving at a walking pace toward the river."

"10-4. Thank you," Griff responded loudly and keyed the microphone, telling the others, "Washington advises the package left the vehicle and is proceeding to the river at walking speed."

Several clicking microphones confirmed they all heard his message.

To Eva, the next ten minutes ground by at a snail's pace. She steadied her breathing and prepared herself for what might happen next. No report came from TechOps of the drone being launched.

The group of task force officers and agents soon grew larger as the teams assembled in the Chicken Little Farms' parking lot. Doug pulled in, followed by a marked SCSD all-wheel-drive SUV. Eva handed Griff his cell phone, and they stood around with the other agents in a tight group by their cars.

Doug introduced Deputy Russell Morris. "He can help us confront our two suspects who are down there by the river."

"Eva and I are concerned about the cleaning crew interrupting our operation." Griff nodded his head toward the plant. "We believe our two suspects will launch an inert incendiary drone into the chicken plant. Timing is critical. We don't want to frighten them until they launch, as we need evidence of their intent."

"I'll be watching for any movement from the folks inside," Eva declared.

"We need to be on our toes and react quickly," Russell said. "Exactly where are the suspects now?"

"In the park along the Suwannee with their two drones." Griff raised an arm toward the river.

Russell looked in that direction. "That park closes at six in the evening. Apparently, the gate isn't locked."

"Good," Griff said. "You have a basis for detaining them for being in the park after closing."

"Detaining, yes." Russell then shook his head. "Arresting, no."

"We have enough to arrest them now." Griff handed the car key to Eva. "I'm riding with Russell down to the river. We won't advance until there's been a launch. Everybody in agreement?"

Everyone agreed, with Doug adding, "I've got binoculars, so will be watching for a drone strike. Be sure to let us know the moment they launch."

# Chapter 40

Griff held onto the portable radio in the front passenger seat while Deputy Russell Morris rolled the SCSD vehicle to a stop at the gated entrance of Little River Springs Park, their lights extinguished.

Russell lifted his hand and explained to Griff in hushed tones, "There's a parking lot down this road. The sidewalk and steps branch off from the lot, leading to the river on each side of the springs pool. I suspect they're launching from the walkway down by the river. That permits them to avoid any trees. They can get a drone high enough and turn it east. It's only about a thousand yards to the chicken plant."

"Do you patrol around this area much?" Griff asked.

"Yeah, in and out of here checking on dopers. They meet down here to buy their supply."

Their conversation was interrupted by the TechOps analyst on Griff's phone saying, "Sir, one drone is in the air. Our modifications to that drone permit us to see the same images as the pilot is seeing."

"Where is the drone now?" Griff wanted to know.

"He's at five hundred feet, viewing the plant to your east. Okay, he's accelerating toward the plant … he's hovering it above the building."

Griff keyed the microphone on the radio, "Drone now above the plant at five hundred feet."

TechOps blared, "Bingo! He's just crashed into the roof."

Griff shouted into the radio, "Drone crash on the roof!"

"I saw it hit," Doug reported. "The roof is arched. I can see the drone, but there is no fire or explosion."

Griff returned to his phone. "Thank you, TechOps. Please stay with us until we determine if the second drone will also fly."

Eva said, "I'm in Doug's car. Do you want any of us to come to you for an arrest?"

"This is TechOps. The remaining drone is now moving at walking speed back toward the vehicle in which it arrived."

Griff broadcast again via the portable radio, "Eva, you and Doug come to us, leaving someone there to observe the drone on the roof."

"I'll stay here on the drone," Crystal answered.

TechOps advised, "The second drone has stopped moving near where the suspect's vehicle is parked."

Griff looked at Russell, "Let's get down there and put some lights on them."

Russell drove forward, with Griff directing over the radio, "Everyone follow us, except Crystal."

When the team descended into the parking area, Eva came on the air, "I'll stay in the SUV. I don't want Dylan to see me."

Deputy Morris aimed his SCSD vehicle toward the Rover in the unlit parking lot. Suddenly, Russell switched on his Mars lights. Red and blue flashing lights reflected off the Rover and also off Dylan Webb and Jesse Kingsley.

Both men spun around and faced the lights. Sitting atop the roof of the Rover was the carton containing the remaining drone.

Griff and Russell hurried from the truck and rushed up to the suspects.

"The park is closed, gentlemen," Deputy Morris declared. "You have a good reason for being here?"

"We aren't doing anything wrong," Dylan replied, shoving his hands into his pockets.

"Any weapons or fishing equipment on you?" Russell demanded.

Griff reached up, removed the box from the roof, and opened it.

Russell flashed his light into the box. "Oh, oh. A drone. Drones are unlawful in the park."

"It's just a toy," Jesse Kingsley claimed.

Griff removed the drone from the box and held it up for Russell to examine with the flashlight.

"No, Sir-ree." Russell held it up to Jesse. "A toy? This thing hanging here on the bottom appears to be a modification. I think it's been weaponized."

The deputy set the drone back in the box and turned to the two suspects. "Good thing I brought some federal agents with me. What do you say, Griff? Want to take these guys into your custody?"

Griff pulled out his handcuffs, proclaiming, "I'm FBI Special Agent Griff Topping, and am arresting you both for possessing a weapon of terror and conspiracy to commit acts of terrorism. Assume the position here on the hood."

As Griff advised his two prisoners of their Miranda rights against self-incrimination, Doug Montgomery and other Florida agents swarmed in to take responsibility for the arrests. Before leaving the area, Doug assigned Crystal and the officer from Tally to remain at the Chicken Little plant and arrange for the Suwannee County Fire Department to retrieve the drone as evidence.

As the team prepared to leave for Tally, Griff shook Russell's hand and thanked him for his assistance.

"What about the Land Rover?" Russell asked, dropping his hand.

Griff looked to see if the prisoners had been placed in cars for transport. "As soon as the prisoners are gone, Eva will drive it back to Tally. It's evidence in the case."

**EVA MONTANNA AWOKE** the next morning in a different hotel. She was in Panama City, not far from her parents and Kaley. At this point, they did not know she was even there.

After the previous night's arrest of Dylan Webb and Jesse Kingsley, the task force agents, along with Griff, had transported the two prisoners back to Panama City, where they were lodged at the Bay County Jail. Eva had followed Griff in Jesse's Land Rover.

Eva and Griff checked into their rooms at a hotel for a couple hours of sleep before meeting with federal prosecutors in the U.S. Attorney's Office. At the same time, FBI Special Agents Doug Montgomery and Crystal Lasher attended the arraignment of Dylan and Jesse, who were charged with conspiracy to commit acts of terrorism, which included assaults on Grass Fed Beef and Little Chicken Farms.

Eva and Griff also coordinated with FBI Headquarters in Washington and the Philadelphia Terrorism Task Force, arranging for the immediate arrest of Dylan's and Jesse's co-conspirators. They then briefed the Press Secretary for the

Department of Justice on what could be released to the media.

Exhaustion threatened to overwhelm Eva, so she drank excessive amounts of hot coffee. It was two o'clock in the afternoon before she phoned her parents.

Her mom answered warmly, "Eva, how nice to hear from you in the middle of the day."

"I just have a moment, Mom. Griff Topping and I are in town for work. You and Dad should check the news for details. Dylan Webb, the infamous guest at your home, has been arrested. I'll advise Kaley."

"Of course. Will you and Griff be free to join us for dinner? I hope Kaley will come, too. We haven't seen her too much lately."

Eva gulped, unsure what that meant. Rather than grill her mother, she simply said, "I'm not sure if we can make it and have to go now. I will be in touch. Give my love to Dad."

Next, Eva sent a message to Kaley, asking her to skip the rest of her classes and meet her at the local task force office, giving her the address. Eva also called Zion Adelman with a quick heads-up.

It was after three o'clock when Crystal Lasher walked up to Eva at the desk where she was sitting and where she'd typed her report last night. Crystal wore her big glasses, and Eva could see her eyes were bloodshot.

Crystal hid a yawn behind her hand, saying, "Eva, look who just arrived to see her mom."

Kaley stepped around Crystal, and Eva did a doubletake. Kaley was wearing her blonde hair in a braid. They looked like they could be sisters. Eva rose to give Kaley a big hug.

In Crystal's presence, Eva told her daughter, "I'm here because last night Crystal and our team arrested Dylan and Jesse for acts of terror. It will be on the news soon."

Kaley opened her mouth but said no words. She blinked her eyes rapidly before staring first at Crystal and then at her mom, as if in shock.

"It's true." Crystal pointed to the drone on her desk. "They tried to burn down a chicken processing plant last night using this drone."

"Ugh!" Kaley exclaimed, folding her arms. "Will they think I snitched on them, Mom?"

Eva put an arm around Kaley's shoulder. "No, honey. They will all be suspecting each other, but none will ever have reason to suspect you. After all, they never divulged to you what they were planning."

"You're right." Kaley let out a long sigh.

"Hey, Kaley," Griff called, emerging from an office and pointing at the drone. "Did Crystal and your mom share with you about all the good you've done?"

Relief washed over Eva by simply watching Kaley's frown vanish. As her mother, she was grateful Kaley was associated with such quality people as Griff and Crystal.

"I have more good news," Eva declared. "My mom knows I'm in town and has invited you to dinner tonight, Griff. Gram hopes you'll come, too, Kaley."

Griff patted his stomach, which gave Kaley a chuckle.

"I'm not one to pass up a homecooked meal," he said. "First, I need to debrief Kaley. I'll need a witness, so Crystal, can you sit in with us?"

Crystal brought Kaley into the office, and Griff closed the door. Eva was okay with not being included. Kaley was his source, and she'd rather not know. Returning to the office computer terminal, Eva accessed her emails. One stood out as important—a message from Trudy Graham, New York supervisor of the ICE cadre that arrested several of the retired FBI agents.

Trudy had written: *Eva. Call me at your earliest convenience.*

Eva found Trudy's number in her cell phone, and Trudy answered immediately.

"Eva, thanks for getting back quickly."

"I'm calling from Panama City. Griff and I have been up most of the night arresting some eco-terrorists." Just thinking about her lack of sleep caused Eva to yawn.

Trudy said she was calling with more good news. "The White House is announcing today the swap with Communist China. Nelly Jin is being released in return for an American businessman and a female Hong Kong banker."

"Yes!" Eva exclaimed. "That's wonderful news."

"There's more, Eva. The retired ICE agent you interviewed, Jordan Clouse—"

"I am surprised by how much corruption he revealed," Eva interjected.

"It's astounding," Trudy replied. "He spilled his guts before a Federal Grand Jury. Yesterday, I met with ICE Director Whidbey and the FBI Director. Based on your questioning of Clouse and what we've learned, the FBI is cleaning house. Several high-ranking agents, as well as retired agents, are being indicted, as well as most everyone in the Lancet Group."

"And the hits keep on coming," Eva quipped, no longer feeling tired but invigorated.

"Wait, there's still more. Regina Spires retired yesterday and is no longer the head of OPR with ICE. She and her husband are being indicted, along with a woman in Citizen and Immigration Service that Regina's husband has been bribing for years to get citizenship for undeserving persons."

"Trudy, you and your team of ICE agents have done a stellar job. You succeeded in keeping your investigation pretty quiet, too."

Trudy deflected the compliment back onto Eva. "Much of the credit goes to you and the Taiwanese source you developed. Director Whidbey was commending you during our meeting."

"I heard Regina was angry because my transfer was stopped, but I've never received an official cancellation," Eva said, her tone revealing her doubt.

Trudy continued, "Whidbey has rescinded the transfer order issued by Regina. According to Clouse, she bore you a grudge for beating her out of the top rank in your rookie class and erroneously blamed you for her assignment to Anchorage post-graduation."

"It's a shame, Trudy," Eva said. "We agents face enough danger on the outside; we need all the support we can get inside our agency."

"Eva, I totally agree. I have my own horror stories but will save that for another time. Watch for the press release tomorrow where the FBI and Attorney General are sure to take all the credit."

"As usual." Eva laughed. "I will notify Captain Ming. He'll be so relieved."

Her call with Trudy ended, and Eva returned to her emails. She was glad she did because she burst out laughing at the message from two days earlier, captioned: *Cancellation of Pending Permanent Change of Station.*

Eva hastily read through the orders, which satisfied all her doubts. She and her family could remain in the Washington, DC area until she and Scott decided they wanted to leave.

She logged out of the computer. Moments later, Griff and Crystal came out of the office with Kaley. Her daughter looked as wiped out as Eva felt.

Griff said, "Eva, you might as well see your folks. We're done here for the day."

"I'm ready to leave. Kaley, give me a ride to Grams?"

"Sure, Mom. We need to make one stop on the way. I promised to buy root beer for the black cows."

Eva gathered the tote that held her badge, cuffs, and gun and said to Griff, "Aren't you coming? Dinner's at six. I texted you their address."

"I can't do that, Eva. It's your family time."

"No way," she objected. "You are family. Besides, you have to come. We're sharing a rental car, and I'd have no way back to the hotel."

"Okay," he relented with a grin. "See you at six, and I'll stop and buy root beer."

**AS KALEY DROVE**, Eva was heartened by how ably she found her way around Panama City. A strange feeling overtook Eva. Here she was suddenly being cared for by the daughter, who had until just recently relied on Eva for everything.

Kaley stayed quiet, focusing her attention on the traffic ahead. Eva savored the peaceful moments after the tumult over the past few weeks.

As they neared the farm, her daughter erupted, "Mom, you've had such an exciting few days. I could tell from what

Griff and Crystal said that your job is rewarding, amazing, and needed!"

"And I sense you're totally energized by the events and seeing Crystal do her job so well," Eva suggested.

"Do you know what she said, Mom?"

"I'd like to hear it."

"That someday, I'll make a great agent like you!"

Eva reached over and patted Kaley's arm on the wheel. "I'm glad you're old enough to discern more about the battle between good and evil. We live in a corrupt world where evil influence abounds. With four more years of maturing and your college degree, if you're still interested, you might enjoy a position like mine and Crystal's. Then, you can bust evil players like Dylan."

"I just did my part in busting Dylan." Kaley glanced over with a wide grin.

"Yes, you surely did. I'm proud of you. And thankful to God for answering prayers."

"Mom," Kaley began, turning down the long drive to her grandparents. "You never told me the government pays rewards to confidential human sources. Have you ever paid people?"

Eva wondered where this conversation was going. "In very rare circumstances. Did Crystal tell you about such rewards?"

Kaley reached into her purse between the seats and pulled out an envelope. She handed it to Eva.

"Read this, Mom. This year's tuition is paid."

Eva lifted out a check. "This says it's for ten thousand dollars."

"Yeah." Kaley smiled at her mother. "I was shocked."

Eva shook her head. "No. No. Kaley, you can't keep this. It's too much."

"Griff told me that you'd think so, but he got it approved at a very high level because Dylan deceived me and put me at risk. And because your team dismantled the drones, it saved lives and valuable property. He also said I helped identify other terrorists."

Eva carefully considered her daughter's reasoning and

changed her mind.

"You and Griff are right, Kaley. I probably would have handled the situation the same way if it didn't involve my daughter."

"I made a decision. I am going to major in criminal justice."

Eva didn't respond, just patted Kaley's arm again. They reached the farmhouse, and in the blink of an eye, as often happened to her, Eva's tired mind recapped the events of the last few days. God had been so good. He'd kept their team and Kaley totally safe.

The Lancet Group was defunct, and Danny Boyd, Regina Spire, her husband, and several retired FBI agents would hopefully be serving time along with Kim Wu. An act of terror was averted thanks to Kaley. Dylan Webb, Jesse Kingsley, and seven others should also be going to prison. Captain Ming's sister was being released, and Eva wasn't moving to Chicago.

Hallelujah!

# Chapter 41

Eva relaxed at dinner with Kaley, Griff, and her parents. All the stress and strain over Kaley's well-being evaporated. It was wonderful to be enjoying together the fabulous meal and black cows. Eva was especially pleased with how accepting her parents were of Eva's work partner and how at ease Griff was with them.

Back at her hotel later in the evening, she had one remaining task to complete and placed a call on her cell phone.

A very suspicious voice answered slowly as if asking a question, "Hel-lo?"

Eva used her caring voice, "Captain, this is Eva Montanna calling."

"Oh, Eva, it is you," he said, sounding relieved. "This phone you gave me seldom rings."

"I'm here in Panama City and would like to meet with you tomorrow after you leave work. We need to supply you with a new and better telephone."

"I can do that. We need to find a place."

Eva scanned the Internet on her phone and, finding a store, told him, "After I hang up, I will text you the address to the Cellphone Shop and time. Let me know if it works for you."

"Thank you, Eva. Yes, I will respond."

"Captain, I have another matter. I don't mean this to be a promise, but I am told our government has arranged a swap with the CCP. If true, it's possible that tomorrow, your sister will be released by the CCP."

Eva waited. But no response.

"Captain, did you hear me?" she pressed.

He answered in a quiet voice, "I am happy, but afraid it might be a mean joke. The CCP not to be trusted."

Eva felt sorrow for him. "I understand but wanted you to know and to have hope. They said it will be tomorrow. If it's not, we can believe it will happen soon. Meanwhile, watch for my text. And you and I will pray for her release."

"Amen, Eva. Thank you. I will see you tomorrow."

**EVA AWOKE EARLY IN THE MORNING,** almost expecting to hear a rooster crowing. Then she reminded herself she was at the hotel and not at her folks. Rather than eat breakfast at the buffet near the lobby, she settled for a large coffee and goodie bag to go, as did Griff.

Eva ate the muffin and banana at the JTTF office in PC. She and Griff spent hours writing additional reports and processing the evidence with Doug and Crystal. She'd texted Captain Yang Ming on her son Dutch's old phone, asking Ming to meet her and Griff at the Cellphone Shop, three blocks from the front gate of Tyndall Air Force Base, at six p.m.

It was nearly noon before he texted back: *See you there at the designated time.*

Eva was about to email her supervisor, Sosa Garcia, back in DC, when Griff walked up to her desk with his brows creased.

"I still have to speak with Kaley," he said. "How about the three of us have lunch?"

"Sure. Anything I need to know about?" Eva probed.

He shrugged. "Routine stuff required of all confidential human sources."

They arranged to meet Kaley for lunch near the campus, and thirty minutes later the trio grabbed burgers and fries from Seminole Sammy's, a block from campus. They were spread out on a picnic table with a beautiful view of Grand Lagoon, the inlet off the Gulf of Mexico.

Eva sat across from Griff and next to Kaley. Seeing her plunk the backpack down on the picnic table's bench seat, Eva grinned. Her daughter already carried the look of a seasoned collegiate.

"Kaley, how do you like being a Seminole?" Griff asked lightly.

"There are some serious football fans here, and even worse on the main campus in Tally, but I'm not much of a fan. I like this campus and the school. Most of the students I meet seem friendly and nice."

Griff set down his iced coffee. "Even the ones you traveled with to demonstrations in Tally?"

Kaley shot Eva a puzzled glance before gaping at Griff. When neither replied, Kaley's eyes sought her mom's again.

With no idea of what Griff knew, Eva stayed mum.

"Um ..." Kaley finally answered. "Not really."

She placed a shaky hand on Eva's arm. "I wanted to talk with you about this. I didn't expect Griff would be around when the subject came up. But that's okay."

"And?" Griff said, holding his uneaten burger between two hands.

She blinked rapidly. "I know I didn't volunteer to help you, and I know it's only because Dylan caused it. I'm really not like him or his people."

"You're right, Kaley," Griff nodded. "I never would have asked you to become involved with such people. In fact, I would have been shocked if you had ever chosen to associate with them. But I thank you for doing what you did."

Eva rested her hand over Kaley's. "Are you saying you don't want to help Griff any further?"

"Yes, and no. I've met the nicest group of people in the church over there." Kaley pointed over her shoulder at a church nearby. "Bay View Chapel is where I go with Ashley and Stephen. You met him and his parents. They are all so nice, like you and Dad. His father, Mr. Wilson, is the veterinarian for the Adelmans. They are lighthearted and encouraging people. I enjoy being with them."

"That's such good news," Eva cheered. "Sounds like you're seeking out new friends who share your faith and values."

Griff ate some of his burger before adding, "And I'm hearing Kaley say that spending time with Dylan's type of friends is draining and stressful."

"Exactly!" Kaley cried. "It's like they don't like themselves or anyone else."

"Kaley, you are sure of who you are," Eva said, lifting her hand. "You've been created in God's image for a relationship with Him. You're maturing to the point where you understand God's plan. You committed yourself to a life of walking with Him, and your life is fulfilled. You're happy—"

"Ashley and Stephen share that same happiness," Kaley

interjected. "We worship and praise God together. We aren't mad at everybody, and we're not miserable. It's too hard being around people like Dylan. Angry people."

Griff smoothed a napkin over his moustache. "Kaley, you have it figured out. Many people get to my age and are still lost and angry. For that reason, I'm glad the Dylan chapter is behind you. It can be closed. There's no need for you to provide me with any more information."

Kaley studied her mom's face. "What if I want to help you? I've learned lots about the justice system and want to be a special agent. By helping you, I'll learn more, and that might help me get hired."

Eva sat numb, searching for what to say. Griff jumped in.

"Kaley, your mom and I both got hired as special agents, and we were never sources. We knew less than you know now. If you're meant to be a special agent, it will happen. Concentrate on your studies and invest in the lives of your grandparents and your nice friends. These other students you've met who are like Dylan, maybe sometime you can introduce them to God who has made your life so fulfilled."

"I agree with Griff," Eva added with feeling.

Kaley dipped a fry into ketchup. "I should do that. Plus, I still have Griff's number. Maybe God will dump another exciting case in my lap."

"Oh no!" Eva raised up her hands. "I'll be praying He doesn't."


**EVA KNEW THAT BACK IN VIRGINIA** Scott and her family would be sitting down to dinner. And she was in Panama City, arriving with Griff at the Cellphone Shop. She could see Captain Ming through the window, waiting inside.

Eva opened the SUV door. "He's here. I'll bring him out so we can talk privately."

"I'll drive around the corner," Griff replied. "So, we're not so visible."

As Eva neared the door, Ming must have seen her because he opened the door for her.

She kept her voice low, telling him she and Griff wanted to speak out in the car for a few minutes before buying his new phone. The two walked around the corner, and Eva placed him in the front passenger seat. She sat behind Griff in the rear seat and reintroduced them.

Captain Ming nodded. "Yes, I remember you, Griff. Thank you also for helping me."

"As I mentioned, we'll buy you a new phone while we're here," Eva said. "First, I have news."

"My sister?" he asked, hope mixed with doubt edging his voice.

Eva retrieved the texts on her phone. "I received this message earlier, around the time you would have left the base. My superior in Washington says, 'Be advised. This morning in Hong Kong, Akina Ming deplaned from a Chinese military aircraft that arrived from China. The missing Hong Kong bank employee appears in good health. She immediately left on a commercial flight to Taipei.'"

Yang Ming's eyes widened, and he gasped, "Is this reliable?"

Eva placed a hand on the front seatback. "It is. In fact, another message states that an American was returned to the U.S., and Nelly Jin was flown from Washington, DC to Beijing. The exchange is completed. Your sister is safe."

Ming clapped his hands together in front of his face.

"So good. So good," he repeated with a beautiful smile. "I thought it would not happen. But God is good."

"All the time," Griff said. "We also considered it might not happen. The CCP is not trustworthy."

Ming nodded his agreement. "You see how ChiComs refuse to fly my sister to Taipei. They pretend it does not exist."

Eva raised her hands and folded them. "Her release is an answer to my prayers."

"Mine, too," he said, a tear running down his cheek.

Griff ended their celebration with cold facts. "Captain, after we finish here and buy your new phone, you must not transfer *any* contacts, pictures, or apps from your old phone to the new one. If you forget and do so, the CCP will again track your every movement and conversation. You must manually type in your contacts and abandon both old phones.

You'll receive a new phone number for Florida, which you can change when you're in Taiwan."

Ming nodded vigorously. Now it was Eva's turn. She needed to ensure her source's good standing with his command and that of the U.S. Air Force.

"Captain Ming," she said in a serious tone.

He turned sideways, focusing his attention on Eva.

"I need to ask you a very important question."

He twisted even more, locking his eyes onto Eva's. "Yes, what is it?"

In her most businesslike manner, Eva probed, "At any time have you disclosed to the people who have been threatening and extorting you, or any persons for that matter, any information you learned while performing your assignment as a military pilot?"

Ming's eyes blazed. "No! Never!"

"It's my responsibility to notify appropriate Air Force officials that there's been an attempt by an enemy state to co-opt you," Eva said, holding his gaze. "You suggested in the past you felt a need to advise your superiors."

She paused a moment for effect. "Now is the time for you to do so."

"Yes." Ming nodded energetically. "I will do so at once."

"Good. I must advise the Air Force of what we did to arrest the ChiComs, but it will look better for you if you're the one to tell them first."

"I agree," he insisted. "I will do so in the morning."

"Excellent," Griff said from the front seat, opening his door.

Eva opened her door and got out to stand beside Griff, saying, "Let's go inside and get your phone settled."

Captain Ming left the SUV and walked around to join Eva and Griff.

Before they went into the store, Eva said quietly, "One more thing. In the next two days, I will prepare a report of what happened. A copy will be turned over to the Air Force, and I hope by then you'll have already notified the authorities."

To Eva, his sober expression and nod confirmed Ming was the real deal. She had no doubt he would be as honorable going forward as he had been in the past.

**THE NEXT DAY, EVA COULDN'T WAIT** to get home. The flight seemed like it would never end. After she landed at Reagan Airport, she quickly texted Scott: *I'm here! Griff can drive me to the office, so I'll see you soon. Love!*

While waiting to exit the plane, she kept checking her phone. Scott didn't reply. She found a cryptic message from her boss, telling her to meet in the morning to discuss a new terrorism plot. As they walked down the arrival corridor, pulling their carry-ons, Eva asked, "Did you get a message from Sosa?"

"Yes, but I have no idea what new plot he means," Griff replied. "It might be nice to stay home for a few days anyway."

"I totally agree."

Eva left the secured arrival area. What she saw amazed her and warmed her heart. Scott was waving at her, along with Andy and Dutch.

"We missed you too much, Mom!" Dutch cried.

She hugged them all, resting her head against Scott's tender embrace.

"What a fantastic surprise!" Tears hovered on Eva's lashes. "No wonder you didn't text me back."

"We had fun planning this surprise, didn't we guys?" Scott's grin spread from ear to ear.

As Griff greeted Scott and his sons, his wife, Dawn, hurried up, looking rattled.

"It took ages to find a parking spot," she said, sounding out of breath.

She fell into Griff's arms.

Scott rounded up his family. "We're all celebrating at our favorite pizza parlor in Vienna. Let's hurry and beat rush hour."

"I know the very one," Griff replied, his arm around Dawn. "Whoever arrives first, order extra garlic knots."

He and Dawn headed to their car. With Scott pulling her carry-on behind him, Eva nestled her hand into Scott's free hand. The boys ran on ahead.

Scott called, "Guys, stay where we can see you."

"Being here with you is wonderful," she whispered. "I love you and missed you."

"Is Kaley okay?"

Eva squeezed his hand. "She's thriving. Hoping we come for Christmas. So are my folks."

"Let's go for two weeks, Eva. Work is taking its toll on us both."

She held his hand all the way to the van. Dutch and Andy hopped in, while Scott stowed her carry-on in the back end. He came around to hold open the door for her.

Eva caught his arm, "With my transfer being rescinded we're free to stay here as long as we want, or until God gives us a new calling."

"We've much to talk over. I'm concerned with new developments at DOD."

She touched his cheek. "I want to hear all about it. A new case is also heating up at the JTTF. Honey, God's fingerprints have been evident from the moment you saw me tackle the Runner. And we've seen, through His intervention, how justice was assured."

Eva buckled her seat belt and, with a smile, turned to survey the new normal. Just her, Scott, and the boys.

# EPILOGUE

Eva and her family reunited for the Christmas season at her parents' farm near Panama City. Spending Christmas Eve in Florida with the people she loved was just what Eva had dreamed of after such a hectic and busy year. Scents of fresh pine boughs wafted throughout the house. The family relaxed in the living room after hanging popcorn strands and homemade ornaments on the Christmas tree.

Gram beckoned them all to the table with a wave. "It's time for lunch. We have to get the boys in their costumes for the Christmas nativity. The program starts at four."

Andy passed the plate of sandwiches to his sister Kaley, asking, "How's college?"

"It's turning out better than I thought in the beginning," she said, helping herself to a turkey sandwich.

"Do you think I'd like it?" he pressed.

Kaley smiled at him. "One thing I know. You'd love living here with Gram and Gramps. I sure do."

"Andy and I are back in the barracks!" Dutch cried.

"Yeah, thanks, Kaley, for staying in one of the guest bedrooms," Andy said. "Dutch and I are having a blast."

Everyone laughed. After dessert, Gram took her grandsons to her sewing room to try on the shepherd costumes she'd made for them. Eva and Scott walked out to the veranda, sipping warm apple cider.

Eva lifted her cheeks into the sun, telling Scott, "I can see that in her three months at FSU, Kaley has become gentler and more caring toward her brothers."

"She's maturing before my eyes." Scott's smile spread across his face. "I'm happy Andy treats his sister more kindly too."

"Yes. Kaley's experience helping Griff has actually deepened her faith and led her to new Christian friends."

"Whom she might not know if she'd stayed in Virginia for college," Scott said, finishing her sentence.

"Just so you know, staying here with you in this never-ending sunshine with our dear family, I couldn't be happier."

They had just finished their cider when Dutch stepped out onto the veranda, wearing his linen shepherd's robe and a puzzled look on his face.

"What about the sheep if I'm a shepherd? Gramps only has cows and goats."

His dad, along with Gramps, soon set him straight, and the Montanna family drove in two vehicles to the church. On her way into the church, Eva took out her cell phone as she'd forgotten to silence it. A text from Griff showed on the screen, so she swiped it open.

He'd written five minutes ago:

*Eva, I know you're on Christmas vacation, but can you phone me right away?*

She dashed outside and made a quick call to Griff. "We're getting seated to watch Dutch, Andy, and Kaley perform in the Christmas pageant. You sounded urgent."

"I won't keep you but for a moment. Bo Rider, our colleague and friend at the Agency, reached out to me. Our same enemy who went after the Runner is at it again. And your name is mentioned in the overseas chatter. Thought you should be aware, change your passwords, and be prepared for strategy meetings when you return."

Eva's mind whirled. "Griff, I'm speechless and need to know more. Perhaps after Christmas, I can get to a secure phone at Tyndall, and you can share more. Meanwhile, I'll do as you suggest. And keep the kids off social media."

"Good idea, partner. And Merry Christmas to you all."

"Merry Christmas to you and Dawn."

Eva hung up and turned off her phone, uncertain of the ramifications of Griff's call. She inhaled deeply. No way she was mentioning this to Scott or anyone until she had more info from Griff. She dropped her phone into her purse, determined to set her mind completely upon the Christ child and His miraculous birth.

She quickly found her seat next to Scott just as the lights dimmed. Shepherd boys Andy and Dutch came striding down the aisle in their long robes belted at the waist, along with several other boys from the church. They each stepped toward the altar carrying a walking stick.

Kaley looked so grown-up dressed in a black skirt and red jacket as she stood down front at a lighted podium. In a melodic voice, she read aloud to the congregation from Luke, chapter 2, "And there were shepherds living out in the fields nearby, keeping watch over their flocks at night. An angel of the Lord appeared to them, and the glory of the Lord shone around them, and they were terrified."

A choir member dressed in a white robe lifted his arms to the sounds of loud thunder vibrating in the overhead speakers. Eva could see her little Dutch drop to his knees and tremble. Andy, too, went to his knees.

The choir angel spoke to the shepherds, "Do not be afraid. I bring you good news of great joy that will be for all the people. Today in the town of David, a Savior has been born to you: He is Christ the Lord. This will be a sign to you: You will find a baby wrapped in cloths and lying in a manger."

Eva sat in awe as suddenly more choir angels in white robes filled the front of the church.

Kaley again read aloud from the Bible she held, "Suddenly a great company of the heavenly host appeared with the angel, praising God and saying ..."

Here the angels all said together, "Glory to God in the highest, and on earth peace to men, on whom his favor rests."

Kaley finished reading, saying that when the angels had left and gone to Heaven, the shepherds said to one another, "Let's go to Bethlehem and see this thing that has happened, which the Lord told us about."

Dutch, Andy, and the other shepherds rushed forward to the baby Jesus lying in the manger with Mary and Joseph. Alongside Jesus and His earthly parents were the wooden lamb and donkey Zion had carved. Even the lamb was looking at baby Jesus with worshipful eyes.

Pastor Dobson came forward, holding a wrapped package in his hands. Lifting this upward, he said, "Jesus Christ is the greatest gift ever given. In the same way you take this gift from me when I give it to you, Jesus' gift of everlasting life is not yours unless you accept His gift of salvation, hope, and peace. Will you receive Him into your hearts tonight?"

Tiny LED candles were passed out. The audience sang

"Silent Night" with the lit candles shining all through the church. On this night, Eva thought about her Savior Jesus being born for her. The light of His life and love filled her, and she knew He would be with her, helping her in everything and for always.

# ABOUT THE AUTHORS

ExFeds, Diane and David Munson write High Velocity Suspense novels reviewers compare to John Grisham. The Munsons call their novels "factional fiction" because they write books based on their exciting and dangerous careers.

Diane Munson has been an attorney for more than thirty years. She has served as a Federal Prosecutor in Washington, D.C., and with the Reagan Administration appointed by Attorney General Edwin Meese as Deputy Administrator/Acting Administrator of the Office of Juvenile Justice and Delinquency Prevention. She worked with the Justice Department, U.S. Congress, and White House on policy and legal issues. More recently she has been in a general law practice.

David Munson served as a Special Agent with the Naval Investigative Service (now NCIS), and U.S. Drug Enforcement Administration over a twenty-seven year career. As an undercover agent, he infiltrated international drug smuggling organizations, and traveled with drug dealers. He met their suppliers in foreign countries, helped fly their drugs to the U.S., feigning surprise when shipments were seized by law enforcement. Later his true identity was revealed when he testified against group members in court. While assigned to DEA headquarters in Washington, D.C., David served two years as a Congressional Fellow with the Senate Permanent Subcommittee on Investigations.

As Diane and David research and write, they thank the Lord for the blessings of faith and family. They are collaborating on their next novel and traveling the country speaking/appearing at various venues.

Check out their website at:
www.DianeAndDavidMunson.com

at the center of power. The Munsons' thrillers are companion books, with characters reappearing in other novels, but each begins and ends a new story.

ISBN-13:978-0982535516
344 pages, trade paper
Fiction/Mystery and Suspense
14.99

**The Camelot Conspiracy**

"The Camelot Conspiracy" rocks with a sinister plot even more menacing than the headlines. Former DC insiders Diane and David Munson feature a brash TV reporter, Kat Kowicki, who receives an ominous email that throws her into the high stakes conspiracy of John F. Kennedy's assassination. When Kat uncovers evidence Lee Harvey Oswald did not act alone, she turns for help to Federal Special Agents Eva Montanna and Griff Topping who uncover the chilling truth: A shadow government threatens to tear down the very foundation of the American justice system. The Munsons' thrillers are companion books, with characters reappearing in other novels, but each begins and ends a new story.

ISBN-13: 978-0982535523
352 pages, trade paper
Christian Fiction / Mystery and Suspense
14.99

**Hero's Ransom**

Could Chinese espionage disrupt your home town? CIA Agent Bo Rider (The Camelot Conspiracy) and Federal Agents Eva Montanna and Griff Topping (Facing Justice, Confirming Justice, The Camelot Conspiracy) return in

Hero's Ransom, the Munsons' fourth family-friendly adventure. When archeologist Amber Worthing uncovers a two-thousand-year-old mummy and witnesses a secret rocket launch at a Chinese missile base, she is arrested in China for espionage. Her imprisonment sparks a custody battle between grandparents over her young son, Lucas. Caught between sinister world powers, Amber's faith is tested in ways she never dreamed possible. Danger escalates as Bo races to stop China's killer satellite from destroying America, and with Eva and Griff's help, to rescue Amber using a unexpected ransom.

ISBN-13: 978-0982535530
320 pages, trade paper
Christian Fiction / Mystery and Suspense
14.99

**Redeeming Liberty**

In this timely thriller by ExFeds Diane and David Munson (former Federal Prosecutor and Federal Agent), parole officer Dawn Ahern is shocked to witness her friend Liberty, the chosen bride of Wally (former "lost boy" from Sudan) being kidnapped by modern-day African slave traders. Dawn tackles overwhelming danger head-on in her quest to redeem Liberty. When she reaches out to FBI agent Griff Topping and CIA agent Bo Rider, her life is changed forever. Suspense soars as Bo launches a clandestine rescue effort for Liberty only to discover a deadly Iranian secret threatening the lives of millions of Americans and Israelis. Glimpse tomorrow's startling headlines in this captivating story of faith and freedom under fire. The Munsons' thrillers are companion books, with characters reappearing in other novels, but each begins and ends a new story.

ISBN-13: 978-0982535547
320 Pages, trade paper
Fiction / Mystery and Suspense
14.99

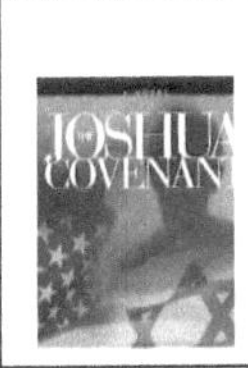

### Joshua Covenant

CIA agent Bo Rider moves to Israel after years of clandestine spying around the world. He takes his family, wife Julia, and teens, Glenna and Gregg while serving in America's Embassy using his real name. While Glenna and Gregg face danger while exploring Israel's treasures, their father is shocked to uncover a menacing plot jeopardizing them all. A Bible scholar helps Bo in amazing ways. He discovers the truth about the Joshua Covenant and battles evil forces that challenge his true identity. Will Bo survive the greatest threat ever to his career, his family, and his life? Glimpse tomorrow's startling headlines as risks it all to stop an enemy spy.

ISBN-13: 978-0-983559009
336 Pages, trade paper
Christian Fiction / Mystery and Suspense
14.99

### Night Flight

When CIA Agent Bo Rider adopts a retired law enforcement dog for his family, teenagers Glenna and Gregg are surprised to discover Blaze's special skills. They put the dog to work solving crimes, but a captured criminal seeks revenge forcing the kids to hide out at their grandparents' Florida home. In Skeleton Key powerful villains connive to stop the teens from discovering their criminal enterprise. As Glenna and Gregg face high stakes, they find courage to keep pursuing justice. In Night Flight, the Rider family learns the true meaning of loving your neighbor as yourself. This is the debut thriller for young adults and grand parents by these best-selling ExFeds who write factional fiction based on their careers.

ISBN-13: 978-0983559023

224 Pages, trade paper
Fiction / Mystery and Suspense
9.99

### Stolen Legacy

*Stolen Legacy,* by Diane and David Munson, tells the daunting tale of Germany invading Holland, and the heroes who dare to resist by hiding Jews. Federal agent Eva Montanna stops protecting America long enough to visit her grandfather's farm and help write a memoir of his dangerous time under Nazi control. Eva is shocked to uncover a plot to harm Grandpa Marty. Memories are tested as secrets from Marty's time in the Dutch resistance and later service in the Monuments Men of the U.S. Army fuel this betrayal. The Munsons' eighth thriller unveils priceless relics and a stolen legacy, forever changing Eva's life and her faith.

ISBN-13: 978-0983559047
336 pages, trade paper
Christian Fiction / Mystery and Suspense
14.99

### Embers of Courage

ICE Special Agent Eva Montanna discovers the world is ablaze with danger when militants capture her task force teammate, NCIS Special Agent Raj Pentu, during a CIA operation in Egypt. She risks her life to defeat tyrants oppressing Christians, and is plunged into a daring rescue mission. Eva's faith is tested like never before as mysterious ashes, her ancient family Bible, and fifteenth century religious persecution collide with modern-day courage under fire. This riveting novel, the ninth by ExFeds Diane and David Munson, is their third linking true historical events with their signature High Velocity Suspense.

ISBN-13: 978-0983559061
336 pages, trade paper
Christian Fiction / Mystery and Suspense
14.99

### The Looming Storm

Tomorrow's headlines leap from the pages of *The Looming Storm* when Federal Agent Eva Montanna uncovers a menacing threat to harm Eva and her family. When daughter Kaley travels to Eastern Europe on a class trip, Eva's Christian faith is challenged, and their lives are altered in the blink of an eye. Tensions skyrocket as Eva and Griff Topping, her FBI partner, use every trick to infiltrate a band of Florida smugglers. The agents are shocked when their undercover charade reveals the criminals have sinister plans for America. Secrets are shredded in the Munson's tenth 'stand alone' thriller, as this spousal duo rips the veil from a labyrinth of covert criminal enterprises.

ISBN-13: 978-0-983559085
305 pages, trade paper
Christian Fiction/Mystery and Suspense
15.99

### North by Starlight

After ten best-selling thrillers, Diane and David Munson launch *North by Starlight,* their first romantic suspense with Attorney Madison Stone racing to Starlight, Vermont from her D.C. law firm to save the inheritance of Jordan Star, sole heir of his late grandfather's Star Mountain ski resort. Maddie arrives in the winter wonderland ready to defeat the claim of Jordan's mystery relative. Instead, she finds surprising struggles and diversions in the idyllic town during the Christmas season when her ex-boyfriend, attorney Stewart Dunham shows up to represent the interloper. Maddie sharpens her legal skills in outwitting him and a greedy mining enterprise bent on changing Starlight forever. She and Jordan form an alliance, and the ensuing legal battle leaves her emotionally vulnerable until Trevor Kirk, a geologist, focuses her mind back to what is important, saving the town and finding her heart.

ISBN-13 : 978-1732582309
291 pages, trade paper
Christian Fiction/ Mystery and Suspense
14.99

### The Breach

Joining forces again, Federal Agent Eva Montanna and FBI Agent Griff Topping battle against a domestic terrorist threat, until their personal information gets compromised. Are they being doxed? And if so, to what end? Eva's Christian faith and family relations are further tested as she and Griff plunge into investigating threats against U.S. Senator Cambridge Easton. When they uncover shocking allegations that the assigned judge is corrupt, it's a race against time to figure out the truth. But Eva's job demands are only the beginning, as she navigates a web of deceit when an intelligence breach impacts her daughter, her daughter's employer, and the employer's adopted Amish son. Who can they trust? Eva and Griff must fight crime and terrorism with their wits tied behind their back. Will they find out in time if the hacker is a determined foreign enemy, or someone with a personal vendetta against them?

ISBN-13: 9781732582323
258 pages, trade paper
Christian Fiction / Mystery and Suspense
15.99